Dark Sea's End
Book One of
Beyond Ash and Sand

Richard Nell

Dark Sea's End
Beyond Ash and Sand, Book One

Author: Richard Nell
Email: email@richardnell.com
Website:http://www.richardnell.com

The following is a book of fiction. Names, characters, places, and events are either the product of the author's imagination, or used in a fictitious manner. Any resemblance to actual persons, living or dead, or actual events, is purely coincidental.

Cover art by Felix Ortiz
Design by STK Creations

Chapter 1

Not one more, Chang thought. Not one more of his crew would die, or be abandoned. He whispered an ancient sea prayer, and swore it by Roa's treacherous heart.

He scraped his knife along the bumps and craters of the prison's stone wall, looking at the men he might make corpses. "Touch him," he hissed, "see what happens."

All around him the remaining crew of the Bahala rose with exhausted groans, their callused hands over shivs and clubs. They all knew their chief's killing voice.

The four marines before them—now prisoners in the same Alaku royal prison as Chang's pirates—exchanged sweating glances in the gloom. They didn't really want violence. All they wanted was a place to sit, and if they squeezed and kicked out a few convicts they'd have a safe, dry patch of wall to rest their backs. It wasn't much, maybe, but better than the alternative—better than being surrounded on all sides by criminals and privateers belonging to rival lords.

"He's a simpleton." The captured marine pointed at Old Mata, toothless now with one white eye, a broken man who stared at the wall as if it were the sea. "Why bother with him?"

Chang shrugged. The truth would suffice.

"Because he's ours."

The marines stared from sweat covered faces. They looked in Chang's eyes and saw what they needed to see. Without a word, they turned away, moments later attacking a smaller gang on the other side. Chang and his brothers waited, and watched—the crew of the

Bahala knew violence. They knew it had a way of spreading like fire, and that you might start it by choice, maybe even for good reason, then watch as your whole life burned with you inside.

This time the fire ended quickly. The well-fed, well-trained marines knocked a few heads and spilled a little blood without killing. The beaten men crawled away and the others left open the space. Just like that, the new order of things was established.

Chang put his knife away and sat with his brothers. Soon the marine captain was squished up next to him, their bare shoulders pressed together in a wall of reeking flesh ringing the wall of stone. Chang didn't mind. The marine seemed right enough and he and his crew would do well. Another time, another place, Chang would have served with men like him. But that's not what they were anymore, not in here. In the young island king's prison, a man had to fight for a scrap of rice or a chair or a moment's respect. That's just how life was. Things were simple, without all the soft lies landsmen used to cover it up. It was difficult for the well-born sailors, no doubt. But it was all 'Lucky' Chang had ever known.

* * *

Time passed slowly in the dark. Chang had lost track of the days and counted by meals. Usually it was a few buckets of rice with whatever meat and sauce was left from the palace scraps. When he heard the guards he rose without thought to make his claim. He and his boys were the second largest crew and so they ate second unless someone wanted to settle it with knives. "Let's go, boys." He was up and pushing, eyes roaming face after face for threat. Finding none, he made it to the bars.

"There they are, coming like good dogs." The guard smiled. "Get your scum, pirate. You're coming with us."

Chang took his moment. He was here for piracy, and a man left the Alaku prison for piracy in one of two ways. Either one involved rope.

"Get your scum, I said." The guard worked at the metal gate as others formed up with spears and knives. Chang still hadn't moved.

"What we doin', Chiefy?" Scab-cheeked Basko shifted his feet at Chang's side and scratched at his fleas. Basko was a lazy scoundrel of a sailor, but a proper brute when things were rough. He bounced on his heels as he palmed his knife, wild-eyed and ready to die.

"Ain't no use," muttered the Steerman, already coming up to surrender. The little islander was as vicious as he was cowardly, and you could never know which for sure.

Basko hissed his contempt, but the Steerman was right. They could fight and hurt or maybe kill a few of the guards, but they'd lose. Even if they won there was no way out of the king's maze.

"We go." Chang stepped forward with his hands to the bars.

"Good dog," said the guard, strapping him with bronze chains. "Now get back you bastards!" More guards waved spears at the growing cluster of prisoners, sticking one or two to make their point.

Soon enough Chang and his crew were rattling their chains through the narrow corridors, led by spear and boot to another holding cell still too small for so many men, but luxurious in contrast to the prison.

"You got a guest," said the guard through the gate. "Asked for you special." He smiled. "I think it's finally time to die, pirate."

Chang didn't much like to talk unless it mattered. He found a wall and leaned, noticing a few shafts of light through a grate near the top of the cell.

"Ain't no execution," said the Steerman. "They'd 'a taken us outside where others could see."

"Might be torture," chimed in Basko helpfully. "Old Mata never did tell 'em where he buried all that silver. Might be they think we know."

"Just listen, and be ready." Chang's voice silenced the rest. "If I say go, we go. Got it?"

"Just listen," repeated the Boatswain, stretching his thinning shoulders. The Oarsmen brothers cracked meaty knuckles, the Pitman stared off at nothing, and the Swabbies nodded with youthful vigor.

They all stunk like filth and death now even more than usual. A hundred days they'd been fighting and running on a broken ship until at last the kingsmen had caught them moored and helpless trying to make repairs. Then it was shackles and guilty this and guilty that and 'so says the king of the isles'. Now here they were, trapped like rats, but from listening to Chang they were still alive.

Soon the guards were greeting a visitor outside, and Chang signaled the men. He didn't know why they'd been brought here but it made no difference. This was the best chance they'd have—one chance to maybe rip off that grate and climb one by one to the fortress above. No one escaped the Alaku prison proper. Not one man in a hundred years. So it was the grate, or it was nothing.

A key fumbled at the door, and Chang's heart quickened as the hinge creaked. A tall man in a dark robe walked inside, his hands calmly tucked into his cuffs.

Chang stared and felt his mouth gape in recognition.

The men's nervous eyes danced across him, waiting for a sign that didn't come.

"Good morning," said the greatest killer in the isles, his smile calm as a Bato breeze.

"Well?" The Steerman licked his lips in the silence, hunched forward like a dog with a scent. Chang shook his head, still unable to speak. *"Well?"* The Steerman said louder, the others lurching with restless panic. Chang managed to say 'no' just as the man lunged.

Their visitor sprung as if waiting. Bone cracked against bone as his hand smashed the smaller man in the chest like a club, dropping him instantly to his knees. He slumped over, coughing and gasping for air.

"You are Lucky Chang," said the robed killer—the dead king's assassin, and terror of the isles for a decade. His almost pleasant eyes gazed into Chang's. "You are the crew who survived the pirate purge?"

The crew stared at their fastest man groaning on the stone, and all thoughts of violence vanished from their faces.

"No," said Chang, doing his best not to show his fear. "I'm innocent. We all are."

The 'spymaster' smiled with what seemed genuine, if tepid, pleasure. "I'm here to offer you a deal, Chang. Honest employment, and afterward, freedom. For you and as many men who would follow you."

Even the injured Steerman perked up at the words, horking phlegm as a few wide eyes roamed Chang for assurance.

"Why should you offer us anything?"

The killer smiled his smile. "Take the evening to think it through, if you like."

"We both know I've got no choice. Just tell me why."

The visitor shrugged and stepped away, knocking again at the door. "You'll do well, I think. I need good sailing men, Chang, that is why. And because no honorable, free sailors would accept my offer."

Chang didn't much like being a prisoner, but he liked being a slave even less.

"Tell me why gods curse you." He felt his hands ball to fists, though he knew just as well that he was trapped like a damn landsman, metal shackles like he'd worn as a boy. The spymaster turned, the same smile on his terrifying, forgettable face.

"A curious pirate. How interesting. You'll soon see, my friend. You needn't worry. You'll soon see."

* * *

Nervous guards had waited outside their meeting, and Chang realized this meant their guest had *chosen* to come in alone. He'd wanted to be locked in a room with ten desperate men who all had hidden scraps of wood or metal tucked away. Which meant he had *wanted* violence, just so he could put it down.

The thought disturbed Chang through the long night and into the morning as more armed guards marched him and his men from their pit. They clattered their chains through long corridors of the palace maze, then into royal gardens where they were stared at by clean, frowning servants. Instead of the gate they'd been inside those months ago, this time they were taken to the coast, to a royal harbor filled with warships.

"Look at that," said the Pitman, awake now that the sea was close, gesturing at a huge rammer. "One of them new coastals with the wider sails."

"Must be five hundred ships," muttered an Oarsman. "Never seen so many in one place."

Chang said nothing, though he'd never seen so

many, either. The guards took them past the dozen swaying docks that led to the Royal Alaku Navy, past the warehouses and drydocked vessels, marine barracks and construction.

A single ship was moored near the beach, a nearby transport weighed down with an iron anchor and lashed with thick hempen rope. The dead king's spymaster stood in front of it, hands in cuffs, frozen smile etched on his face.

"Loa," he greeted them in the island custom with a half bow. "From now on you may call me Captain Eka, or just Captain. This will be your ship for the forseeable future."

Chang walked closer to the vessel, and the more he did the stranger he realized it was. Twenty years now he had spent on ships in the thousands of Pyu islands —twenty years of trading, robbing, and raiding amongst the greatest navies and best ships in the world. He had never seen anything like this.

It was facing them, the angled curve of the sleek but high hull incredibly steep from deck to bottom. A long spar jut from the front like a spear, with countless lines lashed all around it. And the mast! No, Chang realized, there were *three* masts, all built in a row, towering above like castle spires twenty times the length of a man. He found himself staring with all the others, head turned this way and that as he tried to understand.

"Impressive, isn't it?" The killer-turned-captain smiled. "Don't be too pleased. It's complex beyond reason, and you'll need to learn every piece of it."

"How many crew?" Chang managed.

"Ten, ideally. We could make do with five."

"Then it's just us? You've no other men?"

Eka tilted his shaved head. "And the pilot. Does that concern you, Chang?"

"No." He shrugged and met the man's eyes, despising games when they didn't favor him. "But what's to stop us cutting your throat the first night, *Captain*, and tossing you in the waves for Roa?"

The assassin's smile widened, as if he had assessed this threat and found it trivial. "If your moral upbringing fails you, Master Chief, then nothing, save for my own humble efforts. And that of the pilot."

Chang snorted. "Two against ten. You're a fool. I won't board a ship captained by a fool."

Eka shook silently with what might have been a laugh.

"Did you hear that, Savage?" he called to the ship. "I think you're going to like this one."

A form emerged audibly from the hull, his footsteps thudding along the wood. Chang felt his own feet move back. Sun glared off the pale, bald flesh of a hairless scalp, then bare shoulders as wide as a tree. A deformed giant rose next to the closest mast, impossibly tall and lithe for his muscle. His people were known to Chang. He was an 'ashman', from the far South, a people who had killed and butchered islanders for the past two years before the king made peace. He stepped down the gangplank, his strange, golden eyes turning on Chang and his men. His scarred frame gleamed with sweat, and he held what might have been a carving in his huge hands. All his life Chang had survived by taking the measure of violent men, and in his new Captain he had recognized a killer and acted accordingly. In the golden slits before him, squinted almost painfully against the sun, he saw a monster.

"Yes, I heard," spoke the creature, his voice as deep as the sea. "He's right. You *are* very foolish."

"Look at his eyes," muttered the Steerman, rather rudely, turning to the others with something like disbelief. "That's their leader. The sorcerer, with golden eyes. That's Bukayag The Butcher."

Chang remained silent. He had never seen the ashman leader, but he had heard descriptions. A deformed giant with golden eyes, just as was said. Chang couldn't imagine there were two.

"My name is Ruka," said the barbarian warlord. "And I am no threat to you. I lead nothing, not even this ship. Look to Eka, and to yourselves. I will look to the stars."

With that he turned and ascended the ramp with heavy steps, humming as he polished the carving. Eka half bowed and extended a hand.

"Come, gentlemen. There is much to do. We sail West as far as West goes—beyond the far lands of the mountain tribes, beyond the continent, and into an endless sea. I should like to leave with the tide."

Chapter 2

Chang watched the sails of *The Prince* expand, somewhere between fear and awe.

"More mainsail!" Eka shouted from his perch atop one of the masts. Their new 'captain' had exchanged his robes for the typical short cloth shirt and pants of an island sailor. He could clamber up and down the rigging as fast as a born marine, and seemed to know the trade as well as any of the crew. It was, in a word, infuriating.

Chang gestured and the Pitman raced to obey, grumbling curses in some far flung tongue of the Western isles. The Pitman's sole job was the sails, and he was accustomed to being a master of his trade, working largely alone on a single mast. But this ship was too large for one man to handle, and so the whole crew had to learn. Chang looked over at Basko fumbling with a growing cluster of line and growled, running to help him sort it.

"Makes no bloody sense," he said, red-faced, as Chang grabbed an end.

"Rigging is rigging. There's just a lot of it. Here." He threw away three he didn't need and pulled at the highest, which flew off instantly. The day was windy, and the huge cloth sails whipped and curled with tension, thrashing like beasts as they fought their restraints.

"More mainsail," Eka shouted from above. "And what's the bloody problem, third mast?"

Chang stared daggers but held his tongue. 'What problem?' he wanted to shout. '*What bloody problem?* We should have five more men! We should have less sail and more time to practice in safe waters.' But he had already voiced these complaints, and was met first with contempt from the captain, then a baffling explanation from the pilot. In both cases it meant 'shut up and deal with it'.

"It's like a navy ship," Chang explained to Basko. "Like the flagship Old Mata stole from the Molbog. The lines are just thin, use only a hitch knot, the smallest you can."

"Aye, Chiefy."

With that sorted, Chang ran across to the main mast.

"Where's my bloody sail, Master Chief?" the captain barked from the nest. Chang grit his teeth and tried to understand the thick cluster of line just as the Pitman cried in triumph and released more sail, the cloth flapping wide as it unfurled.

"There's your god cursed sail, you bastard," Chang growled as the men laughed and whooped, stepping away. Chang seized a line and moved to the rail, looking out across the bow towards the coast of the continent. As he did he watched the sea. Soon he blinked against the cool air and spray and knew it wasn't just the wind. The water moved away from him far faster than seemed possible. The three sails were full, the huge cups of cloth strained against their spars. And what became clear was a simple fact: this ship could damn near fly.

"Look at her!" Eka cried with the first signs of actual enthusiasm. "Bloody *look* at her!"

Chang's crew gaped at the sea, then at each other, just as amazed as he was.

"True," muttered Old Mata—the only word he could still make with regularity—splitting clumped line with old and three fingered hands.

Chang had sailed on a dozen ships and watched

thousands in his decades on the sea. Never had he seen one move this fast, nor with such confidence. Not even close. Such a ship could sail the isles without fear, for none could catch her. She would be free in all the ways others were bound—to go where she pleased, no matter which king or killer told her the the waters were his, the laws already made.

Chang's eyes turned to the savage pilot standing precariously on the edge of his ship. One push and he would be gone, lost in the sea and leaving one man against ten with no space to run. Only one huge hand gripped the rail as the pilot looked over, watching the side of the hull.

As Chang watched him, the barbarian's head turned, ever so slightly, as if he'd smelled something foul on the air, and met Chang's eyes.

Chang turned and coughed. The man frightened him, though that wasn't why. Even a giant could be killed, and killing both men to steal their ship would lose Chang not a moment's sleep.

But he could wait. There would be less risky moments, more favorable chances for 'Lucky' Chang to earn his namesake. There always was. They were only at the first horn, and still they had to cross a hundred ri of open water, past the Lonely Isles, all the way to the Western edge of the world. In a way, perhaps, Chang was curious. Before he killed these madmen, he wanted to see how far they truly meant to sail.

* * *

Zaya, daughter of Juchi, clutched the rail of a foreigner catamaran, and watched the pirate ship come closer.

"They're still gaining," said the old island captain in

his own language. Then, after a long delay, with something like resignation. "Steady course. We can't outrun them."

Zaya knew little enough of ships. In her own lands she was a skald—a singer of songs, a lifter of fears and maker of joy. She knew how a man felt by the look in his eyes, or the slightest change in his posture. She knew terror when she saw it.

"Can't we toss the cargo? They'll just take it. Let's throw it overboard, aye?" One of the sailors paced and pulled at his clothes and tried but failed to swallow with a mouth drained of moisture.

The captain snorted and rolled a hunk of root in his teeth. "Do that and we're all dead men. At least with the pirates, we have a chance. Fetch weapons! Ready the hooks! Prepare to be boarded!"

Zaya stood paralyzed on the prow. When she'd first decided to make the crossing, her fear had been the sea, and maybe what traveling men might try in the depths of night. She hadn't even considered pirates.

The great eye of Volus—the 'sun' in these lands— bore down from above with heat she had never known; the clear, blue waters of the Alaku sea sprayed as the strange, three-hulled ship turned straight towards the Great Continent. She put a hand up her shirt, fumbling to hold the knife tied to her chest. She had never used it. Her mother had trained her with spear and bow, but she had never killed anyone.

In her own land, the land of ash, she would be the safest person on the ship. In the Ascom men did not harm women. To do so was to burn in the fires of hell forever, trapped with the mountain god until the stain burned clean. But here, in the Pyu isles, they had no such belief. As far as she knew, men slaked their lusts whenever power allowed. A woman could be bought, owned, abused and discarded. Zaya knew she was

15

young and beautiful. She was foreign. And she was the only woman on this ship.

She flinched and turned to find the youngest member of the crew—a boy of no more than twelve—who had apparently tugged at her sleeve. "Sorry, miss, you're to go down below now." He gestured, clearly unsure if she understood. "Safer. Down below."

Zaya looked one last time at the approaching vessel, then did as she was asked.

She stepped over barrels of cloth and silk, loaded along with supplies in the cramped space of the transport, until she'd reached the back. She felt the rocking of the waves, and in that strange moment of waiting, was reminded of the much longer and more frightening voyage from her homeland. There had been storms that seemed to consume all the world, but her ship had weathered it. Now perhaps she was to die before she even reached her destination. It was what she deserved, perhaps, for her stubborn foolishness. Her head had been so full of great tales like Haki the brave, or the great shaman of Noss.

When the war with the empire had ended, and many ships full of adventurers and pioneers began their journeys to the new world, Zaya had decided to go with them. All her life she had only ever wanted to see her own grand adventure, to see the heroes and make the stories for herself. Her father had tried to warn her.

"They never put hunger, boredom, or the shits in great tales," he'd said without his customary humor. "They never say you'll near break your back on some damned horse, and eat the same rotten potatoes for weeks." He'd sighed and met her eyes. "They don't tell you about the waiting, or the fear of what will happen. There's no songs of the helpless terror of not knowing how the story ends."

She'd smiled and comforted him, told him she'd be

careful and that she loved him, but she had to go or else her music and stories would become a lie, and she'd grow to hate them, and then herself. He'd patted her hand.

"I know, child. Now be gentle with your mother. She'll never understand, and she'll rage, but she loves you as much as I."

She'd hugged him, then she'd told her mother and forced herself not to match the angry, disappointed words.

"Why? Why would you do this? Do you think all I've done has been to send my daughters into danger, alone? All your father has done? All your father has *suffered*? For you?"

"I will be forever grateful, Mother. I love you, and thank you, but I must live and see what this world is or else I will never love my part in it.'

She hadn't said it, and perhaps couldn't until she'd sat for weeks on a ship and thought on her mother's anger, surrounded by sweating families and the sounds of the sea. Instead she'd left the home she loved, and turned away without another word.

She was older now, in spirit if not in body. She had waited, and feared, as her father warned her. But she did not understand, not truly, until this moment, as she sat in a foreigner's hold, her hands shaking on the formed handle of her father's blade in the dark. Zaya had not known what terror was until she heard the sound of arrows whistling like shepherds, and the first brave sailors screamed.

* * *

"Look, there, Chiefy! I told you. Two ships fighting off the coast."

Chang frowned but stepped to the rail and squinted. They'd been practicing rigging all morning, making loops around the seas outside of Sri Kon. He wanted nothing more than to fall down in his bunk with maybe a bottle of rum, but the day was yet long. He glanced at Eka watching from the prow, and by his face, the captain felt the same.

"Those aren't Alaku colors," the captain shouted, almost as if were trying to convince someone. "They're not our problem."

He turned his head towards the giant pilot, who leaned against the heavy door of his cabin, eyes downcast as if bothered by the harsh light. Eka shook his head, and sighed.

"Damn you, Savage, very well. We might chase them off if we get closer. Six degrees port and maintain sail," he shouted. "Arm yourselves while you're at it."

The Steerman glanced at Chang, who raised a calming hand before shouting up to the prow. "With what, Captain? We've got nothing save a few cobbled knives."

Eka gestured below. "There's bows, hooks and spears. Go and get them."

Again the Steerman looked at Eka with wide, incredulous eyes, and Chang merely shrugged. "You heard the man. Go get armed."

Basko went first, as always. Behind him the pirates went in twos and three, coming up with fine spears of carved yew and bronze tips, short bows and a pile of well-made arrows. Not a one intended to fight, of course, save to kill their hosts. But it was still nice to have them.

Chang found Eka's eyes roaming him and his men. He clearly noticed the surprise and pleasure—the comfort and familiarity with tools of death. Chang cleared his throat to cover his own excitement, sensing freedom drawing ever closer. Still, he couldn't help but notice, the captain did not look afraid.

They sailed in relatively tense silence. The outline of the two ships came closer, and Chang soon recognized the first as a mid-sized merchant catamaran, likely an island trader from the outskirts of the isles. The other was a military scoutship—sleek and fast and no doubt belonging to some island lord, filled with marines out of uniform, robbing any vessel they could catch with tacit approval. Such men were not considered 'pirates' like Chang and his men, though that's exactly what they were. After all, these 'pirates' were sanctioned. They killed and robbed on the approval of some rich man in a fortress, and that made all the difference in the world.

"They aren't running." Eka said flatly. "There's at least fifteen crew, maybe more."

The barbarian hadn't moved from his position by the door. His golden eyes had taken on a kind of glow, his dour expression darkening by the moment.

"I will not kill," he said at last.

"Admirable," snapped Eka, "but unhelpful. When we started this venture you claimed to be pilot and I the captain. Well as captain I suggest we steer clear."

The giant's eyes snapped to the smaller man. He seemed almost ready to lunge from his rest, but he calmed. "Yes," he agreed, "you are captain."

"Good." Eka took a breath and gestured away from the ships, still circling and loosing arrows. "Turn West. We'll get out of sight, then move at half sail throughout the…"

"*Help us!*"

A feminine voice crossed the waves. It was rich, and strong with a strange accent Chang couldn't place.

The giant blinked and surged forward, his head turned like a dog with a scent. He disappeared into his cabin, and Eka sighed.

"Change of plans," he called to the crew, then stepped down to meet Chang's eyes. "We're going to help that ship, Chief. If I were you I would tell any of your men who would like to see the dawn not even to whisper of betrayal. For as frightening and violent as looks our good friend the pilot, I assure you, the reality is worse. Do you understand?"

"Of course, Captain." Chang smiled. "We wouldn't dream of it."

Chapter 3

Zaya spotted a ship from the only window in the cluttered hold. At first she was seized with dread, assuming it another enemy vessel filled with pirates. She felt what little hope of resistance she had fade to nothing, and nearly fell back to wait for doom on one of the many barrels. But she forced herself to look. Though the light was fading she soon saw the new ship's sails were enormous—angled and curved forward, almost like triangles. Her heart pounded as recognition came—these were not island sails. They were the sails of her people. Could the vessel be from the Ascom? Was that possible?

"*Help us!*" she cried in the island tongue with all the strength in her considerable voice. She watched, and waited, then cried again in the Ascomi tongue.

Above she could still hear arrows and men crying out in triumph or agony. The merchant vessel twisted and turned, no doubt trying to prevent the attacker from being able to board. In one such turn she caught sight of the enemy vessel in close pursuit, and with resignation, she realized their potential savior was still too far away. They would be boarded soon, slaughtered long before it could arrive.

She took deep breaths, then looked for a weapon. "Gods curse these people," she muttered, rummaging through the endless crates and barrels of fabric and spices, lumber and iron nails. As she prepared to use a long piece of wood as her weapon, she remembered how the sailors from her own people had bound their weapons to the hull itself with nets. In the gloom she felt her way along the swaying ship, hands running over the many objects stored in the same manner. She cried out in surprise and relief as she jabbed something pointed and sharp, then struggled with the ropes and tipped a bundle of short spears at her feet. They were too small and blunt, and perhaps had been made for fishing or whaling, but they would do.

Zaya hummed a low song of war to steady her nerves. She heard hooks scratching against the hull, then clattering as they threw planks and rope and who knew what else to bind their prey. She felt her breaths turning ragged, and rose her voice to sing of Haki the Brave as he fought the giant Omaka. How many times had she sung of the great heroes? How many times had she told the stories of warriors in battle?

Now she knew she must put deeds to words. Perhaps then the goddess Edda might hear, and bring her honor.

Men screamed as metal and wood clanged in the sounds of combat. The door to the hold broke open, the dim light from a clouded sun showed the silhouette of an islander. Zaya roared, and lunged, ramming her spear through the first pirate's gut.

* * *

"More sail!" Eka called from his perch, and Chang motioned at the Pitman to obey. He wasn't much concerned about the handful of marines in the scout. He was *concerned* that when they realized they were under attack, they would have enough sense to start firing their arrows, and if they were lucky, they'd burn down Chang's future ship.

"Damned stupid fool bastards," he muttered to the men at his side.

"Heavy in the water," said the Steerman with a grin.

"Might be a tidy haul, Chiefy," Basko agreed, "if we

play it right, could be just like old times." He grinned, and Chang pushed him towards the masts with a scowl.

"Just do what he bloody says 'till I say otherwise, and don't get killed."

"Aye, Chiefy." Basko went with a chuckle, his mood finer than it had any right to be. But then Scab-eyed Basko always did like a fight.

The Prince barreled down on its target with disturbing speed. The manouevering of the merchant and her pursuer brought their movement to almost nothing, and despite their good sails in the mostly headwind, *The Prince* pursued like a monstrous wolf.

"We're nearly on them, Savage!" the captain called, and for a moment Chang wondered exactly what the hell the barbarian intended. Then his cabin door opened, and the warlord stepped outside. Chang forced his mouth to close.

Gone was the half-naked barbarian, replaced by a metal giant clad in rings of iron from neck to knees. "I will not kill," the giant said low and fierce, as if to himself, his eyes staring out at nothing.

"Spirits." The Steerman muttered as he stared, the rest of the crew gawking in turns. Chang managed to turn away long enough to glare at the fast approaching enemy ship, which was now nearly stationary and half attached to the other vessel with grapples.

"We should slow," he called to anyone who might listen, thinking *you're going to ruin my damn ship!*

The giant blinked and looked at the enemy, then shrugged. "This hull is more iron than wood. *The Prince* does not fear such little things."

Eka looked at Chang, and bloody *grinned*. "Hold course, Chief. That should get their attention."

Chang stood with the other men on the foredeck, for

a moment too stunned to react. *Madmen!* he wanted to shout. *And so stupid to name your ship. Even worse to give it a masculine name to strike the sea-god's ire! Damned stupid fools.*

But he held his tongue, and shook his head. "Rope, lads. Get yourselves bound to the ship. *Move!*"

The men realized their predicament and scrambled to obey, most tying themselves to the masts, a few dashing down to the hold. Chang might have joined them, but he wanted to *see*.

He watched the profile of the scout ship grow and grow, then the gloomy water churn around the fighting ships, cutting aside to permit *The Prince* on her deadly course. Some of the privateers realized they weren't turning and began to shout and cut ropes and raise sail, but all in vain. If he'd had more time, Chang might have prayed to Roa. And if he had more time than that he'd have tried the good spirits and the rice-king's gods, or even the damn sun god of the empire. A good pirate knew anyone who'd spare him would do.

Chang had been on many ships in a ram, on both ends, and could have gone his whole life without another. But such was the way of things. He cringed and held to the mast as the ship struck, and for a few terrible breaths Chang wasn't sure if he'd flown forward or stood still. The screech and crunch of the huge weight coming together became his world, wood splintering and crushing as *The Prince* slowed itself on the corpse of her enemy. Chang coughed from the pressure of the ropes digging into his chest. Whether from fear or instinct, he was soon on his feet with a knife in one hand and a spear in the other, racing towards the doomed scout ship.

"Come on, you bastards!" he roared at any man insane enough to follow. Basko was already at his side and snarling for blood, the Oarmen brothers on his flanks. The Steerman staggered behind kicking off rope and taking aim with a bow, apparently a killer today and not a coward.

Ahead of all, the giant charged, a metal shield in one hand, a strange club in the other, his size and gleaming iron armor making him look like a statue come to life.

The few marines still on their own sinking ship tried to stop them at the edge of the hull. Ruka swiped the first from his feet as if he kicked a rabid dog. Chang ducked behind him for cover from an arrow, then leapt at the closest man and just missed his throat with a spear thrust. He dropped and followed with his knife, sinking the blade deep into the man's side before knocking him back with his knee. Basko caught a spear beside him and tossed it away, matching the strike with his own into a fleeing marine's thigh.

More of the enemy charged back from the merchant vessel, which they'd seemed to already secure. The captain leapt from his perch—an impossible jump that should have broken his legs, instead he rolled and flung two knives that lodged firmly in two sailor's throats. Before Chang had time to gawk, he heard a woman's voice singing words he didn't understand, the sound rhythmic, and harsh, like a marching chant. At the sound of it, the giant went mad.

Ruka roared and smashed smaller men aside, barreling through three without bothering to block their blows. Spear thrusts deflected and bounced from his armor as he crushed a man's arm with his club, swatting another into the sea. A few broke in panic at the sight of him, fleeing mindlessly to the far side of the ship.

For a moment Chang felt in a dream, wondering how the hell he was even here on this bizarre creation, with these insane men. But he supposed it made as much sense as anything.

"Stay with the barbarian!" he called to the others, then leapt forward and stabbed a man too distracted with the giant to fight back.

At first he had hoped neither the captain nor the pilot would survive the encounter. But watching them fight, in the midst of chaos and a mortal struggle Chang didn't even understand, he knew it wasn't possible. He followed, his sense of survival loud and trusty as always, telling him the truth, no matter what he wanted. Today the truth was this: behind the giant was the only safe place to stand.

* * *

Zaya stood in the dark at the foot of the stairs, and breathed. One of the marines had bounced a throwing knife off her scalp, and she felt blood dripping down her ear and shoulder. His corpse lay at her feet. Another pirate huddled in the corner, his hands covering exposed guts.

Zaya wasn't much of a warrior in the land of ash. Women didn't duel like the men, and her mother was far better, all her sisters had more interest and skill with both bow and spear. But it seemed these islanders were untrained. They had attacked, though trapped in a narrow passage, against an opponent with superior reach, while trying to descend stairs. So she had stabbed and skewered and let the men tumble. It seemed the only reasonable thing to do.

"Get inside! Get down there!" yelled another foolish voice from above. Zaya could hardly believe their stupidity, but as she prepared for another kill a group of the islanders pushed frantically at the man at the top, and several fell clustered down the drop. Zaya cried out and stabbed the first, but the reckless charge knocked her from her feet, crashing her into the barrels.

Her ears rung and her head throbbed from striking something hard. She'd lost her spear, but couldn't see well enough to try and find it. She stood with a hand on one of the crates, then screamed as a man gripped her wrist and slashed a knife just short of her face. His eyes were panicked, terrified, like an animal caught in a trap. She kicked the crate and knocked out his legs as she pulled away and reached for the knife under her shirt. At least five of the pirates stood in the hold now. She backed away watching them, knife raised and mouth twisted in a sneer.

Whatever fear she'd felt was gone. There was only now, only the next man, the next deed, and Zaya's heart sung with the knowing at last what it meant to be a warrior in the legends. She only wished she could have known and lived.

"Guard the stairs," one of the pirates growled, and two others groaned and stood at the bottom. He clutched a hand to the shallow wound in his side, and met Zaya's eyes. "You're going to pay for that, you bitch."

Zaya lunged, and smiled as the man pulled back.

"Come die, coward," she hissed in the island tongue. "Tonight you burn with the mountain god."

The man's surprise buried quickly beneath his rage. He tossed aside a barrel and came on, knife dancing back and forth in a clearly practiced grasp. *Watch the arm*, Zaya heard her mother's voice. *The blade follows the arm. Don't be distracted by the blade.*

The pirate attacked, and Zaya met it. She caught his wrist and held it, stabbing down with her own but just scraping the top of his shoulder as he dropped it away. She pulled back for another stab but the pirate lunged and bashed his head into her chin. She stumbled but kept her feet, feeling more blood dripping from her lips. "I'll kill you," the pirate glared with hate-filled eyes. "I'll fucking kill you."

Zaya felt light-headed as the fear returned. He was shorter, but very strong. Catching the knife had been lucky. He was too fast and too confident and she needed her spear, or a distraction, anything to keep him away.

Both their eyes turned as something huge struck the pirates at the stairs. An armored giant leapt into them, ignoring their blades as he clattered across the hold with a man grasped in each iron fist. Zaya needed no further sign from the gods.

She charged silently for her enemy, plunging her knife deep into his chest before he grabbed her and spun her to the floor, roaring in rage. They grunted and fought over the blades, twisting and pulling, clawing and thrashing with their legs.

The pirate won.

With a cry of triumph he pulled the knife from Zaya's grip, struck her across the face with his hand, and drove the knife towards her heart.

Before he could finish, a fist seized his hair and pulled him away, his blade waving in panic at whatever attacked him.

Another island pirate stood at his back, and unceremoniously slashed his throat. This new pirate tossed him aside and sniffed as if bored. He was thick and dark, with shaved stubble like cut wheat over his face and scalp. He met Zaya's eyes, and smiled.

"You have a beautiful voice," he said, his own dark baritone made of smoke.

Then the giant was standing over them both, and the pirate held up his hands in a sign of peace as he stepped away. "She's alright," he said. "Calm, mighty pilot."

Zaya blinked in the gloom of the hold, seeing spots in her vision from maybe the pain or maybe the terror. She looked up at the giant hoping it was one of her people—somehow a great warrior of the Ascom, miraculously here, to rescue her in her moment of need. She stared at the giant's golden eyes and blinked because, like any in the Ascom, she knew them.

There was only one warrior—only one man in the Ascom who could see in the dark with the sight of a wolf. It was the prophet of Noss. The Godtongue. The man who Zaya's father had served longer than she had been alive, who had taken her people across an endless sea to paradise, won a war against an empire, then just as strangely, disappeared.

She knew then it must be the imaginings of a panicked mind, and stopped fighting the dark spots that had all but swallowed her vision. She heard her blade rattle against the wood beneath her, and accepted oblivion.

Chapter 4

Zaya dreamed of music and a perfect hearth fire. She sat next to her brothers and sisters while her father sang and played his lyre, and her mother swayed at her side. The roof creaked with heavy snow, but their home was still warm, and safe. Her mother's swaying grew stronger and stronger until Zaya became annoyed and pulled away. When she looked, however, it was not her mother she found, but the golden eyes of the prophet, staring from a dark hallway.

She jerked upright and woke from her dream in a long cot that stunk of sweat. Her body pulsed with pain, rippling up and down her arms and ending in her head. She heard a woman moan and realized it was her, then closed her eyes to steady a dizzy wave.

"Slowly, *Macha*," said the voice made of smoke. "Your countryman comes. He is very clever, but even more ugly. Prepare your beautiful eyes."

Zaya risked a squint to find the pirate who'd saved her standing in the cabin. His dark eyes matched the smile on his lips, but faded as heavy footsteps appeared behind him.

"Move."

The deep voice swept the pirate aside, and Zaya almost gasped as the Godtongue filled her view.

"It's really you," she mumbled, then nearly wept in relief. She hadn't dared to believe. There could be no doubt now—the gods, fate itself had brought her here.

"Lay back and stop moving." The shaman knelt at her bed and scanned her with his strange gaze, speaking in the tongue of their homeland. He had removed his armor, and was dressed much like the island sailors.

His shirt was open and his chest bore many more scars than Zaya remembered when she'd seen him in the capital. Even his face seemed as if it had healed from terrible burns. "Your wounds are superficial," he said, removing a glass jar of oily paste from his pocket before slathering it over her scalp. "You will heal quickly if you do as I say."

Zaya smiled and nodded, a great burden lifting from her shoulders as she closed her eyes.

"What madness brought you to that ship." The shaman's voice soured and he whispered so only she could hear. "Does your mother know you are alone on the sea?"

"I…" Zaya was surprised to hear the shaman speak like a nursemaid. "I go where I will. I wished to see the new world."

"And your parents?"

"Didn't want to leave Orhus."

She opened her eyes to see his frown. "Your place is with them."

"My place?" Zaya sat up, feeling a bit of blood rise to her face. "Was it not the great son of Beyla, who sailed into an endless sea on little more than a raft? I came through known waters on a proper ship, and you call *me* reckless?"

"Call me Ruka, that is my name." The shaman sighed and wrapped a piece of white cloth around Zaya's head. He met her eyes, which was not common for men to do in their culture. "If we had not come as we did, Zaya, you would be dead now. And your father's heart would be broken."

"But you did." Zaya took a calming breath and put a hand over Ruka's. "This is not mere chance. My father was your skald for decades, and now here, in a wide sea, you find his daughter in need? I don't think so. The gods brought us together. Nothing could be clearer."

Ruka snorted. "Such arrogance. Am I not the Godtongue? If the gods had such a plan, would I not be the one to know?"

"Perhaps you've been ignoring them in your… absence." Zaya said with more anger than she'd intended. "Perhaps they sent me to remind you."

Ruka rose and gestured to the man at the door, switching to the island tongue. "Stubborn child. This is Chang. Call, and he and his men will attend you, with the utmost respect and care." The way he said this seemed directed more at the *pirate* than at Zaya. "I will guide us to the coast."

"What coast? Where are we going?"

"You are going to the colonies. And then *we* are sailing West."

"I'm coming with you."

Ruka shook his head. "I will not reward your father's service by taking his daughter to her death."

Zaya kicked off the thin blanket and stood on trembling legs, taking a stride towards the Godtongue. He frowned and lifted his arms as if prepared to catch her, but stayed where he was. Zaya fought a wave of nausea and stood until she'd steadied against the swaying of the waves.

"I am a daughter of ash," she said as she gulped saliva. "I don't need your permission, nor my father's, or anyone's else's. Edda hear my words, the gods brought me here to bear witness. Now tell me where we're going." Zaya felt lightheaded and for a moment could hardly believe she was lecturing the prophet of Noss. He smiled with what she thought was more contempt than warmth, but turned away.

"As you say, *daughter of ash*. Eat, and rest. The man who died to save you had no name, for these islanders are superstitious, and fear their sea gods will find them. But he was a young, competent sailor, and fought bravely." At this she thought she saw the silent pirate's eyes flicker with emotion, and stay on the shaman in surprise. "You replace a man whose life was at sea and could perform many tasks. You will be expected to do the same." Ruka stopped at the door and looked at her again. "Where we *go* is once again an endless sea, ready to swallow our little raft. You may find the stories more enjoyable than the truth. Perhaps later you will remember this moment. When you do, know that it was *you* who chose, not the gods. It was always you."

Zaya waited until he'd left, standing proudly for as long as she dared before collapsing to her bed.

* * *

Chang waited patiently for the angry giant to leave. His hands fiddled with a bundle of feminine clothes, then left them alone when he realized. Save for this foreigner, he had not even *seen* a woman in two years. Women were rarely reckless or desperate enough to choose life on a ship, and often unwelcome in any case. Alas the same was true of prisons.

With his best and most disarming smile, he stepped deeper into the young woman's cabin holding an armful of her things. Despite the puffed lip, the soiled and disheveled clothes and bandages, she was unassailably beautiful. Her light hair and skin, her pale green eyes, all were most exotic in the isles. Her curves, on the other hand, were most familiarly welcome, and Chang was pleased for any opportunity just to look at her.

"Out!" came her melodic voice, too light and pretty to be harsh. "Out and to hell with all of you!"

"Aye, *Macha,*" he soothed. "But first I have your things from the ship. I thought you might like them."

The girl's eyed widened as if galled to be disobeyed. She turned and scanned Chang from feet to face before her eyes lingered on her belongings.

"I could not be sure, of course," Chang shrugged and stepped closer, placing the bundle on a chair. "It could be the marines who wore this." He lifted a long, cloth dress, then withdrew what he assumed was the barbarians small clothes, and waggled his brow. The girl finally grinned, but banished it as she snatched the clothes from his hands.

"Thank you." She turned away, running a callused hand over the wooden instrument Chang had saved from a rotting crate. She turned back and met his eyes, frowning almost shyly when he didn't look away. "My name is Zaya, not *Macha.*"

"No, no, you must not use your name, dear girl, for one day Roa will hear, and take you down to the sea. Only good Chang and his trusty First Mate Basko are protected." Chang sighed then smiled for the girl. "*Macha* are sea-spirits, beautiful and terrible. They are fierce she-beasts who drown men in the sea when they are angry." When she blushed he gestured at the instrument. "You play this? You sing?"

She nodded and he rubbed his hands together as if in anticipation. "I too am a teller of stories, a singer of songs." Here he shrugged. "Admittedly, my audience… they applaud like children at most anything."

The girl smiled but to Chang it seemed mere politeness. He bowed and withdrew. "Rest, *Macha.* If you are in need, sing your siren's call. As before, I will come running."

He closed the door without glancing back, then chided himself. He was rusty, no question, and would have to do better. With a sigh he put the pleasant distraction of the girl from his mind and turned for his crew. Already he had failed and lost a man. Now there was one more dead brother from a once strong pack of twenty free men on two ships, picked down to ten slaves, now down to nine. Chang did not blame the girl for the young Swabbie, whose real name was Afa though none of the men ever used it. No. He blamed his 'captain', and the strange giant. And though they frightened him and did not seem evil men so much as careless with his crew's lives—one day, perhaps soon, they would pay most dearly.

Several days passed with a peaceful sea. The incredible *Prince* caught fine winds in her sails and flew like a sicklebell, past the ends of the Tong and the colonies of the Southerners, around the horn of the peninsula men called the last civilized lands to the West, before the long, jungle beaches that followed. There they stopped and bought supplies at the only remaining port, nearly as West now as West went before the Dark Sea, where only gods and spirits lurked to take men to the depths.

Every day Chang brought Zaya her meals and apologized for the meagerness of sailor fare. Every day she shook her head and said her people ate very plainly.

"How do you come to speak our language so well?" he asked on the third, lingering at the door.

"My father taught me," she answered. "He and the shaman came to these isles many years ago."

Chang bowed. "They have my thanks. To hear your voice speak my people's words is most appealing."

"Is it common for your men to speak to women like this?"

"Like what, *Macha*? To compliment?"

"Yes." The girl winced but Chang thought the discomfort only temporary.

"You are a beautiful woman, *Macha*. And like all women you make a plain, ugly world a little brighter. Why should I not say so?"

Zaya put down her barrel-lid plate and released a breath.

"A man of ash who wants a woman…he would boast of himself, of his deeds. In that way he lets a woman decide if he is worthy."

Chang grinned and put a hand to his chin. "Then I must tell you, it is well known I am one of the richest, most dangerous, most successful pirates in the entire world."

The girl expertly hid a smile, and raised her brow.

"Like the men who attacked me?"

"No, *Macha*! Those were mere brutes and servants. I am a free man who lives by my wits, no need or desire for laws or kings."

"Ah," the girl's face soured, though it held a subtle humor. "We have a name for such men in the land of ash. You are a chiefless bandit."

"Is it customary to interrupt a man's boasting?" Chang raised his voice in mock offence, and the girl smiled and gestured for him to continue. He cleared his throat. "I have killed a hundred men with my own hands; I have outwitted admirals and storms and traveled a thousand ri in every direction."

At this Zaya lifted her plate and took another bite of rice before she shrugged. "Where I am from, lies are judged by the goddess of words. Any man who utters them are cast down to burn with the god of the deep mountain."

Chang nodded and stepped closer with his warmest

smile. "Then I am fortunate. Here in the isles, the gods never listen."

The humor in Zaya's exotic eyes reached further down her face as she smiled. Chang considered something as bold as sitting beside her and touching her hair or hand before a voice from nowhere snorted in disapproval. Chang jumped and turned to find Captain Eka watching him with those deep, treacherous eyes.

"Good morning, Zaya."

The girl rose and bowed with a grunt of pain. "Good morning, Captain."

"Ruka tells me you'll be joining us." He pointed to the shore. "That is the last scrap of land on the coast. If you've changed your mind, you've one more chance." His eyes turned and bore deep into Chang's, as if he were not truly speaking to the young musician.

"I go where the shaman goes, Captain," the girl said bravely. Chang smiled politely and said nothing. The captain continued to watch him, then turned away without another word. Chang waited several strides before he called after him.

"On that point, Captain, I've been wondering—where exactly *does* the good pilot go? My nose tells me there is a storm coming from the West. Perhaps we should wait on the coast."

Eka looked out at the sky as if without a care in the world, though already it swelled with dark clouds.

"We won't be stopping anymore, Chief," he said. "Were I you, I'd make sure the girl learns how to secure herself. If she goes overboard, the pilot may throw us both in to get her. He's not much of a swimmer."

"As you say, Captain." Chang bowed, then turned to the girl to find her eyes hiding fear. When the captain had gone, he whispered. "Not to worry, *Macha*. Chang is very good with rope." He then waggled his eyebrows,

but by her blank expression, she had missed his joke
entirely.

Chapter 5

As the captain promised, they sailed straight into the storm. Zaya went with the increasingly agitated Chang, who told her to wait while he spoke with his men in the hold. She listened at the top of the stairs, and heard muttering about madness and bad luck and an ill-fated journey without a sacrifice. "There's a woman aboard!" rasped a voice. "And the damned pilot's a monster himself."

Chang soothed all. His smoky voice rose and fell and made promises and assurances, and soon they came from the hold with fake smiles and bows. Chang clapped her on the arm like a man as he pointed to the mast.

"Alright, *Macha*. Let us see what you know."

She followed and did her best, but they both quickly learned the answer. Chang smiled politely at her fifth failure to tie a simple knot.

"So," he said, "you are very green."

"Yes," she admitted, feeling blood heat her face. "I've never lived on the sea." She wanted to explain that her parents were wealthy and that she'd never had to do much save for her music and around the house. "But I can cook and clean," she added, rather lamely, which did not help with the blush.

Chang's swarthy smile matched the glimmer in his eye. "Not to fear, *Macha*. I will teach you many things."

As usual she detected the lewd undertone and ignored it. The man was handsome—in a dirty scoundrel sort of way. But he was too confident and aggressive by far, and nearly his every word and gesture made her uncomfortable. She suspected if he ever touched her the way he spoke to her, she'd break his nose as soon as smile.

"The Captain says you must replace our Swabbie, and so you must. On a ship, the captain is God, neh? You're a mate now, responsible for many things, and I am your chief. The captain orders me, and I order you. When you are given orders, this is not the time to ask questions, it is the time to obey. You hear your chief, you act. Understand?"

Zaya nodded, and Chang smiled.

"Much happens on a ship and things must be clear. You say 'aye, chief', or 'ka, chief'."

"Aye, chief," Zaya said, feeling silly.

"Very good. We'll make a sailor of you, have no fear. But not today. Today this is yours." Chang lifted a bucket from a cluster beside the mast. He stepped beside her and looped a rope around her waist, knotting it several times with such speed Zaya couldn't even follow with her eyes. He tied the other end to the mast and gestured to the hold. "When the rain comes, *Macha*, you take your bucket, you scoop the water, and fling it from the side. You do this until your chief tells you to stop, but you move careful. You stay near the wall, always. It will be slippery, and dark, and the deck will angle back and forth, understand?"

"Aye, chief," Zaya said, hoping she kept the tremble from her voice.

Chang nodded and stepped away, barking at another man in an almost gibberish version of the island tongue, too accented and quick for Zaya to follow. She stood there feeling ridiculous, holding her bucket and watching the darkness grow.

She watched Ruka as he tied several barrels to the masts beneath the sails, then stood at the front of the ship, ignoring the scrambling of the crew. He had hardly

40

spoken to her, or anyone, since she'd joined the ship. Dark bruises had formed under his eyes, as if he had hardly slept since the day he rescued her. The Captain, Eka, stood near him, stealing glances at both Ruka and the crew.

As she watched them, Zaya began to feel entirely out of place. The sailors were moving faster now, taking down sail and stowing everything with rope or tucking into nets or down into the hold. She wanted to help but felt she'd only be in the way. She stood with her bucket, questioning her own story of finding this ship and whether it was fate or just dumb luck and no closer to the truth of the epic tales.

The first drops of rain felt cool in the warm wind. The sailors seemed to stop together without a word, all eyes turned to the sky as if reading a book Zaya couldn't understand. It grew dark, then darker still as the rain fell fast and hard. Lightning flashed in the distance, revealing a swollen sea like a moving desert of black dunes. As she watched it in terror, Zaya felt further from home than she had ever been, lodged in a dream world that only existed when the lightning fell. Soon there was only the sound of the wind and the waves.

Chang's voice woke her from her reverie. Whether it had been a few heartbeats or half the night, she did not know.

"Start bailing!" his rasping shout covered the ship. Zaya closed her hands around the iron loop on her bucket. She followed the wall down below, soon sloshing water with her boots and finding men doing the same. She scooped with her pail, which was heavier than she expected, then tromped up the stairs, following the swaying deck with her shoulder against the wall of the cabin. With a grunting heave, she tossed it overboard, then turned back to do it again.

Every lumbering, awkward trek down and up was

difficult. Soon she had thrown five, then ten, then she slipped and fell hard to the deck and lost count. Once or twice she heard Chang's voice to hurry up and she cried out 'aye, chief', but moved no faster. She heard him call others by their made-up names but never hers, so she carried on. Her arms began to tremble at the weight, her fingers slipping on the slick wood, once or twice spilling the water on the deck with a cry, only to turn back and try again.

Her legs went next, cramping and threatening to fail her on the stairs, then on the moving deck. She tripped twice over her rope. She bashed headlong into one of the crew, and was shouldered away many times in the dark. Sometimes she had to lean against the wall and rest, nearly weeping from exhaustion. But she remembered Chang's words. She stayed on the wall, she watched her feet. She took smaller amounts of water but she didn't stop. She never stopped.

Later, much later, there was light. Chang's voice rose with the dawn, like a bird of paradise greeting the sun.

"All hands rest," he shouted, his voice hoarse but strong. Zaya slumped against the wood that had meant life. She held her bucket in numb fingers as she squinted at the sky, and slept where she lay.

* * *

"You did well, *Macha*," said Zaya's father by their hearth.

He gave his warm, black bearded smile, but his voice was wrong as he stroked her forehead with a callused thumb. "Roa swam, spirits curse him. But he didn't find us. Not today."

She smiled, and slept, and later she heard him hum and sing, but his voice was mist in cool night air, and she fought the heavy lids of her eyes.

When she woke it was in a cabin, her legs covered with a cloth blanket. Watery rum and some salted pork lay beside her in bowls, and she took eagerly to both. Her raw hands trembled on the cup, the strength in her fingers nearly gone. She realized the singing from her dream had not ended.

Men's voices sang in harmony, and she stood with a groan on aching, feet, her back lancing with pain. She opened her door and found Chang beside it in a wicker chair, the crew awake and working. Some cleaned and scrubbed, others sealed off barrels set out in the rain, or picked scattered supplies and bailed water. Others fussed over the sails, or sat at the edges of the hull with oars. Chang sat and watched all, singing a rythmic sort of chant that the men answered, back and forth.

'We'll row-y-o.'

'*No carry me below!*'

'We'll row-y-o.'

'*No carry me below!*'

'We'll row-y-o!

'*No carry me below!*'

'Then we'll all hang down the line!'

Zaya leaned against the cabin as she listened and watched them work shirtless in the sun. Chang smiled when he saw her, clapping a man on the back before he leapt up the deck and took Zaya's arm.

"Good morning, *Macha*. No time for idleness, there's work to be done."

She nodded though her body sagged in horror, and the man Chang had tapped sang in a strong, practiced voice, in his place, answered as one again by the crew.

'We'll be *all*-right.'

'If we make it round the isles!'

'We'll be *all*-right.'

'If we make it 'round the isles!'

'We'll be *all*-right!'

'If we make it 'round the isles!'

'Till we all hang down the line!'

Chang took her to the furthest edge of the deck where a pile of rope seemed laid out for practice. As the men sang he showed her a 'bowline' knot, and a 'figure eight', and a cleat and a clove, an anchor and a square. He showed her where to tie off in a hurry, where the water left the deck and how to open or close it, until Zaya's head spun and he left her to tie her own knots.

All day the islanders sang and worked. It was as if the long night and storm hadn't phased nor slowed them, as if their hands and bodies were made of stone. They slept in turns, and ate in turns, never leaving the ship with less than a handful of working men.

Zaya collapsed much earlier in her bunk to rest to the sound of their voices, then woke to them. Again Chang left her food and water and she found him outside her door, grinning as he saw her.

"I receive special treatment," she said awkwardly, and the pirate chief shrugged.

"You *are* special, *Macha*. Not to worry. All are born on land, save for your loyal chief, whose mother was a sea snake. But we'll make a sailor of you yet."

Zaya nodded, then followed him to her hated pile of rope, beginning again with fumbling hands. When Chang left she looked out on the empty sea, blue now and a perfect line in all directions, no trace of the night's violence, or a single speck of land. She hummed as the men sang, too shy yet to raise her voice with theirs.

She worked all day and nearly cheered as her hands tied her first bowline correctly twice in a row. Though she was weak she could still manage, and felt a warmth at the beginnings of competence.

"Very good," said Chang from behind her, as if he'd sensed the moment of success, before wandering off to some other man to bark orders.

Zaya kept at it, sometimes humming or adding her own words to the simple but beautiful verses of the sailor's songs. She tied a hundred knots and for a long time didn't think of where they were going or why, nor of her family or her mother's disapproval.

Much later, Chang came and sat beside her and smiled without words, gesturing at the horizon. Together they watched the sun set, and Zaya saw the orange light consume the world, spilled like paint across an endless blue canvas, reflected in a mirrored sky. She felt as if she floated, alone but not lonely, lost in something true and beautiful and so much greater than her. Next to it, her own desires and problems, hopes and fears, felt suddenly insignificant. Almost silly.

"You see it." Chang's dark eyes were glazed as if with a drug, his face angled as if he heard music on the waves.

"Yes," said Zaya, because she did, and Chang nodded and smiled with his thick lips.

"As I said," he sighed, "we'll make a sailor of you yet." With that he rose and tossed the last bit of rum from his cup to the sea. "For Roa," he winked, then turned away, humming as he went below, leaving Zaya alone with the night, and the sea.

Chapter 6

A beast roared as the sun fell.

Zaya flinched on the rail, ripped from her peaceful reverie and the beauty of the open sea. She waited, trying to understand, or hear it again, but there was no new sounds from the water, and she couldn't tell where the noise had come from, or even how close it was. Then it roared again.

The sound was deep, beastial, a half painful moan, half challenging shout. And it was close, not even in the water. It was on the ship.

Zaya turned to see several of the crew awake and panicking on the deck. They spun back and forth, wide eyes staring at the Eastern cabin, then at each other, seeking *anyone* who had an answer. Zaya stepped closer, a fearful sweat prickling her skin in the warm night air.

"What from the hells...?" Chang came roaring shirtless from below. The men calmed in his presence, in turns pointing at Ruka's cabin at the far side of the ship. Zaya was almost glad for the distraction as her eyes roamed Chang's dark and scar-slathered skin. A series of lighter colored lines crossed his back, framing thick muscle like the grooves of a brick wall. She blinked as the roar sounded again, this time followed by a crash as the cabin wall shook.

The captain was suddenly before the door and facing the crew, his hands raised for calm.

"A nightmare, gentlemen. Go back to your rest. There's nothing to fear."

Another crash split the night, and even the captain flinched as wood splintered from the side of the cabin.

"Spirits preserve us," said one of the men, some kind of charm held tight in his fist as he stepped away. Chang stared hard at the captain.

"What's wrong with him? What *is* he? Dear gods that *voice*!"

As if on cue, a roar again shattered the still night. This time the cabin door burst from its hinge, and half the crew cried out and fled as Ruka staggered from his room. He dropped to a knee before the assembled crew, shirtless, huge yet lean body of muscled bone angled like a beast on the hunt, hands covering his face.

Behind him, flickering in the moonlight, a shadow loomed. Great black wings seemed to sprout from its back, skeletal arms extended with jagged claws. It was darker than the night save for two red spots that must have been eyes, leaking smoke like chimneys.

Ruka's face contorted. His body heaved as he clutched at his sides, until at last he looked at the men and opened his mouth, eyes wide in fear, speaking a single word in an almost whispering rasp.

"Run."

* * *

"Down to the hold! *Now!*" Chang grabbed Old Mata and pushed him ahead, then spun and looked for Zaya. She still held her rope at the edge of the rail, gawking with the rest at the giant. *"Go!"* he seized her arm and yanked her towards the hold, which seemed to knock her to her senses.

His men were scattering across the deck in panic but rallied at his voice. Chang left Zaya at the stairs and tried not to look back, but couldn't stop himself. He glanced again at the barbarian pilot, who grasped at his own flesh as if trying to contain something within.

"Go you damned fool gawking bastards!" Chang pushed more men below as they reached him, still unable to look away. The captain was circling the giant pilot with a blade tucked against his forearm.

"Ruka?" he called calmly above the din. "Tell me what to do."

Then it was only Chang, Eka and apparently Zaya, all standing on the deck with the monster. The rest of the crew jammed themselves below, hopefully trying to seal the entrance with crates and oars.

"Damnit, Macha," Chang said, not sure why he himself hadn't run down screaming. Her jaw was clenched and apparently she'd found a spear.

"I have to see."

Ruka's groans continued, a deep, inhuman sound that bellowed like a dozen beasts locked in mortal peril. Chang pulled the knife from his belt and stepped forward, locking eyes with Eka. The captain shook his head but shrugged at the same time.

Finally the roaring ended. Ruka rose looking sick and even paler than usual.

"I think it's over," he mumbled, swaying on his feet.

His shadow seemed to disagree. It *stepped* from the cabin wall, nearly the size of the giant, emerging from the man like darkness made flesh. A small golden chain bound its ankle to the pilot, the metal glowing as if hot, disappearing into the pilot with a ghostly pallor. The creature snarled and dashed forward, clawed feet clattering across the hull as it charged straight at Eka.

Zaya acted first. With two long strides she met the creature just as Eka leapt from its path and struck. The metal tip pierced its body, and an acrid stench filled Chang's nostrils. The nightmarish creature howled and snapped the spear shaft as if it were a toy, turning on

Zaya before Eka's knife plunged deep into its back. With a howl of rage, the creature spun and slashed its claws, black blood oozing from its wounds, but the captain leapt away.

Chang rushed to Zaya's side though he knew this was all madness. He thrust his knife into the shadow, and it swiped a gangly arm without looking. He fell back just avoiding the frightening claws.

Finally, Ruka seemed to blink awake, and rise. He was unarmed, but he grabbed the creature's head in his huge hands and wrestled it to the deck. Zaya seized the broken piece of her spear and attacked again, ramming it into the creature's leg. Chang followed, slicing and spraying the wretched blood in arcs across the deck.

The shadow roared in fury, trying to push Ruka away, long arms waving fumbling slashes that once or twice raked his back with shallow cuts.

"*Kill it*!" Eka was stabbing with abandon, Zaya and Chang attempting to do the same, though every wound seemed to accomplish little more than spill more darkness over their arms.

The giant pilot pulled his 'shadow' close—foolishly close, considering the creature's row of sharpened teeth. Chang feared the creature would rip a chunk from his face with its teeth, but Ruka bit *it* instead. He lunged for the creature's throat, chomping and rending the shadow as they both tumbled to the deck. Chang stepped away and pulled Zaya with him, feeling his arms burning slightly from the oil-slick blood. The shadow thrashed, and stilled, and soon all that remained was the sound of Ruka's chewing.

When it was over, the pilot panted and looked up at the moonlit sky. Darkness dripped down his jaw like blackened blood, and Chang stood with the others in silence, too horrified and confused to speak. For a moment Chang thought it might be best to take his knife and plunge it into the man's heart.

"You can't kill me," the giant breathed, as if he'd read Chang's mind. "There's more, much more. They will escape if I die."

Eka nodded and clenched his jaw, putting his knife away. *"They*, Savage? Is this why we're on this ship," he said, his voice tight. "To keep...*this*, away from the continent?"

"No." Ruka spit darkness as he shook his head. "I didn't know. It must have been...I killed a...spirit, near your monastery. A boy that was not a boy, worshiped as a god. The flesh perished, the spirit remained."

Chang cleaned the filth off his knife with an angry tug, having no idea what they were talking about. He'd have thought them mad were it not for a dead shadow at his feet, and he glanced at Zaya, feeling his anger build now that the danger seemed passed.

"I didn't agree to this," he felt his voice rising with every word. "You didn't say we'd be trapped with a *monster*. On the sea! With nowhere to go!"

"Then we'd best find land." The giant stood, his face still grotesquely stained with the black blood of the creature. He lifted the corpse and staggered to the rail as if to throw it overboard, but it crumbled to dust and vanished in his hands.

The captain watched with hard eyes, then frowned, turning them on Chang.

"You didn't *agree* to anything, pirate. I scooped you from a hellhole where you'd have been executed if you were lucky, left to starve if you weren't. So let me make the situation clear: you and your men serve me, or you die. That is the bargain."

With that he turned towards his cabin, then called over his shoulder. "And get those trembling fools up here. I want that deck cleaned before morning."

Chang's arm burned both with the monster's blood, and the need to kill the bastard. But he had not survived the unfairness of his life by being stupid, so he saluted as a good marine would to his worthy captain, and turned towards the hold.

Before the dawn, Chang sat with his brothers below drinking rum.

"We could tie 'em up," said Basko. "Kill the captain, tie the monster, then sail all the way back to the continent."

"Aye," said the Pitman and most of the others. Though the Steerman rolled his eyes.

"Don't need to bloody tie 'em up. We just dump 'em in the sea, and let him drown."

"I bet it's a clever lie anyway," said an Oarman. *"Course* he says we can't kill him. That's what I'd say! We should just cut his throat and toss 'em in the sea, like the Steerman says."

A few eyes turned to Chang, who sat silent at the table drinking.

"Ain't right," said the Boatswain. "He's a demon. A godless monster. He'll be the death of us if we don't do something, Chief."

Chang snorted and drank his rum.

"What the hell do you know of it," he said as he stood, casting his gaze over the crew. He held up his arms, which had burned red from the creature's blood, though he'd doused them a hundred times in sea water. "That thing came from a shadow. It came from *him*!" he pointed up the stairs. "Who will be the man to cut his throat? Aye? You Basko? You?" He shook his head and sat. "I watched that man hold a demon with his bare hands. He bit out its damn throat and spit its blood in the sea. Blood that almost burned my flesh from my bones, and yet where is he? Sitting up there. Alive. So sit down, and don't be fools."

"True," said Old Mata, eyes on a port hole, staring out into the dark.

The men quieted after that.

"We wait," said Chang nice and slow. "We do our jobs, we survive the sea. When we get our chance, when *I* say, we take it. Not before. Now go to your bunks."

The men had been sullen, but they'd gone. When he was alone, Chang walked the deck and stood in the cool breeze to burn off the rum.

"Why me," he said to the cursed gods and the evil spirits, which before tonight he had believed in but not as much as he believed in foul weather and squalls. Now it seemed evil spirits truly lived in men and emerged from shadows, and the world reformed before Chang's eyes.

"You were very brave," said Zaya's voice behind him, and though he knew it was her his hand went for his knife before he could blink.

"I'm sorry." She half-turned away. "I didn't mean to startle you."

"No trouble, Macha." He let her see the man instead of the pirate. "Come and join me. The night is fine."

She came and stood beside him, but neither spoke for a time.

"The captain...," she said with caution, though he didn't know why. "He said you were in prison. To be executed? For what crimes?"

Chang snorted, feeling the man try to run, try to hide. "My life is a crime, Macha. I was born beneath the tattered banner of a toppled king. And so I was a boy with no family and no home. I was a slave, until one day other kings who were not mine said I was a pirate. I suppose I am."

He felt bitterness he had long buried enter his words, but couldn't stop it. She didn't seem to know what to say, and Chang regretted speaking so honestly. Better, as ever, to joke and speak of the now. Women did not want to hear of a young man's terror—that he had been forced to steal and kill and lie or else he would have been used and slaughtered, another bloated corpse beneath the waves.

"You sent your men below, but you stayed," she said after a time.

"They are my men." Chang shrugged.

"But why did you stay?"

"Curiosity, maybe. Who knows such things."

They said no more for awhile, and Chang felt a rare compulsion to silence.

"I overheard you. You and your men," Zaya said, and the skin on Chang's neck prickled. "You mustn't try. You can't kill him. Ruka, I mean. He has killed kings, Chang, and stopped armies. He's a legend, a man of the book. I'm a storyteller, and I know this is not how his story ends."

Chang snorted and shook his head, hating the pirate thoughts that told him to kill her and dump her for the waves. "I wouldn't try, Macha. I know you're right. Somehow, yes I know. Anyway, I think I like him. I prefer to kill men I dislike."

She nodded, and for the first time Chang realized her hand was stiff in her shirt, perhaps holding a knife. "And the captain, what about him?"

"Oh, the captain I could kill. Several times, and sleep soundly. With a happy smile."

He turned to see Zaya matched his look, and they both grinned.

"I prefer you like this," she said.

"Like what, Macha?"

"Honest, maybe. Less sure. You should get some sleep. Perhaps tomorrow we'll have to kill another shadow."

Chang bowed his head in the island way. "You are a strange woman, Macha. But enjoy this Chang while he lasts, for each dawn I am renewed. Tomorrow, I will be twice as sure, and half as honest."

She smiled and showed her teeth, the sight as beautiful as any sea-stretched dawn. "I thought you pirates didn't use names."

"As in so many things, I am different. Roa need not find me, beautiful girl, he and I have an understanding. He always knows where I am."

"As you say," the girl's brow quirked before she turned. "Goodnight, *Chiefy*, or *Lucky*, or whoever you really are."

A slave, he thought but did not say, *a wounded reed in the wind, trying only not to break.*

"Goodnight, Macha." He returned the smile.

She went to her cabin, and Chang to his bunk. He lay amongst his brothers and flinched at the raw skin still burned by the shadow's blood, and failed to sleep. He doused even the hint of a life of memories better left buried, holding to the sounds of the water and the sway of the ship. "One more day," he whispered to Roa, who owned his body and soul, and would one day collect. And though he had told Zaya the dawn would renew him, when he closed his eyes, as ever, he was never entirely sure.

Chapter 7

Chang woke before the sun with a drop of rum. He felt his way to the mess, where he found both oarsmen eating salted eggs in silence, eyes downcast and despondent.

"And a bloody good morning to you, too," he said loudly.

"Morning, chief," they muttered and blinked but didn't rouse.

"Where's the Boatswain? And why isn't the sail raised? I sense a breeze."

They said nothing and for now Chang let it go.

"Well go and bloody get them," he kicked one of the men's chairs, then hauled himself up to the deck and examined the masts for cracks. There was still black stains from the fight with the shadow on the deck, but worse, it was damn near empty. There should have been five men working but Chang saw only two. He winced to cover the anger but soon saw Ruka fiddling with one of his contraptions in the sun and understood. The pilot's eyes were tired but otherwise he seemed for all the world as if he hadn't been spewing monsters the night before. Chang saw only one thing to do.

"Morning, Pilot. How are we feeling today?"

The giant looked up and seemed to search for insult, then shrugged.

"Today the captain says we fish." He raised his contraption as if this were related, and Chang nodded happily.

"A fine plan. I'll have the men fetch nets and take turns."

"Only the nets," Ruka said as he stood. "We will

trawl. The winches should do the rest."

Again Chang smiled as if he understood. "As you say, pilot."

Ruka grunted, and Chang walked back down to the hold, whistling as he took two steps at a time. At the bottom, he looked up to find nearly the entirety of the crew waiting in a cluster. He stopped whistling and met the eyes one by one.

"We been talking, Chiefy." Basko started, which meant this was serious. "We ain't going to sail with that monster. Ain't right. We got a captain who sails into storms. We got a woman aboard, and a beauty at that, who don't know our ways and tempts Roa, brother, you know it. It's a doomed voyage, Lucky, we all know."

Chang raised his brow, tilting his head with a hand to his chin. He said nothing and waited until the men were awkward, meeting every eye. "Doomed, you say?" He frowned. "We all know, aye? I'll tell you what I know. This ship weathered that storm better than anything any of us ever seen. It wasn't close, boys. Who'd say otherwise?"

The Steerman spit and several of the others shook their heads. "See how the chief talks? I told you," said the Pitman. "Harbris."

"It's hubris," Chang corrected, and the man stared.

"It's mad talk is what it is. And not a word about the beast. We're bloody doomed."

"You think I don't know about the creature?" Chang snapped. "Who was it who stayed and fought with nought but a knife? Eh boys?"

The men looked to the planks like scolded children and Chang knew he'd have them for now. He sighed and shook his head, putting a hand on Basko's broad shoulder.

"We'll trick Roa as we've always done. We'll learn

this ship. We'll watch this monster and see what he does. We'll smile and follow the captain's orders. And when the time is right, as I *keep saying*." He jabbed his finger in the Steerman's face. "When the time is *right*, lads, and not a moment sooner, then we'll do what needs to be done. Ka?"

"Ka," the men muttered in disgruntled spurts, and Chang took a breath.

"Well then. If the bloody mutiny is delayed. The Captain wants fish, and the monster thinks he'll do the work, so there's that. Now get to your damn posts."

* * *

Zaya listened to the men discuss their betrayal, then returned to her cabin. She sat at the single table looking out the window crack at the Godtongue fiddling with some tool she didn't understand. She had no conception of what to do.

Surely, the shaman and his ally recognized their peril? Their confidence against ten angry pirates seemed at the least misplaced. But then, it was the *Godtongue*...perhaps the gods themselves would whisper of the men's treachery when and if it arrived. Zaya had no idea.

She had slept in fits and starts all night after the shadow emerged, lost in nightmares of its claws and eyes, and the howling of the shaman. What had the day before made her feel unquestionably safe aboard this ship, had now become the greatest source of danger. All her life, like most of the others her age, she had thought of this great man, this mighty prophet of the gods, as nothing but a hero of the book.

Her father had never encouraged such talk. Instead he had listened and warned in gentle tones and in different ways throughout her life, that with great light came contrast; that beyond the reach of light there was always, *always* darkness. For the first time Zaya understood.

Still, it was the *prophet*. The great shaman who had given her people a dream of paradise, and lifted them from their frozen tundra, taking them across the sea. The heroes of the book of Galdra were not pious priests or gentle things, but warriors and killers. They fought mighty beasts and paid the price for the good of all, losing their hands, their lives, or even their souls. It's what made them heroes in the first place. Zaya's task as skald was not to judge them, but to understand, to record. The thought gave her strength. She had been brought here by the gods, of that she had no doubt. So she must do her part to help the man, and perhaps, the crew. Surely that was her task. With a breath she stepped into the morning light.

"Good morning, shaman." She smiled for him and walked without fear, feeling the eyes of half the crew on her back. The shaman looked at his tool and at the sea, but bowed his head in greeting.

"Good morning, Zaya."

As she heard his voice, and looked on the furtive movements from a man who always seemed so purposeful, she realized—he was ashamed.

That she had not thought of this made her feel a fool. Sometimes she forgot he had once been an outcast— rejected for his deformities by his kin, living in the wilds, a rebel and outlaw long before he was known. She felt pity, then, more than fear. She turned and faced the crew who yet watched her, knowing this must not be ignored. Men's strength could sometimes make them brittle. She knew someone must break the tension built of fear and strangeness.

"The night was long for all of us," she called. "Tonight,

I say we feast." She gestured to the crew. "I've been listening to your songs for weeks, gentlemen!" She looked at Chang and smiled. "Tonight I'll sing the songs of your valor, and teach you how a real singer sounds."

A few men at least grinned, and even the shaman smiled politely. Captain Eka looked on from his perch, his face as ever a neutral mask of nothing. It was a start.

"It's too high," one of the pirates growled, stepping away from the shaman's device. To Zaya it looked like several hooks on ropes with a wooden block that held some other device, and at first she couldn't understand the benefit, especially with so many able-bodied men to hold the nets. But the shaman insisted, and soon attached the vast netting to his hooks, and began hoisting them up or down into the water, letting them dangle out from the ship in huge amounts as the ship continued with a bit of sail.

"The breeds of fish I expect this far to sea will feed near the surface," the shaman answered calmly. "They will feed in the day. The elevation is correct."

"How he talks," said the red-faced sailor, an eye cast to the others. "Where'd you learn to speak, eh? From some island princess?"

The others smiled or snorted but none of them laughed. They had been required to help more than the shaman let on, extending the netting around the hull and ensuring nothing was caught or torn. Zaya stood with her rope pile working on knots.

Such comments had been swelling all day, from small complaints to what seemed to Zaya now outright mockery, the point cruelty not jest. The shaman tolerated it, and said nothing. Zaya could hardly believe as she watched. Amongst her people, words mattered a great deal. *Honor* mattered. A man who tolerated such things rarely kept respect. But even more astounding was that men would even hint at insulting the shaman, who had been seen as a holy man, a great warrior. It was almost intolerable, but not her place to interfere.

The men kept on extending the netting, the captain guiding the ship with the wind at the helm. Chang was with them but uncharacteristically silent. He watched on, taking his turns with the nets, stopping occasionally to grunt mild approval over Zaya's knots.

Morning turned to afternoon, and as the shaman told the sailors it was time to check the nets, a loud pop sounded from the device. Before Zaya could do more than look, Ruka had leapt across the deck, seized the closest sailor, and pulled him aside as the wooden box snapped from it's place on the deck. The apparatus flew off the ship, straight through where the man had been standing.

The crew watched in stunned silence as the netting drifted away, though much was still held by the crew.

"Too much weight," Ruka said as he stood, brow vaguely furrowed. "We must have...caught something large. Or perhaps it's a raised bit of land..."

"Or it's a stupid fucking contraption," said the same red-faced sailor, rising up and stepping away from the shaman as if from a snake, his face pale.

"Just get the damn netting," Eka yelled from his perch. "And lower the sails."

Chang and a few of the sailors left shirts and pants on the deck, with a glance back at Zaya, who looked away. The men made filthy jokes Zaya was glad not to hear or fully understand, then they dove into the sea.

The others did what they could from the deck, reeling

in armfuls of slippery rope at a speed that beggared belief. Zaya did her best not to watch the strong, shining arms and backs. Amongst her own people, men and women rarely interacted except in families and formal occasions. They were modest, and covered most of their skin because of this and the cold. Every day she wore her overdress that felt too hot and already she longed to strip down to something else but couldn't bring herself to do it. On top of the discomfort of the heat, being surrounded by these working men gave her feelings she'd rather not have. She focused on her hated rope, trying to pull it in the same manner as the sailors. They'd returned much of the netting now and the few sailors were clambering back up as Zaya heard the yell.

"Get out of the water! *Now!*"

The strength of the call alone shocked Zaya back to reality. Ruka ran to the rails shouting, grabbing one of the climbing men and tossing him up like a child. Zaya abandoned her rope to move closer.

There were only two men left in the water, swimming with hard strokes towards the ship, their clusters of netting released. Behind them, a slender triangle, like a dark sail, jut from the water.

"They won't make it," the giant whispered, then ran towards his cabin.

The dark sail rose higher, until the huge body of some monstrous creature shimmered beneath the waves.

"*Swim!*" the men were calling. "It's nearly on you! *Move your arses!*"

Both Chang and his man swam with incredible speed, but next to the creature hardly moved. Zaya felt her hands clutching the rail. She knew her people hunted whales and that there were some that killed men, but she had never seen one. Her own helplessness trapped on the sea, in this creature's element, filled her with the same terror she'd known trapped in a storm. She could only imagine what the men in the water felt.

"Pirate!" Ruka's voice carried across the deck as he emerged. He threw a jagged spear point first, and—amazingly—the captain stretched out a hand and seized the shaft harmlessly from the air. Two more in his other hand, Ruka reached the rail and raised one back to throw.

As if pulled, Zaya ran forward and grabbed the other. Ruka met her eyes, then looked to the sea.

"Wait until the last moment," he commanded. "Aim just before the head. It will swim to the spear."

Zaya's heart pounded and she tried to get a feel for the weapon. It was solid iron, perfectly smooth, the weighting incredible. She had trained with spears all her life but never held such a thing.

"Soon." The shaman's arm drew back. "Don't throw with me. Wait. Be sure."

Then he growled and released, the javelin sailing true, sinking instantly into the water then sticking as red stained the blue. The captain threw his own a moment later. Zaya stepped back, lurched to the rail, and roared as she followed.

Both struck. The beast turned and thrashed beneath the water, diving away from the attack. Chang and the other man swam the last few strokes to the deck and safety, pulling themselves up with ropes to collapse panting at the other men's feet. The crew erupted in cheers, lifting them and laughing as if it had all been a game.

"A fine throw." The big man named Basko bowed to Zaya with hands together, and many of the others nodded or called their agreement.

"True," said the toothless old man with a grin.

A few thanked the captain in similar words, and Chang rose up with a stretch as if he'd never been worried. He was almost naked, and the water dripped down his body as he extended his limbs. Zaya forced herself to look away.

The sound of metal clattering and a man's grunts interrupted, and the crew soon realized Ruka had bound his own spear with a chain. He staggered with the weight, warring with the creature perhaps as he pulled across the deck and wrapped the chain around a mast. The crew watched him, then the sea, until more red stained the water, and finally the beast rose to the surface, pulling uselessly against the ship's weight.

"There is your feast."

The shaman released a long breath, then walked alone to his cabin, closing the door without another word. No one, including Zaya, thought to thank him.

Chapter 8

Chang took great pleasure dragging his would be killer from the sea.

"Look at that big bastard," he yelled, arms straining at the chain as the other men heaved and whooped. Between the nine of them, they just managed to lift it over the rail, where it flopped dead across the deck.

"A right monster," said the Pitman with a whistle. Then the Steerman, who butchered animals as well as he butchered men, went to his work. He chopped the fins, then opened the creature with a clean circle cut around its head, and a line down its back. The crew helped peel back layers of flesh as he sliced down the flanks, and revealed the feast.

Sea-shark wasn't much good to eat, but a good pirate had to be practical.

With Basko at his side, Chang took his time inspecting the harpoons lodged in the creature's flanks. One was stuck angled just below the animal's fin; the next was directly lodged in the back, close to the spout. But the third—which was really the first—was deep and buried into the bastard's soul, narrowly scraping the heart.

Both men glanced at the giant's cabin, then met each other's eyes. "Good throw," said Basko. Chang winced and nodded in reply.

That the pilot had just saved his life was not lost on him. A man like Chang, a man who started with nothing, remembered those who helped him, because few ever did. He stood and wiped moisture from his hands.

"See they clean up their mess. And you can make a small fire on the top deck for cooking, but you watch it.

Don't let those drunken bastards burn my ship."

"Aye, chiefy."

Chang went below to his bunk, ensuring he was alone before he closed his eyes and clenched his hands, forcing out the terror as if he squeezed it from his veins. He took short, ragged breaths before he calmed, banishing the memories of youth—of being dangled over the sea with sharks circling, sport for pirates as a slave.

The giant had saved him. He found the thought lodged deep in his brain already, seeping out to reform the picture of the world. The giant had saved him when his brothers were unable. That was the truth. Though Eka was the captain, it was also clear that the giant's will was what brought them here—*his* purpose that had freed Chang and his men from that rotting prison, where they'd been destined for the rope, or worse.

All his life Chang had remembered his friends, and his enemies. Never had they been the same man.

When the shaking stopped Chang opened his eyes and took long, calming breaths.

"It will pass," he whispered, until it did. "It will pass."

When his strength returned he stood in the dark belly of the impossible ship, and put a hand to the strongest hull he'd ever seen. The giant built this ship. He knew that, too. When he'd first met the man, he had looked into the monstrous eyes and seen a thing that knew what it was to be a low-born slave. Once nothing, then a famous man loathed by many. Chang could relate.

Then when the netting broke, Ruka had saved the Steerman's life. He had saved Chang and Basko in the sea, and not as a master protecting his property, but a bastard son who saved his brothers without a thought.

"Gods curse him." Chang said, then laughed. He felt his mood returning, bolstered by the sway of the sea and the sound of the wind. So it was decided, like it or not. The giant was one of theirs. And so Chang would earn his trust and bring him close and see him through the waves. And maybe even back again.

As he considered the dangerous man or creature, and the alternative of being only his enemy, Chang had to admit—the feeling was relief. It soon passed, and Chang hummed a sailor's song. A good pirate had to be flexible.

"Smells good, doesn't it, Macha?"

Zaya took a breath and cracked open her door. Chang had apparently washed his clothes and shaved. He stood outside Zaya's cabin with some kind of stringed instrument and a bottle of rum, pretending to breathe in the fumes of cooking meat.

"It smells like fish," Zaya answered, opening the cabin door fully. Chang grinned and withdrew, his gaze sweeping her overdress, lingering on her now untied hair, which had grown long enough to spread down most of her back.

"Your beauty is like the dawn."

As ever the man's manner made her uncomfortable. Tonight, however, she would tolerate such things—she would play and sing for the men as her father would have done, and raise their spirits. They needed it, and so did she.

"Thank you." She smiled politely and stepped onto the deck, almost groaning in the heat. The heavy fabric of her overdress already made her sweat, and she prayed the evening would be cool when the sun fell.

"What shall we play?" Chang leaned closer, as if they conspired. "Do you know any sailing songs? Or songs from the isles?"

Zaya shook her head.

"No trouble. Do you prefer ballads, or jigs?"

She stared because she had no idea what he was talking about, and Chang frowned as he scratched his chin with the back of one hand.

"What would you suggest we do?"

"*We* needn't do anything." She nodded her head in respect. *"We* eat. Then *I* will play and sing for the men."

Chang made a scoffing sound in his throat, then blinked when Zaya met his eyes.

"Macha is serious. Oh sweet, sweet Macha. If only your wisdom matched your beauty. As you wish. But when the time comes, I will be ready. You need only summon me with your siren's call, I will come to your aid, without a word of satisfaction."

"That's very decent of you," Zaya rolled her eyes to hide her grin, then stepped carefully towards the roasting bits of whale-shark.

The sailors stood around a metal bowl that held the fire, scampering like rabbits if they noticed an ash or spark get too high. Zaya took a seat on one of the long benches brought from the hold, then took a bowl of the shark meat from a cook with a thankful nod. She stared without a shred of appetite. It looked like a bowl of black fat, and reeked like fish. She was prepared to fight the impulse to gag, but realized the color was some kind of sauce, and forced herself to spoon a piece of the rubbery meal. The taste, at least, was better than the scent.

All around her the sailors shoved fatty meat into their mouths with abandon, chewing like children and slavering over their rum cups, the prying eyes of their captain and pilot far away on the upper deck.

When their stomachs were full, and the sun had dipped into the far horizon, Zaya took up her lyre, and began to play.

She started with the song of Zisa, which was slow and beautiful and fit the quiet evening and the tiny fire. She lost herself in the swaying of the waves and the rising and falling of the song, until she opened her eyes knowing it had been perfect.

The men were mostly silent. Some, Zaya realized, had gone off to other parts of the deck, to play dice or sleep.

"Do you...know any sailor songs?" The big brute named Basko leaned beside her with hopeful eyes, his breath reeking like rotten meat and rum. Most of the others that remained seemed rather bored, looking off into the sea.

Zaya nodded, knowing the answer to this question was always 'yes'. She wracked her mind for a sea song, but could only remember the tale of Nertha, a half god, half man, who had tried to swim to the spine of the world, but had gotten lost and froze in the ice.

It was fast, at least, and full of glory before the fall. In the land of ash the men who heard it would stomp their feet or their cups as they roared approval, and perhaps even the women might clap along.

She played and sang the words in her own tongue because she didn't have the skill to translate and play, and still the sailors mostly just stared. By the end, Basko stepped away with a hopeless look without even a word of thanks. Zaya felt her face reddening. Her father was the greatest skald in the Ascom. He had taught her well, and she had played many times for matrons and warriors in the halls of several chiefs to raucous approval. That she was skilled was not in question.

"Give us a song, Lucky!" One of the more drunken sailors spilled a bit of his rum on the deck as he staggered away.

Zaya forced herself to look at Chang. He stood as if disinterested along the cabins, a most annoying twinkle in his eye. He shook his head and swore he was too tired, too drunk, too shaken from the shark that nearly claimed his life, until the men were begging as they laughed, as if it were a ritual. All the while Chang held Zaya's eyes, outlasting the men and Zaya's increasing discomfort, until at last she nodded. He took up his instrument with a dramatic sigh.

"You belly-aching bastards. Well, alright. If our lady of the sea will have me." He wiggled his brow to another roar from the men, then stepped beside her and whispered. "Just follow along. You'll soon know what to do."

He strummed a very simple sound with his equally simple instrument, then called in a strong voice.

"Oh the work was hard, and the pay was low."

Men spilled rum and whale meat as they rose to sing.

"*Leave her*, Lucky, *leave her*!"

"Oh the seas are rough, and the kings yet come."

"Then it's time for us to leave her!"

Zaya felt the weight of their voices in her chest. Unlike as they worked in the day, their voices came together in harmony. Hair stood on her arms and neck at the sound, as it had only rarely when she sang with her father. She closed her eyes and listened to the verse repeat again and again, the words changing but the refrain repeating. Finally, she joined in.

"Oh the rats are gone over we the crew."

"*Leave her, Lucky, leave her*!"

"Oh the seas are rough, and the kings yet come."

Oh it's time for us to leave her!"

She sang for verse after verse, matching her higher pitch to the others. After ten or more it became like a prayer, the men drunk but still drinking, embracing as they sang. Some moved about the deck, hopping from foot to foot.

Chang seized Zaya's hands and forced her to leave her lyre and dance while he sang. When he paused to take a swig of rum, he handed it to her, and she drank deep as the men cheered. From the corner of her eye she saw the captain and even Ruka watching with grins on their faces.

"Oh the seas are rough, and the kings yet come."
"Oh it's time for us to leave her!"

Zaya danced as sweat poured down her body. She was taller than most of the men, so she hunched to stand at their level. As the night wore on the songs changed but retained their simple words and verses, higher and higher in pace. Zaya drank, and sang, and later seized Chang's knife from a scabbard and cut the hated sleeves from her dress as he laughed.

"What did I tell you, Macha?" he cried, "We'll make a sailor of you yet!"

When she finally collapsed on the bench, most of the men fell to the deck with their bottles or comrades, their laughter sweeping the ship. She lay there upon the creaking wood that still reeked of fish, staring up at the swirl of foreign stars with the sound of the waves, her hand still holding Chang's.

Such things were not done in the land of ash. She shouldn't have allowed him to touch her, and all her life she had been taught a chiefless man was unworthy of such an honor. These men were 'pirates', contemptible at best, bandits and outlaws at worst.

But here in their company, breathing hard from the song and dance, she knew she felt more free than she had in her entire life. And if that's what it was to be a sailor, she thought, she only hoped Chang was right.

* * *

"You're a very good singer," Zaya whispered later, standing at the rail. Chang hunched nearby, lighting a plant he called tobacco in the tiny remnants of the fire. Most of the crew had gone to their bunks or passed out elsewhere, and Chang stepped beside her at a comfortable distance. He smoked and looked out at the waves, his eyes far away.

"Tell me of your homeland, Macha. Are all the women as beautiful as you?"

Zaya shook her head and watched the black sea. "If I say yes, will it make me less special?"

"Never." Chang blinked and seemed to return slightly from wherever he'd gone.

"I lived in the capital of my people's lands," Zaya said, picturing New Orhus in her mind. "Though it's on the coast it would be considered very cold by you islanders. My mother was a priestess, an important woman, though to me just mother." She shrugged. "In the winter she scooped cups of snow from our yard and mixed it with sugary sap bought in the square. My father was a famous man, and well respected. He told me and my siblings stories every night by hearth light. We were very happy."

She blinked and found Chang smiling, though perhaps more with his mouth than his eyes.

"And yet you left this happy place for the sea," he said, breathing in a mouthful of smoke. He offered it, and Zaya shook her head.

"I got older. All my life I wanted only to live the great tales my father told. I did not choose my childhood."

Zaya caught the judgment or maybe resentment before Chang buried it away.

"No," he said quietly. "None of us do."

She wasn't sure she wanted to ask. Low-born men of the Ascom could live lives of such misery it was hard for her to understand, and harder still to hear the details. No doubt the same was true in the isles and the continent. Chang took a long breath and his smile returned.

"All that matters is what we do now, Macha. I have chosen my family. I would die for them, and they for me. That is enough."

"Yes," she agreed. "What we do now is what matters."

Chang lifted a bottle of rum to his lips, and offered this too. After a moment of hesitation, Zaya took it.

"And yes, I am a very good singer." Chang said with a smile. "I was born a slave, Macha. Do you know this word?" She nodded, understanding it well enough though her people had none. "My master's ship was attacked by pirates. They killed everyone, but in my fear I sang, and they decided to keep me. That was many years and ships ago."

"A slave. A pirate. Yet here you are." Zaya smiled. "A beautiful woman at your side."

Chang laughed, the sound as melodic as his singing.

"True. And a jailor as my captain, and a monster as my pilot, sailing into the great, wide sea."

"Is it truly endless?" Zaya decided to let the monster comment pass.

"So they say." Chang shrugged. "The islanders call it the Peaceful Ocean." He smiled. "The name is a joke, for it's as peaceful as the grave. My own people have another name."

Zaya realized he was saying he wasn't from the isles, but let that pass too.

"The sailor's graveyard," Chang's eyes lit as he

smoked. "Roa's toy. The dead, dark sea."

Zaya leaned on the rail and said nothing for a time, sipping again from the sweet, but potent island drink.

"My people once believed our North sea was endless," she said. "We were hidden from the world because all agreed it was so. Yet here we are."

"True." Chang smiled. "Though I suspect a few ships were lost before the discovery."

Zaya nodded, having heard the stories. She handed the bottle back and Chang made an obvious attempt to touch her hand in the exchange. She didn't stop him, and met his eyes. "Do you know how we found your islands? What brought my people here?"

He shrugged, stroking her hand now with his thumb. Zaya gestured towards the cabin with her head.

"It was that *monstrous* pilot, singer. It was Ruka who crossed the endless sea, younger than you are now. He crossed it alone. And because he did I speak your language, and lived a happy childhood with enough food and a united people, when my forebears struggled against hunger. Like you he has born hardship and done dark deeds. But you're right, it's what we do now that matters. If any can lead us across this sea, it is him. Goodnight, Chang."

Zaya left him and walked to her cabin without looking back, hoping he did not follow her. Despite her words and attitude, as she took off her dress and lay sweaty on the bunk, she feared if he did, she may not turn him away.

Chapter 9

Days and weeks of sailing passed. Every movement away from the lands Chang knew swelled a nameless fear inside him, so he kept busy, and he kept his men busy. Then the wind died, and they floated listlessly in nowhere, nothing but sea on every horizon, with little to do but wait.

The captain did not help morale. When there was nothing to do he stared out at the waves like a statue, sitting like a monk with his eyes half closed, as if one step from a corpse. The pilot, at least, had stopped screaming in the dark. He stayed to himself, in and out of his cabin muttering, maybe sleeping, maybe toiling on some secret project. Zaya's presence became the problem it was.

A woman on a ship was more than just ill luck. Idle men had the bad habit of considering their fortunes— what they had, what they didn't. Hungry eyes soon roamed the foreign girl every moment without toil, remembering a night of rum and dance. Chang made them clean and polish the wood until it shined, had them fish, and repair barrels, re-organize the hold and re-fasten the rigging. But he knew nothing was enough.

The men soon complained about anything but what they really wanted. The food was stale; the rum was low; the work was useless and the bunks no good. None dared say 'Where's our mutiny? Where's the end? And if there's no end, why don't we at least make use of the girl?'

Zaya herself did not make things easier. Every night she sat with the men and joined in their singing. Since the first night, Chang avoided being with her alone. True, he was not often rejected and felt it strongly with her. But he was not immune to the same desires as his men. He liked the girl's company, but he knew his mind must be clear and strong to protect them both, so he kept his distance until he approached her on the twentieth morning, and explained.

"I see," she'd said, after his long, red-faced rambling. She shrugged. "I will wear my overdress as before, and tie up my hair."

Chang snorted, wondering how so few women understood the depth of men's desire.

"Macha you could wear a barrel and the men would lust after your ankles. They won't hurt you, neh? But they are driven mad, they make other problems. Best stay in your cabin most nights, and come out in the morning."

The look she gave him could have burned water, but she did as he asked. It helped a little.

On the twenty-third day the wind returned, and with it a renewed spirit in the crew. Still the days were long, the nights longer. None of the men had ever sailed so far and long without a glimpse of land, and even for Chang it made a man feel as if the world did not exist, as if all movement made no difference, as if nothing ever changed.

"We are roughly here," explained the pilot in the captain's quarters that night, pointing at a huge map with a stick. Chang had seen many maps in his life, but none so large or as detailed as the giant's. It showed the entirety of the continent, four coasts with every lake, river and nation, and hundreds of islands drawn in Pyu. He pointed to an empty grey space off the West coast of the continent, and Chang looked to it and all the space that remained as he blinked.

"Why is there so much nothing on your map? And on every side of the continent?"

The pilot's strange eyes glittered in the gloom.

"The world is very large. At our present speed, and assuming no sign of land, it would take hundreds of days to circle the sphere, and reach the Eastern coast of the Tong empire."

Chang looked from the giant to the captain, who said nothing as he smoked a cigar.

"That's...impossible." When the giant said nothing, Chang put his hands to his face, scraping over the stubble as he tried to process it. "How can you know the size of the world without having crossed it? How can you *know*?"

The pilot shrugged. "I measured shadows, the curvature of the world, and the speed of the sun. I don't expect you to understand. That I know the size is sufficient. My hope is that we will find new land, but with luck, and continued fishing efforts, we should be able to survive a full crossing."

"This is madness." Chang felt as if his head weighed more than it should. He staggered and felt strong hands grab his arms, then carry him to a chair.

"He's not wrong," said the captain's voice, as if from underwater. "His men will react no better, and maybe worse."

"I told you the size, pirate. Nothing has changed."

"It's one thing to *hear* the size, savage. *Looking* at is something else."

The conversation seemed at a standstill, and Chang blinked his blurred vision away as he groped at a glass of rum on the desk.

"How are you feeling?" said the giant's voice. Chang grunted.

"I want a ship," he said in answer, then forced himself to meet the giant's eyes. "For me and my men. If we survive your mad journey, I want a ship. I want *this* ship."

The pilot's lopsided mouth formed in what might have been a grin. Chang forced himself to stand.

"I've spoken to your...*skald*, pilot. She says your people honor words. She says your goddess is listening. So I want you to bloody say it."

The giant's smile widened. He stood to his full, ridiculous height, head touching the roof as he met Chang's eyes.

"As you wish. For your aid, I, Ruka, son of Beyla, will give you this ship. This I vow. Does that satisfy you?"

Chang tried to think of some flaw in the wording but could see none. He nodded, and the giant bowed his head in the island manner, then turned for the door. Chang found the captain's eyes boring into him, and waited as the pilot left and closed the cabin.

The Batonian killer rose and released a breath of smoke, his other hand lifting a blade from behind his desk. To Chang it looked disturbingly natural—as if without it he'd been somehow...naked. His hand blurred, and the knife crossed the room with a hiss until it sunk deep into the wood by Chang's ear.

"You should have asked me first," the ex-assassin said, as if he'd commented on the weather. A silence lingered while the captain smoked, and Chang returned the man's rum to the table with slow movement, his heart pounding in his chest. He searched for the words, and decided he would indeed ask, but before he could the captain spoke again. *"Talk* of mutiny doesn't bother me, Chang. But keep your men in line, or I will. This ship doesn't need ten crew."

With that he gestured for the door, and Chang bowed and fled.

* * *

Zaya grumbled as she practiced her knots. It had been a long, hot night and she hadn't slept very well. She was tired of the swaying bunk, tired of her cabin, tired of fish and salted whale meat and squatting over her bucket and being stared at constantly by lustful men. She was tired of this ship.

"Why goddess," she muttered. "Why send me to the shaman on the *sea?*"

The work, at least, was getting easier. After weeks of monotonous practice, Zaya could tie a dozen kinds of knots, climb a mast and even help with some of the rigging. Her hands were rougher, her balance on the deck more natural, and the feel of rope had become familiar, almost comforting.

From her spot on the deck, she had watched Chang and the shaman head into the captain's quarters. She watched them leave, and then Chang gather his men in the hold below. As they went, they had the now typical dour expressions of men who didn't much like their lots. But as they came up, they looked like new men. Almost all wore plain smiles, some joking with their comrades as they took the stairs two at a time. Chang caught her eye and smiled across the deck.

"Good evening, Macha." He inspected her knots and nodded with approval. They hadn't spoken much in the past weeks—not since the night they had drunk and danced, and she had ignored his touch. To have called this rejection would have been wrong, and more accurately a last ditch resistance. She was both relieved and disappointed he'd stopped trying.

"Your men are in fine spirits," she said, and Chang shrugged. Then his face turned more serious, and he stepped in front of her almost formally before he spoke.

"I must apologize, Macha. I have made awkwardness between us. I was stirred by your beauty, but, that is no excuse. From now on I am your chief and that is all. You are free to sit with the men at night or do anything else, and the others will keep to themselves or face me. The problem is mine, not yours, neh?"

"Ka, chief," she smiled, still feeling awkward and not sure what to say.

"Good. I miss your singing. Join us tonight." Chang smiled, but it was the smile he would have given to any man, and not just for her. He turned away, and again Zaya felt relief, and loss.

As usual, she went to her work, which today was cleaning fish and skinning old potatoes enough for twelve to take three meals. She ate her hated fish, and tried to find some combination of clothing that didn't suffocate her nor reveal too much skin. That night she sat with the men and sang along, and they at least were in finer spirits than they'd been since the journey started. Even the shaman joined them, sort of—sitting at the edge of the gathering with his far-away eyes.

In a lull while the men walked or rested, Zaya found her courage, and moved next to the shaman.

"May I join you, God-tongue?"

He nodded, though he seemed uncomfortable. Zaya sat and tried to find something to say. Men and women of her culture rarely socialized except for kin, but as his skald she thought surely she must find a way to speak to him. Men liked to discuss their deeds, so she thought she might start with that. Her father had told her much of his earlier years as an outcast, and she knew of many of his exploits.

"Will you tell me of your battle with the emperor of Naran, shaman? I have only ever heard it from my father."

The Godtongue's jaw flexed. He looked out into the darkness, pupils moving back and forth, as if the battle were before his eyes.

"Then you have heard the best version."

Zaya almost swore at the failure, but tried another angle. "The men seem very pleased this evening."

"Yes." Ruka blinked and turned until his golden eyes bore into hers. "They think they're getting what they want." Zaya felt as if he was trying to look inside her very soul, and shivered at the sudden attention. "And you, Zaya," his head quirked like a bird of prey. "What do *you* want?"

"I...to see the world. I have only known life in Orhus. I wanted to see where the gods would lead me."

"Don't speak to me of gods. Tell me why you are here. *What do you want*?"

"I don't know." Zaya had not expected to be questioned like a prisoner when she'd sat beside the man. She felt an anger rising at the rudeness, at the unnecessary questions. "I don't want to just sing of heroes in a book. I want to *be* one. Like you."

He looked away again, the intensity like a flash fire that could fade in an instant. "Most heroes are myths," he said quietly. "Or corpses."

"But not all," she answered without pausing, wishing she could explain. How did you tell a man that because of him your life had been transformed? That a whole people had become something different, something hopeful?

"No." He agreed after a time. "Not all." He sighed as he looked at her again. "I came to this sea to leave the past behind, Zaya. I would like to be just a man, not a shaman, or a prophet." He stood, and she felt herself compelled to stand as well. "I have been cold and distant, for that I apologize. I admire your courage." He smiled, and though his face was deformed by the touch of the mountain god, she found it warm. "Perhaps we are not so different, you and I. Perhaps, on this ship, we will both find what we're looking for. But do not call me shaman, or Godtongue. Call me Ruka. That is my name."

Zaya nodded in respect, lost for words, but the intense gaze remained, waiting for an answer, and she smiled shyly. "I will try."

The corner of the thick lips quirked in a smile that Zaya thought was not for her. "That is all any of us can do, Zaya, daughter of Juchi and Egil. Good night."

"Goodnight...Ruka."

The legendary shaman turned for his cabin, his gait she now realized holding the hint of a limp, no doubt some injury earned in a glorious battle he'd not speak of. With a sigh, and a last glance at Chang singing again with his men, Zaya did the same.

Chapter 10

Before morning on the twenty-fourth day, a perfect wind began to blow from the East. The captain roused the men with his shouting. "Fill the rigging! Extend the halyards, I want every scrap of sail!"

Chang blinked the sleep from his eyes and woke the Pitman and Old Mata, who had already mastered the new sails better than any man on the ship. By dawn the *Prince* stretched her arms to the sun, cloth snapped taut and full on every mast until Chang was worried her bones would snap.

But the monstrous pilot walked the deck grinning. He glanced at the sea and the wide-eyed men as he laughed. Chang stood on the prow, the wind surrounding his scalp and snapping his shirt full like a sail, wondering if this was how birds felt when they flew.

It was only the beginning of a long and blessed streak of fortune. The wind carried them for days with little tacking, then on the fifth the Steerman called *land ahead!*, and the crew scrambled with unhidden joy at even the prospect of an island.

As the outline stopped growing they realized it was tiny, but still, they stopped and fished, and made a great bonfire of the trees. The pilot returned grinning with pots filled with soil and a few plants, and several crabs and other shellfish in a bucket. "Tonight," he'd shown them, "we eat like kings."

Leaving that small patch of land had been hard. Chang and his men returned to the monotony of life at sea, fishing and scrubbing, tacking and repairing. When a sail tore they replaced and stitched it, when a board broke they fitted another before caulking it with fat and glue. Zaya had returned to their nightly singing, and the joy of their reward kept everyone civil.

If anyone suffered from the ashlander's beauty, in fact, it was Chang. He did his best not to watch her. She had stripped down to a sleeved version of a sailor's clothes and let down her hair, which to Chang looked the color of twilight on the sea. She laughed more easily now, her smile carved by benevolent spirits, her growing competence bringing her a pleasant ease.

Chang focused on his work, and his men. In the evenings, to get away from Zaya, he had begun to sit with the pilot. At first the giant was uneasy but cordial, but made it clear he had no desire to speak of his past. When prompted, though, he soon went on endlessly about his plants or his maps, his gadgets or the stars. As a lifelong sailor of the isles, *stars* was a thing Chang knew a bit about.

"There," he pointed on a cloudless night with half a moon. "We call that the Fisher's Hook, see how it curves? And there is the line. You see?"

The giant smiled with his long, jagged teeth. "It is clearly the head of a sheep."

"Damned fool barbarians," Chang shook his head. "In the summer pattern? If it were a sheep it would be sheared. And where are the ears?"

"It is *winter* in the land of ash," the barbarian insisted with the same smile. "That is why the body is so round."

Chang smoked his tobacco, which often summoned the captain as if from nowhere, who would accept one with a nod and sit with them in silence. Chang thought it best to ply the frightening man's vice and perhaps one day buy himself a few moments of mercy, if the moment came.

Nights as ever became days, and days turned dark again in an endless loop of toil and renewal, movement and stagnation—the unforgiving rhythm of the sea. After two more weeks the sheen of the great prize began to wane. The distance from land became more than an abstraction, more even than the knowledge that for each day at sea they must go back again the same distance. The grand adventure became a trick—a fool's errand, a madness which would never see them home or able to claim their prize. The grumbling began, inevitable as the tide.

"How much further, neh chiefy?" it didn't much matter who started it.

"Yeah, Lucky, you sit with the pilot. What's he say, neh? Where's the landfall he promised?"

"Soon enough." Chang answered, day after day, question after question, watching their little dark speck move so slowly across the endless grey of the pilot's map.

A storm came, and went. The *Prince* danced across the waves with little enough help, save for a few hardy men to bail. A calm came after, and it was this Chang truly feared. A few fights broke out over nothing. An oarman and the Pitman came to blows over who'd made the deepest scratch in the breakfast table, frothing and ready to draw knives until Chang and a few others held them down so long they wept and embraced, their madness forgotten.

Time carried on. Some mornings Chang had to force men from their beds to take their shifts, and once roused some would stare at nothing, mostly useless save for the single task before them. You could learn a lot about a man at sea, and Chang had learned his brothers well. Basko did his work, but otherwise vanished into his own mind. The Oarmen and Pitman did nothing if not in each other's company, playing dice with stakes no one else could discern. The Steerman, of course, became a lunatic. His temper exploded over nothing, his violence only subdued by two or three men after a few cuts and bruises.

Zaya sang her songs and seemed so at ease Chang truly wondered if she were a spirit of the sea. The pilot did his work in silence, strange eyes glassy and far away, like a mirror of the growing madness that overtook the crew.

The captain watched all like a predator.

After a long, hot afternoon, when the Steerman shouted and cursed any man who crossed his path, pacing across the deck with a knife, the captain appeared at Chang's side without a sound. "Deal with him," he whispered, "or I will."

Chang had him forced below and locked like a prisoner until the madness passed. But the Steerman wasn't alone. Chang felt it, too—as if he were stretched like old rope, fibers pulling away one by one until the line snapped at its weakest point. A part of him wanted the captain to end it, the same part that wanted it over, wanted off this ship no matter how, to lay down and never to rise, or to walk into Zaya's cabin and take her.

With every dusk her beauty grew, until Chang could see her hair lit by sunlight even as he closed his eyes. She did her work and hummed her songs or played her lyre, eyes sure and smile quick, like driftwood floating in the wreckage of his madness. He knew to touch her was death. The captain was watching, and the pilot too. And even if they hadn't, he knew to touch her was to take on water, to crack the last strong surface of his mind, and drown.

"Are you alright?"

Chang looked away from the glaring blue horizon as he heard the voice of a good spirit made flesh. He blinked and blinked until he saw Zaya, and it seemed he was not looking out to sea at all, but standing at her cabin door.

"You look a little pale," she said. And then Zaya was beside him, easing him to the lone chair in her room. It was her private place, he knew that, as he knew he shouldn't be there.

"I'm alright, Macha," he lied. "Just tired is all. I thought...I'm sorry, I think I've wandered in my sleep. Is it morning?"

"Lie down," she said, helping him to the bed that smelled of her. The scent of her sweat brought him closer to the shore—to good things and away from a monstrous pilot and a killer captain, a crew of madmen and an endless sea. He pulled the lone sheet to his face and turned on his side as he closed his eyes.

"Just tired, Macha," Chang heard himself mutter.

Then there was the sound of a woman humming a child's song, and Chang floated light as air, far away from the *Prince*, and from prison, from a hard life on the sea.

"I'll be alright come morning," he muttered before the end. "It's Roa's promise. I'll wake anew with the sun."

* * *

Chang dreamt of slavery, or maybe freedom. He'd lost track of which was which. First he was a boy in shackles held by iron and hard men with harder tasks that bound his life in endless work. Then came Roa, the great kraken god, and a bargain struck in the hopeless dark. And so with his patron, Chang had survived the sea where so many others fell. He grew to a man, coiled now in ropes made of gold, surrounded by others who needed him, who needed hope and the right words and the right songs, souls like hungry stomachs with only Chang's words to fill them.

"Land!" called a man in his dream, and Chang knew it was a lie.

"Land, he says." Chang rolled his eyes and winked to his brothers, who laughed like children without a care.

"Land, due West!" called the dream again, until Chang blinked and lived both in a dream and a sea-world with a slaver captain and a madman pilot.

He wiped away sleep and tried to wet a cotton-stuffed mouth, rising in a bed that wasn't his in a cabin he didn't recognize. It was Zaya's, he realized. Zaya the sea spirit. How did he get there?

He reached the door and stumbled onto the deck to find the crew lined up and staring out to sea.

"Another island?" He coughed and moved beside the Steerman, wiping the last bits of sleep from blurry eyes. The little islander grinned and gestured with his chin— the men of his lands never pointed with their fingers, else the gods might look too.

Chang blinked and looked out to the horizon, which he now saw was filled from end to end with wrongness, with a color that did not exist because only blue existed. Half the sky was green.

"Hell of an island, chief," said Basko with a grin.

Chang nodded, and looked between the men's wide smiles, a few looking to him now as if only his words might make it true.

He took his moment. The captain stood on his deck with a cigar, puffing with one hand curled around a rope as he looked out, as if lost in thought. The pilot stood at the rail grinning like a child, Zaya near him.

"Land ahead," Chang said with some finality. When the men didn't move he stomped and slapped the rail. "I said land ahead, you lazy bastards. Reduce the sails.

Ready the anchor and the transport. If the captain means to land I want barrels and flasks ready to move. Bloody ka?"

"Ka, chief." The men roared, even the Steerman, as if he'd never held a mutinous thought in his cunning little mind.

They sailed onward with a mild breeze, eyes straining as every man did his best to see more than the green glow of glorious land. It seemed further than expected, and to reach it took the *Prince* most of the afternoon. All the while the captain stood still and silent, smoking, and watching. The pilot went in and out of his cabin, muttering and frantic like an excited child.

Soon enough, the line gained shape. Thousands of trees covered the foreign coast, their strange trunks growing mixed together so close they looked like a wooden wall. Far beyond them, vast hills and mountains challenged the sky in jagged rows. Birds swooped over the sea, calling in challenge and annoyance at their kin.

"It's beautiful," said Zaya, moving to Chang's side. He smiled and fought the water forming in his eyes.

"Aye, Macha. A damned miracle."

At last the captain seemed to come alive, stepping from his watch and turning on the crew. He stepped from the elevation of the captain's deck to the pilot, handing him what looked like a coin, then looked out over the crew.

"Make ready for landfall," he said needlessly. "We'll anchor and explore, then camp on the closest beach."

When the men failed to cheer, the captain's mouth quirked with a rare smile. "The thing about explorers, gentlemen—the first to find new land, they usually end up rich."

"True," said Old Mata, and even the Steerman

grinned.

"Let's go boys." Chang clapped and readied for landfall, a happy smile plastered in place. In his mind he remembered the names of lost ships and lost captains, devoured by their doomed ventures for foreign lands. Some became rich, no doubt, just as the captain promised. But usually, oh yes most usually, they ended up dead.

Chapter 11

Zaya dipped sandaled feet into water as clear as any she'd seen in the isles. The beach was shallow and filled with tiny stones that rested comfortably beneath her feet. The men beamed as they pushed their transport onto the rocky beach, loaded down with weapons and supplies. When they struggled at the end to push it from the water, the shaman seized it and lifted it half off the ground, as if perhaps he might have been able to do so alone.

"Come, cousins," he said, smiling so wide he exposed jagged teeth. "A new world awaits. Who knows what secrets it might hold?" He dropped the boat and raced to the closest patch of trees, running his hands over the bark as he inspected the rounded canopy above.

The captain and his men went more slowly. Zaya walked beside Chang, whose dark eyes roamed the long shore with an expression too difficult to read.

"How are you feeling?" she whispered. He blinked and smiled, though it was not the genuine expression she had come to crave.

"Well again, Macha. As I promised, the dawn has renewed me."

Still, Zaya saw strain in the man's face. He looked out at the land as if more afraid of *it* then the sea behind.

The crew of the *Prince* made their way into the unknown forest that the islanders called 'jungle' for reasons Zaya didn't understand. The heat was oppressive as ever, but Zaya had become used to that. Insects buzzed, chirped and hissed all around them, some settling on skin to sting or bite, leaving the party swatting constantly at themselves as they marched.

"We'll walk awhile," said the captain. "But stay together, and if it's all dense trees like this we'll move the ship and try somewhere else."

They soon found patches of berries and strange fruits which the shaman wrapped in cloth and stuffed into a sack. "Eat nothing," he commanded, but with good humor, his eyes wide and restless as they roamed every plant, great or small. He removed some from the ground, along with patches of dirt he stored in wooden containers in his heavy bag.

The party walked on. When it seemed this whole world were made of thick vegetation, at last they came to a clearing, and for a moment feared they'd found the end of another island, for they heard a sound they thought was the tide. Instead the clearing revealed a pool of water, surrounded by rock and green life, ascending a step-like pattern of rock up the side of a mountain. Water fell down it, hundreds of white cascading rivers mixing into a lake and splitting off as rivers below. The crew beamed, and ran to the water.

Some filled waterskins or cupped their hands in the river to drink. Others took off their clothes as if they meant to leap in for a swim, and Zaya averted her eyes, still embarrassed at the display despite her weeks with the men.

"If you wish to bathe, Macha," Chang pointed at a smaller pool, somewhat secluded in the trees. "I will stand guard, and ensure you are alone."

Whether the offer was genuine or another attempt at seduction Zaya had no idea. She rarely did with the man, and still worried at the madness or sickness she had seen overtake him, and most of the crew. Even the shaman and the captain had seemed disturbed, sometimes wandering with eyes that saw some internal world, and consumed them.

"Thank you," Zaya smiled politely. "Perhaps later."

Chang nodded and removed his shirt, then followed the men into the water.

The shaman and captain had moved closer to the waterfalls, so Zaya stepped carefully along the wet stones to join them. The shaman moved closer along the stone until he came to the bottom of the waterfall, then yelled over the endless din, his hand on the wall. "It looks almost cut, pirate, as if by men. Not so different to the weir in Sri Kon."

Zaya had no knowledge of such things, but the view was breathtaking. Some of the spray from the water was hitting her now, and she closed her eyes as the cool moisture washed over her in steady waves. Her desire to jump into the water with the men was strong, but a lifetime of such things being forbidden was not so easily ignored.

"Get the men out." The shaman's voice changed.

Zaya turned to see his eyes roaming the trees, something palmed in his hand. The captain asked no questions. He barked at the men to get their clothes and weapons and rally to him, clapping his hands as he stepped to the pool.

Zaya looked but couldn't understand the sudden panic. She stepped over a slight rise and saw a number of objects abandoned by the waterfalls. They looked too oddly shaped to be natural, and she squinted to understand before it was clear…there were clay jugs and buckets beside the water, with bundles of rags in heaps. She knew then what had concerned the shaman—there were people here. Others had been at this very spot, and by the looks of it, had been washing clothes before they abandoned them.

Then she heard a scream from the trees.

"Quickly!" The shaman took the steps two at a time,

lifting two surprised men from the pool, their legs kicking like children. "To the ship! *Now!*" he roared.

Zaya stared at the woods, trying to understand. The shouts and screams were growing in number, moving through trees. She began to see colors emerging from the North side—first blues, reds, then yellows in almost circular patterns. After a long delay, she realized, they were shields.

Dark skinned men emerged from behind them, shouting and hollering, their bodies and weapons painted with strange shapes. Others emerged from the cliffs above, yet more from the hills to the South. They carried strange, hooked spears, as well as nets and long ropes.

"There's too many." Zaya barely heard the captain yell over the sound of the waterfall.

"Go pirate. I will not kill," the shaman answered. Incredibly, he raised his hands and settled to his knees, as if in surrender.

The captain took one look at his eyes, and ran.

Only the Western path to the woods remained free. The strange warriors had already began to circle as the sailors emerged from the water, grabbing clothes and weapons as they squished into their boots or sandals.

"What are we doing, chief?" yelled the big brute, Basko, eyes wide as the shouting continued.

"We do what he says! Back to the ship!" Chang yelled, grabbing men and pulling them on.

Zaya did not follow them. There was still a little time. The foreigners were not running, but staying in a kind of formation as they approached, and she looked at the great shaman waiting without a hint of fear as the foreigners came. She knew as ever the gods gave her a choice, as they gave all living things a choice, if not in the manner of their lives, then in the facing of it. She clenched her jaw and dropped to a knee beside the shaman. He looked at her and perhaps sighed, but she saw no judgment there.

She watched Chang at the back of his fleeing men. He turned and met Zaya's eyes, and his hands curled as if even now as the warriors closed, he debated charging back. A surge of warmth for him went through her, but she simply nodded, and gestured towards the woods. With a final look, Chang turned and disappeared into the trees.

* * *

"You should have run." The shaman's words held as little emotion as his expression. He inspected the armed men approaching with cold, fearless eyes, and Zaya tensed as at least ten of the painted warriors circled them on the wet stone. "Not all men treat women honorably," he added, eyes following the spear points now held near his face.

Zaya's heart wouldn't stop racing. "I'm not afraid," she whispered, forcing her limbs to relax as the men wrapped rope around her arms. They were much the same size as the islanders, if perhaps slightly taller, with a range of skin tones like the diverse peoples of the continent. As they grabbed her they seemed strong enough, but next to the shaman, they looked like skinny boys with sticks. Only his lack of resistance allowed them to bind his hands with their rope.

Hands lifted Zaya to her feet, and two of the painted warriors spoke nonsense, repeating words she didn't understand over and over before gesturing for her to be taken. As the shaman stood and went with them, the men again began to whoop and shout as if in some kind of celebration.

With the foreigners around them, they were marched North around the base of the waterfall, to a small path of paving stones that seemed to lead up into the hills. Zaya said nothing. She tried to calm her uneven breaths and keep her feet while the men pushed her onward. The difficult climb somehow helped, and returned blood to her limbs. As they finished the steep rise, she looked out beyond the waterfall, and her breath caught in her throat.

Tan buildings emerged in layers from a rising mountain, row upon row like steps into great peaks that met the afternoon sun. It was the largest city Zaya had ever seen.

She forced her gaze to the shaman, whose eyes moved back and forth over everything, excitement now clear on his face. Their captors forced them onward, down into rich squares of crops that surrounded the city in the same layered pattern as the buildings. Farmers and shepherds stared, flocks of scraggly sheep and goats in vast numbers along the fields. Some bowed to the warriors or thumped tools against the earth.

When they reached the city outskirts, the warriors again began to whoop and holler, the ruckus rising as townsfolk came to watch, adding their own voices to the sound. The people wore little clothing, much like the islanders, yet styled with many colors, jewelry hanging from necks and ears, their hair often immaculately kept. Many gaped in open awe at both Zaya and the shaman, some daring to touch them as they passed.

Zaya felt suffocated, and vulnerable. Hands grabbed at her hair, her clothes, or rubbed her skin. Near naked children fought for a place near her legs, laughing and groping anything they could touch. The warriors seemed unbothered, even encouraging the crowd to come and fawn over their prize, until the shaman growled and sent the foreigners scurrying back.

"Indok, kay tawaha. *Tawaha!*"

A group of men in thick gambeson armor waited in an open square along the road. An older, grey-haired man at their front shouted and the crowd dispersed, the warriors pushing Zaya and Ruka onwards with obvious pleasure. One of the warriors stepped out and spoke in the same gibberish, gesturing dramatically at his men, then at Ruka, thumping his chest and gesturing to the sky.

The grey-haired warrior smiled. He spoke to the crowd before gesturing to the warriors, and the whoops and shouting filled the world as hundreds cheered, and the men puffed their chests.

Their treatment was rougher after that. The new warriors nearly dragged Zaya and the shaman through the crowd, pushing people aside if they got too close. Still, the mood seemed celebratory. People cheered as they passed. They hurried down a series of flawless cobblestone streets, past buildings made of huge blocks of brown stone, that rose up in both square and triangular shapes, connected by steep paths up the mountain-city.

The sun and the warmth of the bodies was unbearably hot, and between the heat and the fear Zaya felt herself panting, desperate to have her hands free. Suddenly the cool spray and endless sea on the horizon felt like paradise.

"Alakwa." The older warrior led them beneath a bridge, then gestured through a narrow corridor of stone. It was small and dark inside, and Zaya felt herself pull away. The men pushed her onward. At first she thought the shaman wouldn't fit, but he stooped and managed, and if he could stand it then she knew so must she. They were led to a stone bench where their bonds were cut and a kind of prison erected at the doorway with a grate made of something like the islander's bamboo.

Then just as quickly, the foreigners were gone, and Zaya and the shaman were alone. She could see his golden eyes exploring the dark like the mirrored lenses of a cat, reflecting the tiny remnants of sunlight.

"What will they do with us," she whispered, hating her own weakness. She knew she should be focused on everything she saw and heard so that later she might tell of the tale. But in this moment, it did not seem natural to think of song.

"I have been imprisoned twice," answered the shaman, his voice disturbingly calm. "The first time I nearly froze. The second, I was fought in a pit like an animal for a king's amusement."

He said nothing more. Zaya almost laughed at herself for seeking comfort from the prophet of the mountain god. Her hands trembled so she forced them closed, and held them hard on her thighs. A little later she heard the shaman release a breath, or maybe a sigh, as if he sensed her mood. He spoke again, his words forced and utterly without enthusiasm.

"This time might be better."

Chapter 12

"Damned bloody fools," Chang hissed and drew his knives. "Stay together! Due East! Away from the sun!"

He had no time to consider Zaya and the pilot. He had to get his men back to the ship, back to freedom, back to life.

"Lead them on." The captain turned away and stopped. He drew a black cloth from his pocket, which apparently was some kind of mask, then ripped off his robe to reveal a tighter layer of the same dark material beneath. His face disappeared as he slipped the mask over his head, even his eyes impossible to see. "I'll distract as many as I can."

With that he moved into the trees and vanished from sight. Chang had no time to consider this madness either. He wiped sweat dripping from his brow, and ran, Basko and the Steerman right at his side.

"What should we do if they catch us, neh chief?"

Chang looked back towards the trees, seeing nothing now but still hearing the shouts and high-pitched shrieks of the unknown warriors. "Whatever you have to," he barked, then counted the men he could see but knew some had likely run ahead. "Leave no man behind," he said, and pushed his officers forward.

The crew that remained stayed together—perhaps frightened to leave each other's sides. They swore as they tripped over tree roots or took a face full of tropical leaves or branches. Birds and monkeys shrieked at them from above, the high pitched sounds mixing with the enemy's, making it sound as if they were surrounded on all sides. Chang began to wonder if that was the point.

Still, the sounds of the main group of the enemy seemed further and further away, and Chang thought perhaps they were outrunning them.

"Keep going you bastards!" he shouted. "No rest until the coast!"

Time became ragged breaths and muscles burning in waves of exhaustion. They reached a small clearing Chang didn't remember passing the other way, and for a long moment he feared they'd turned. Basko saw an Oarsman at its edge, three enemy warriors jabbing spears and trying to tangle him in rope. He held his long knife high, weaving it back and forth and keeping the men at bay. Chang and the others took one look at the colorful warriors, and charged.

Two of the three saw them coming and ran. Three others emerged from the trees, as if they'd just been watching.

"Basko, hold them off!" Chang pointed at the newcomers then circled the lone warrior who hadn't run. He was short, and thin, with a nearly hairless body. To Chang's eye he looked young—no more than thirteen or fourteen. But he held a wicked looking cudgel of wood and sharpened stone, and stuck out his tongue as he growled some kind of war chant.

"Hurt mine," Chang matched the growl with his own, "I hurt you more."

He advanced with one knife ready to stab, the other to deflect. He was used to close-quarter brawls to the death with a swaying ship and all the chaos of boarding. By comparison, this seemed rather straight forward.

His young enemy waved the stick like a torch, as if simply trying to hold his opponent back. Chang waited for it to swing, then lunged. In a moment's work he sunk a knife deep into the lad's chest, sliced his forearm, then kicked him over. He looked away from the boy's wide, startled eyes, grabbed the heavy looking weapon and threw it away before he turned.

His men fared worse against the other three. They were older, and wore a kind of padded armor over their torsos, as well as wooden helmets and vambraces. Two held long spears and wielded them well, but like the youth, seemed more interested in holding their opponents back than killing them. The third man wore an elaborate headdress of feathers. He chased Chang's men with a weapon much like the dying lad's, shouting wildly as if in display.

"Kill him!" Chang pushed his way closer. Four of his men stood near the fight with something like confusion, unable to get past the spears or figure out how to attack their enemy. Chang put himself directly in the path of the more aggressive warrior, and held up his bloody knives. "Come on," he snarled, "follow your comrade."

The warrior met his eyes, and smiled. He changed his stance and leapt forward in a frightening display of athleticism. Chang barely managed to pull his head away as the vicious club swiped, backing further and further away until his opponent left his spearmen guard behind. Suddenly, he was very alone, and exposed.

"Take him."

The pirates converged with their knives, and though obviously surprised, the strong foreigner still managed to bash the Pitman in the arm, his jagged weapon slashing flesh in several bloody lines. In answer, half a dozen bronze knives sunk into his body, and the sailors pulled him down to keep stabbing.

Chang enjoyed the horrified expressions of the spearmen, and with a last look at their fallen leader, they turned their backs and ran.

"Keep moving." He panted and watched the trees for more, hoping he didn't sound as terrified as he felt. Why these men had come in such small numbers and fought so strangely, he had no idea. He was just glad they did.

The jungle soon moved with shadows as the sun dipped towards the horizon. Chang and his men moved as quickly as they could in the direction they'd chosen, hoping they weren't far from their original path, and would end up on the beach close to their ship. The Pitman clutched his arm, but seemed right enough. Two men half-carried Old Mata, whose scalp was red, his face pale, but otherwise seemed alert.

Chang still felt enemy eyes in the flickering light of the canopy. He heard warcries in the calls of creatures in the trees. It began to feel like a dream, a terrible nightmare of life as a landsmen, hunted and trapped like an animal.

"It never bloody ends," cried the Steerman, his spirit flagging first as usual.

"Maybe it's some damn peninsula, and we've missed the coast," said an Oarsmen.

They went on because they had no choice. When they found the sea it was almost dark, and for a moment Chang stared out at an empty beach and a gentle tide lit red by a sliver of sun, with no idea where to turn, or what to do.

"There!" The Steerman pointed down the coast to a dark bump in the sand, and Chang stared until he saw the outline of an unnatural thing. It was the transport.

"True," Old Mata gaped with his toothless mouth, and the crew laughed realizing they'd live.

"Go! *Go!*" Chang forced his numb legs onward. The men's sandals slapped against the wet sand, their ragged breaths caught only to spit or vomit from exhaustion. They found two of the crew waiting at the transport. They hadn't lost a man.

"There they are!" the Boatswain shouted, and the pair whooped in encouragement as Chang and the others made the final distance. Several collapsed on arrival, but the others heaved the boat into the water, lifting their comrades with their hands or just words of abuse.

"A little further you lazy mongrels," Chang lifted Old Mata, dumping him inside once the transport was off the sand. "We're nearly free."

"Where's the captain?" The Steerman almost whispered, and Chang looked back to an empty treeline with no sign of movement. The hollering of the foreigners had apparently stopped, and he saw no sign of anything at all save a few dark wings in the trees.

"We can wait a little while," he decided, then met the unhappy eyes of the men. "We can wait," he repeated. "I'd rather not cross that damn sea without the pilot. And I don't leave men behind."

"You won't need to." A shadow appeared from the gloom as if from nothing, sending the men for their knives in a panic. Captain Eka removed his silk mask, which—like the rest of him—was now greased with the wet trails of men's blood.

The pirates silenced as he climbed onto the transport. The Oarsmen pushed off and fought the tide, angling the small but heavy boat to the side of the Prince, where the last swabbie waited.

"I was about to bloody swim out, you greedy bastards! What took so damn long!" He called before he got a better view of the ragged, exhausted men, then quieted when he noticed some missing. He helped them tie to the transport and haul them up with ropes to the deck.

"Thank the spirits," the Steerman dropped to the rail. Two men helped carry Old Mata below, while the rest went wordlessly to their bunks or posts. The captain met Chang's eyes.

"Come with me, Chief. We've decisions to make."

* * *

"Why didn't the damned pilot run? Surely those bloody tree stump legs are good for something."

Chang dropped heavily into the only chair set out for guests in the captain's quarters. The captain snorted and removed a box of long, thin cigars from his desk, offering one to Chang, which he took as gratefully as the rum poured from a fine glass bottle.

"Running implies fear," said the captain after a long pause and a sip from his glass.

"He didn't want them to think he was afraid?"

"No, Chang. He *wasn't* afraid." The captain shrugged. "Maybe he was curious. Maybe he didn't want to risk killing someone in his flight. The motives of the man you call 'pilot' are best deciphered by wiser men than I. Now tell me, why did you pause and not leave me there on the beach with pleasure?"

Chang met the man's eyes. He inspected his long limbs, his perfect posture, thinking on his fine accent and expensive clothes. No doubt he was some noble-born landowner's second son, raised in a palace in a family loyal to the king. That a royal assassin should look down his nose on a common man who did what he had to was not shocking, but it still rubbed Chang the wrong way. When he spoke it was with more of a tone than he should have.

"There is more than one kind of honor. *Sir.*"

The captain stared, and eventually smiled. He rose with a nod to a cupboard at the back of his quarters, and began stripping the now bloody black silks he'd been wearing beneath his clothes. The body beneath was like a sculpted statue of bronze. "And what of our now captured crew, chief? Does your kind of honor allow us to abandon them?"

Chang had been considering that since he fled the jungle. By any reasonable estimation, both Zaya and the pilot were dead or imprisoned somewhere impossible to find. That so many of the natives had managed to attack them, and so quickly, implied these lands teemed with warriors and tribes. "We could maybe survive the journey home without the pilot," he said, and shrugged.

"Yes, maybe," agreed the captain.

Chang glanced up at the man's near nakedness and saw whip scars coated his back. His arms, legs, and chest held scars from blades and gods knew what else. Chang felt his estimation changing, and forced himself not to stare as he cleared his throat.

"I don't leave men behind, Captain. At least not without a fight."

The captain covered himself with a plain sailor's shirt and pants of linen cloth. He quirked his mouth as if amused at the answer, then returned to his seat for another sip of rum. "You surprise me, pirate. I expected you to try and convince me to run."

The man was getting on Chang's nerves now and he leaned slightly in his chair. "With respect, you know nothing about me. I'd kill you and a hundred other kingsmen to protect my own. And maybe the two we lost aren't strictly mine, but that man is one of Roa's guides, whatever you might call him, and Zaya is a spirit born of the sea. So yes, I'll help them, and not because you asked."

With that he threw back his rum and would have stormed from the quarters if his legs didn't feel like limp noodles from his flight. Captain Eka was grinning now and poured Chang another glass, the fingers of his other hand outstretched in a gesture of calm.

"I didn't mean to offend you, Chang. I merely suggest you're a practical man—a man who judges what he sees. And I suspect, like me, you saw a whole land filled with savage killers. Does the thought of facing that not frighten you?"

Chang felt his eyes drooping from the day and the rum, thinking of all the years of survival at sea. Lucky Chang, they called him, because he'd survived two shipwrecks and a hundred things others hadn't. Survived, even thrived under the iron boot of the sorcerer king, when so many crews had died or fled, surrounded on all sides by kings and laws that told them and everyone there was no such thing as a free man on the sea. But Chang knew the truth. He wasn't lucky. He was a killer, and long ago he'd made a pact with the dark god of the sea. He belonged to Roa, and only him.

"You just tell me your plan, Captain, if you've got one, and my boys and I will see it done. When we're home and safe we'll expect you to keep your word and give us our prize, or we'll see that's finished too."

The captain leaned in his chair, no more trace of amusement or judgment that Chang could see. "You have my word," he said, then grinned. "After they've had their rest, tell the men we sail on the dawn. I think we're going to be here a little longer than expected. We've got some exploring to do."

Chapter 13

Yacat, son of Mar, stood on the temple steps as a batch of the Chichi tribe were cleaned for execution. As a military commander, and a member of the Mar family, it was his responsibility to ensure these men were treated honorably, then presented properly to the gods.

"Warprince Yacat?"

"Hmm? Yacat blinked and looked to the prisoners. The speaker stood at ease with the others as the slaves washed him, and though they were young, strong men, Yacat had no fear they would attack, or flee. They had fought with honor.

"My name is Nahu. I fought you at the Orino river," said the prisoner. "It is a privilege that it should be you who sends me to Centnaz." He put a hand to his forehead then waved it forward with respect.

"The privilege is mine." Yacat nodded. "Your tribe fought like tigers. Had you not been betrayed by the cowardice of your neighbors, you may have beaten us. Their men were killed, their corpses left rotting for the crows."

Nahu snorted. "Then you have my thanks." He stood straight and proud, as was his right and duty as an honorable captive, and Yacat liked him. That he should be sacrificed seemed in that moment such a stupid, useless waste, Yacat felt a lifetime of revulsion fester like an open wound. He found he could no longer watch.

"Please excuse me, Nahu. But I will be at your side for the ritual. You have my word."

The prisoner nodded lower than honor demanded, and Yacat turned from the temple platform, leaving a scowling High Priest in his wake.

The citizens and warriors of Copanoch bowed or saluted as Yacat passed, only the priests refusing him the honor. His father was not popular with the temple of Centnaz, the Devourer god, but Yacat himself was openly reviled. This didn't bother him, and was entirely deserved. He had mocked their rituals and beliefs since boyhood, and nearly killed one of their priests over a woman. *One day*, he thought as he stared, *I will find a way to destroy you. You and all your false, lying priests, and your wasteful, foolish sacrifices.*

His personal guard swarmed around him as he moved, watching the citizens for weapons or any threatening move, ready to disarm or kill any who got too close. Yacat himself felt little concern. He was largely loved by the citizens of his city—a proven warrior, and a great hero of many battles. Because his mother's blood was common, they sometimes called him the Peasant Prince, for he was not a viable heir to the throne. But no doubt this also helped, for it was always easier to love a man who would never rule you.

It was mid-day of the second week of the sixteenth month, and the holiest festival of the divine calendar in Copanoch loomed. It was for this reason alone Yacat's father had sent him East to defeat the armies of the river tribes, and take prisoners. The people loved victory, and they loved the spoils. Now the city hummed with activity. Rich and poor prepared paints, food, clothes, and jewelry, readying for family feasts, and sacrifices to the gods. The landowners and noble classes would be bringing their tenants and laborers to dine with them, or visiting their houses with gifts. Allied noble families from the two other great cities were arriving with their entourages to cavort and plot with relatives and allies in war. They would prepare for months to host a week of ritual and celebration, but Yacat did not share his people's joy.

With his men encircling him, he hurried through the lesser temple grounds, climbing without pause to the noble houses and the palace. He returned the gestures of respect given by the royal guard—the Wolf, Puma, and Fox warrior-priests that were his kin by deed.

"What is my father's mood?" he asked at the heavy stone entrance to the king's inner court. One of the three elite warriors there cleared his throat.

"Mixed, I would say, *Tahana*," the big man answered. He used Yacat's unofficial military honorific, which literally meant 'spirit of war'. This was technically not allowed for living men, but all knew Yacat would be known as such in the histories when he died. Most who had fought with him used it, unless the royal family was in earshot.

When Yacat said nothing the older warrior winced. "His bowels have been running like the Madje river. And he has been meeting with Centnaz priests."

Yacat swore and took a breath. He looked at his uncle more seriously. "Are you not the *Silent* Guard, Anatzi? Do you betray all your oaths so easily?"

"Yes," Anatzi answered. "All but one, *Tahana*."

Yacat remained serious, and held his ground. "Were you not so ancient and feeble, Old Goat, I should kill you where you stand."

"You could try, Young Yack," the old warrior shrugged, and Yacat finally grinned.

"If you hear me raise my voice in there, be merciful, and come save me."

His uncle nodded most austerely, and Yacat pat his shoulder as he walked inside.

The royal chamber was as bleak and boring as ever. His father and brother hovered over a table filled with documents, three royal scribes exchanging pages with feverish effort. His brother noticed him first, giving a small wave as he rolled his eyes at the work. The king turned and grunted.

"So the prodigal son returns."

Yacat's brother, and the heir to the throne, hissed air.

"You called *me* the prodigal son mere moments ago, father."

"All my sons are prodigal," King Etzil Mar muttered, then hissed air and scattered papers as he stepped from the table. "Embrace me, boy. And tell me what sins you've managed since this morning."

Yacat went to his father's strong arms without discomfort. When it was over he winced because in fact he *had* been rather undisciplined. "I insulted High Priest Citla," he admitted. "A small matter. But I left him at the main temple of…"

"Heavens *tremble*, boy, I was joking. Oh nevermind. Leave us!" Etzil gestured at the scribes, who rose and saluted as they left without concern, despite the bluster. The king of Copanoch's rages and temper were both famous and well known to be more act than emotion. When the three of them were alone, the king's face changed, his eyes and tone matching the truth of his nature—restless schemer, brilliant strategist, and the pure ambition of a man who had expanded a city into a kingdom.

"I have two pieces of news and neither of them are good."

Yacat sighed and sat beside his brother. "Shouldn't your other sons be with us before we start belly aching?"

"No." The king sat, and for the first time Yacat began to worry. Meetings with only his father and the heir were rare and serious. "First, we've captured strange prisoners from the coast. Some kind of albinos—a giant of a man with demon eyes, and a woman the size of

110

Uncle Anatzi."

Yacat looked from the serious faces of his father and brother, and burst out laughing. "You were starting to worry me, father. This is why we're having a secret meeting? Because you captured a pair of freaks?"

"There's more of them," the crown prince added. "Some farmers fled when they spotted them in the jungle. Our men say they ran to the coast, and took fishing boats to a strange warship they couldn't recognize or explain."

Yacat shrugged. "Send a fleet. You're always whining our navy costs too much and has no purpose."

Etzil waved a hand in dismissal. "Of course I have. But I'll want you to see the prisoners. Speak with the men who saw the vessel, and have your best men ready if I call. We can't afford any surprises. Not now. There's to be no feasts, no rituals, no raids or patrols or *anything* until I say otherwise."

"You make me very happy, father. I despise all those things."

"This is serious, Yacat." The king released a breath and sat back in his chair. "I've been speaking with High Priest Nahua."

The name brought heat to Yacat's face and gut, for it was the brother of the priest he'd killed as a boy—and he had risen greatly in power in the temple since. "And what brilliant insight did the head fool have for us this time," Yacat refrained from spitting on his father's floor.

"*High Priest Nahua*," the king emphasized, "told us not only to expect a dangerous omen before the festival of stars, but that both the other great cities have been in discussions without us on *the matter of main concern*."

By this the king referred to the only thing he had been thinking of since Yacat could remember—the alliance of the three kingdoms of the valleys, and the discussion of an emperor. Yacat rolled his eyes. "So these strange slaves are your dangerous omen? You think he predicted it? No doubt the priests of Centnaz tell every family their allies are excluding them. They prefer us divided. They don't want an emperor. They want power for themselves."

"Whether or not he predicted it is irrelevant," said the heir. "It has been announced. This will enter the minds of every family from here to the sea."

"The priests of Centnaz have nothing against an emperor," said the king, and Yacat found he couldn't look away from his father's eyes. "They merely wish an emperor they consider a friend. An emperor they can *trust*."

"Well that rules out the three of us," Yacat said plainly.

His father took a long and disquieting breath, then released it. He leaned forward, which seemed some signal to Yacat's brother who did the same, taking a pitcher of oven-cooked agave and pouring it into three untouched cups set out by the heap of papers.

"Our treasury has never been wealthier," said Etzil more quietly. "Our allies are loyal, our enemies are weak. The strength of our crops is second only to the strength of our army, and thanks to you my son, our borders are secure." When Yacat said nothing, the king met his eyes and held them. "If an emperor were chosen, our family would be all but certain to succeed."

Yacat snorted. "The devourer's priests will never..."

"Save for the priests." The King finished, and drank his cup. Both men waited until Yacat did the same. The heir refilled them, and the king went on. "But I have obtained certain assurances. The festival of the stars is coming. It coincides this year with holy dates on both the divine and civil calendar. This time more than ever will be seen as the truth of a family's commitment to Centnaz, and to their piety. We must therefore choose a sacrifice."

Still Yacat said nothing. His mind seemed unable to comprehend his father's intention, save that he himself could be offered. Yacat had spent a lifetime disrespecting the new priests and their temples, preferring at all times the old gods and ways. He withheld tribute, he mocked their priests openly, he praised the other gods, and even beat a few of their disrespectful warrior-priests in his army when the moment arose. His life in offering would be logical, and if so, he would obey without objection.

Death had not frightened Yacat in war, and it did not frighten him now. He had lived all his life honorably and for duty, and would die a hundred times for his family's dynasty, if that was what was required. Yet he did not think this was the answer. Yacat's father was not a wasteful man, and he knew his son was the most feared general in the valleys—that he was whispered of by their allies and enemies alike, loved and respected by the army. To discard him was to throw away his main weapon before a battle.

"Your brother and I have discussed it," the king's tone had become neutral. "We have decided. An offering of royal blood will demonstrate our seriousness. If it was done well, if it was given the piety it deserves, with a single loss and a single night's work we might make our family emperors for two generations before another vote."

Yacat nodded, his throat constricted in anger. Common or noble, he had reviled the practice long before he witnessed it. So many lives, so much needless death, the unnatural surrender of life to a silent god. The decision surprised him, but as he accepted his own death he found he was not unhappy.

He had long tired of war, yet knew because of his family he would never be allowed to live in peace. *Let it end now*, he thought, *let me die in service to my family, in honor, and be done with all the death.*

"We have decided to give the gods your eldest son, Yacat."

The words seemed like some terrible magic that turned the air to water. Yacat found he could not move as they continued, like stones rippling through a pond.

"I will honor my grandson," the king's words echoed through the water, forcing their way to Yacat's ears. "I will honor my family and my people and give up a boy I love. And in so doing, your brother will be emperor of all."

Chapter 14

When he again trusted his legs, Yacat stood and returned his cup to his father's table. "The priest," he whispered. "It wasn't your idea was it. It was the priest who asked for my son."

The moment of silence was enough. Yacat sneered and turned to the two men he loved more than any others in the world—men he had killed for, men he would die for. "You know as well as I his brother wanted my wife, that she rejected him. He knows what this will do to her. Does this seem to you the request of a god, father, or that of a bitter, angry man?"

The king shrugged as he stood. "It makes no difference, my son."

"*It does to me*!" Yacat felt the killing urge itch his sword-arm, the hated call to blood he had always felt and always reviled. He heard footsteps and Uncle Anatzi stood behind him, a hand on his shoulder. "Did you know of this?"

Yacat met the man's hard eyes, and found them waver.

"I...nephew..."

Yacat closed his eyes and dropped to the cold stone. His kin came to him, putting their hands on his face and arms, reminding him he had more children, that he was young and would have many more. He heard his father promise him more wives, more wealth, more lands— that he could embrace this moment, embrace the new god of Copanoch and the valley, discarding his past sins against him.

"So many gifts," Yacat said when he could speak, feeling a rage beyond reason, an indignation he couldn't articulate. But understanding came. "Which of your gifts will give me back my honor?" he whispered. "Which will cleanse my betrayal of my child?"

They had more useless words but Yacat didn't listen. He stood and pushed off their hands, and perhaps saw the first signs of concern in their eyes that he would rebel against them. His uncle wore his knife, and Yacat laughed as he saw his hand ready to seize it. He strode forward and grabbed his uncle's arms with all his considerable strength, holding the blade sheathed.

"A man is nothing without honor, uncle, without devotion. Not in a hundred lifetimes, not after a thousand tortures or for the promise of eternal life would I disobey my king, would I strike him down." He met the man's already diminished gaze, then his brother's, then his father's. "All I have is yours. That includes the life of my son. But no stranger, no *priest* will do this thing. So I will be the one to give his life to your god."

The king of Copanoch nodded slowly. Though it was clear he also felt sadness, he was unable to hide his pleasure. "He is all our god, my son. That is a truth you must embrace. When you give your boy, I will be there, standing beside you, with all my support and love."

* * *

Yacat walked the halls of his father's palace, feeling in a stranger's home. He saw the same scuffed porcelain tiles where he played with rubber balls with his brothers. The same beautiful artwork of painted murals and walls remained, the same sculptures of great men and old gods, the same breathtaking view of the city. None of it brought him comfort.

Two hallways and a guarded gate led to the royal

quarters of the king and his family. There Yacat would find his sisters by blood or marriage and their children, the harem and the favored extended family. His wife, Maretzi, and their children would be sleeping through the hot afternoon sun, perhaps snacking on fruit, or playing lazily with their kin.

Yacat had once met two great warriors on the battlefield, a broken sword in his hand, and a war-dart through his arm, and he had charged without hesitation. But he found now he could not face his wife.

Centnaz, the god of sacrifice, The Devourer, was a disease of the mind. He was destroying Yacat's people, and yet he felt powerless to stop it. When Yacat was a boy he remembered many more rituals and holy days for other gods, their priests near as influential in the court and temples. It seemed their moon had waned. The cult of Centnaz had spread amongst the noble families first, encouraging their young men to hate their neighbors for their impiety, then to war and glory as the remedy. At first it had seemed almost boldly political, full of contradictions and nonsense, without proof of result. Yet it seemed even his own kin had accepted it, and not merely because it was useful, but because they now believed in power more than tradition and honor.

Yacat turned and descended through the palace halls and stairwells, trying to think of one person in the world he might sit and speak his mind with safely. He knew there was no one. The faith of The Devourer had spread until it consumed Yacat's world. Many now worshipped one god alone, and of those who did not, all considered him the chief amongst all others. To sacrifice to him had become natural and obvious. The greater the sacrifice, the greater the honor. And though Yacat's people had long sacrificed the present to be given gifts in the future, it was no longer chickens and goats to be eaten when the ritual was over. It was men.

It was *children*.

Yacat walked on, further and further until he found himself beneath the earth in the palace underground. Soon enough, he supposed, he would be there forever. Guards at the cellars saluted and stood at attention as he passed, and so dark were his thoughts, for the first time in his life he failed to return it.

"Your father said you'd be coming," said the captain in charge of the prisoners. Yacat knew his name but found it was buried in a fog. "Right this way, *Tahana*. But you should take a weapon—they aren't bound, and though they haven't fought, they certainly could. They look very strong."

Good, Yacat thought, *I hope they kill me.*

But he discarded this thought because it would not save his son.

"We've had the priests and scribes in with them for a day or two," said the guard. "Seems they don't speak a word, just gibberish."

"Have they been tortured?"

"No, *Tahana*. 'Honored slaves', are my orders. Not to be harmed."

Not today at least, Yacat thought. But such exotic specimens would never survive the ever-hungry glory of The Devourer, not with so many holy days so close.

He took a knife from the guard and stuffed it into his tunic. "I'll see them alone," he said, more on whim than anything.

The guard's brow quivered and he looked to his men before he managed to respond. "My lord, I don't think... surely, the king would not..."

"I am prince and General of the Border," Yacat's impotent rage spilled like rancid water from a cup. "You call me *Tahana*. Now do as I say before I show you why."

118

The Captain paled and half-saluted as he fled with his warriors behind him. Yacat waited until the trembling fury in his hands relaxed, then stepped into the prisoner's domicile. Nothing could have prepared him for what he saw.

The 'albino' warrior was truly a giant. He stood on the far side of the prison with the woman behind him as if for protection. He seemed ready for violence, perhaps in reaction to Yacat's shouts. Though the roof had been built high, near thirty hands, the strange warrior was hunched. He was deathly pale like a corpse, his eyes gold and slanted like a beast. Yacat drew his knife as he met them.

Most of his life he had been a warrior. He had killed before he was twelve, captured dozens in battle, long ago earning more honor than all but the highest ranks of soldiers; he had fought beside honorable knights, and base killers, and learned to spot the difference between the two. The man before him was neither. In his strange, golden eyes Yacat did not see a warrior weighing the threat of another man—he saw a tiger inspecting its prey. Yacat slowly put away his knife, and laughed.

"A fitting end to Yacat, mighty hero, and *Tahana*," he said, sitting on a bench across from the prisoners. "To die quietly in his home by acting a fool." When he'd put away the knife, the woman emerged and took her own seat. Her skin was as pale as the man's, but her hair was long and golden brown and beautiful. Yacat had seen albinos before, and nothing about the man or woman's consistent pigment or eyes or hair were similar. He laughed again, though this time even he recognized the desperation in the sound. "You'll be from the far North," he shrugged, "which it seems my father didn't even consider. So deep is he now in his hunger for the throne, he loses even simple reason." Yacat reached in his pocket for a flask of agave wine, and drank deep. "As he loses his morality."

The prisoners said nothing, but Yacat didn't care. He felt here in their presence was the only place he might speak words he had held deep inside for almost the entirety of his life. Whatever else they were, they were true, but his people no longer valued such things. "My family have lost their way," he managed before he felt his voice break. "They destroy children in their games for power." He felt the tears follow. "My people have lost their way."

* * *

Zaya sat on the uncomfortable stone bench and listened to the foreigner mutter nonsense. Ruka seemed enthralled, as if carefully noting every sound and intonation, as if he could understand.

"Do you know what he's saying?" Zaya whispered. The shaman frowned, saying nothing until the foreigner stopped speaking.

"I will learn. So must you. To be without words will make us animals to them."

Zaya leaned forward, her excitement growing. "Do the gods speak to you? Do they tell you this?"

The shaman's eyes narrowed and he looked away. "I tell you what is true of all men. These ones will be no different."

The way he'd said 'I will learn' had been so matter of fact Zaya had almost assumed it was boasting. Where they came from, men were always boasting of their deeds and abilities, though a shaman like Ruka was outside such things. Still, there were legends of his skill with words—he was not called the godtongue without reason. Men said he could remember everything he'd ever seen or read—that he'd sailed North to the new world and returned speaking every tongue of those lands. Zaya was a skald and heard exaggerated tales often, and so she did not believe this. But still, he did speak several languages fluently.

The foreigner disturbed Zaya's thoughts with a kind of groan, his body drooping across his bench, eyes downcast with his head in his hands. His limbs were long and thick with muscle, his body a dark statue of carved oak. Even his face to Zaya was strong and handsome, and he looked like a warrior. But his weeping and defeated demeanor was not appealing.

"Perhaps he is some kind of advocate? To stand for us in a law circle? His depression does not bode well if so."

The shaman grunted. "Animals have no advocates. I don't know what he is. I suspect a kind of nobleman, perhaps a prince."

"Then what is he…"

The foreigner rose and paced across the room, muttering more of his nonsense with growing volume. He gestured with his hands, his face expressive and ranging from rage to sadness, his voice rising with drama. Zaya smiled as she watched him. The notes of a warrior's song echoed in her mind, and she wished she had her lyre. When the foreigner stopped and stared she realized she had stood and come closer to inspect him. Like the islanders he met her eyes directly, and though this made her uncomfortable she held his gaze and smiled. He was clearly taken aback, so she did what she had been taught all her life to do when others were dejected. She sang.

The sad warrior reminded her of the tale of Avik, a mighty chief who served in the army of Imler the Betrayer. Avik was the only chief amongst hundreds who had turned on his master, helping the prophetess to destroy his army. But before his victory, all he'd loved was destroyed, and even those he had saved considered him a fallen man. A statue of him yet stood in the capital, his dejected eyes much like this stranger's.

As she sang the foreigner stared as if frozen. When she was finished he stared as if he'd forgotten where he was, the stillness finally broken with a blink of his dark eyes, and he spoke words Zaya didn't understand. The tone was familiar, however, and she smiled and bowed her head, then sat again by the shaman. The dark warrior made a gesture with his hand over his heart, then turned and left them alone.

Zaya felt the curious gaze of the Godtongue, and shrugged. "Animals can't do that, now, can they?"

The shaman shook, and for a moment Zaya was alarmed before she realized he was laughing. The sound came after, a loud chuckle that seemed almost painful for the man. "No," he said as if in admission. "The birds of paradise can sing, but not like you, Zaya, daughter of Egil. Not like that."

Zaya nodded in thanks, and did her best to hide her pleasure. "What will they do with us?" she asked, though she wasn't sure she wished to know.

The shaman's good humor faded, and he leaned against the stone and closed his eyes. "They will take us, sooner or later. Make use of what time you have. Watch. Listen. Remember. We must understand this place. Its existence may shake our already trembling world." He lifted his head and met her eyes. "We do not control the future, Zaya. But I do not wish war and sickness and death as our people brought to the isles. I wish to avoid it. You say you have come to me with fate. You say you are my skald, as once your father was. There is a task now before us, if we've the courage. Will you help me?"

For a moment Zaya could not speak, feeling bathed in the warmth of sunlight. If ever there was a moment she knew she had been right to leave her home, and brave the sea, knowing the gods were watching, it was now. Her fears drained away, pushed out with purpose —the great shaman, the godtongue, *needed her help*! She took a deep breath and nodded.

"I swear on the mother, and the mountain, whatever is needed. I will help you."

Chapter 15

Though his family and people had...disappointed him, Yacat was reminded he still had things he could do. He had brave soldiers to pay, rituals to organize, an army and navy to keep in check. Then when his obligations were complete, and all that remained of his duties were to himself and to his Gods, perhaps, yes perhaps, he had a great deal of priests to kill.

"Move the prisoners into my guest rooms," he commanded the guard as he found them. "They are to be attended by palace slaves and kept fit and healthy until I instruct otherwise." When he saw the man's terror prevent his questioning Yacat sighed and put a hand to the man's shoulder. "The king will want whatever knowledge they have. He has left the task to me. All is with his blessing."

The captain visibly sagged with relief, and saluted. "Apologies, *Tahana*. It's just...I'd feared for your safety, if something should have happened..."

"You've done your duty, nothing more. Continue that wisdom now and do as I ask."

"Lord." The captain and his guard saluted again as Yacat left them.

He walked along the palace corridors, smiling as he thought at the difference a few moments could make. First he would see his wife. Together they would weep for the fate of their son, but Yacat knew he must be strong. The festival of stars was not for three months. This meant he had sixty days to test the loyalties of noble sons he had commanded in war; he had sixty days to gather his most loyal troops, confound and flatter his enemies, then slaughter them. So much time was a gift, as music and health and strength were gifts. Strange that it took a beautiful slave to remind him.

"Cuexta, the legend of Trist," Yacat half-embraced the royal bodyguard who held the entrance to the harem. Though his eyes smiled, Cuexta did not return or even flinch at the affection, as was his way. "How many men did you kill on that bridge?"

"Six, *Tahana*, as you well know."

Yacat looked at the ceiling as if lost in thought. "I know nothing. I wasn't there, was I? Perhaps you dragged the corpses before you and declared yourself a hero?"

The man loosed his signature growl, which had been a delight since childhood, and Yacat laughed as he released him and walked past. A dozen royal children played in the enclosed garden. The hot afternoon sun kept the women and servants along the walls in the shade, drinking fruit juice and playing tablegames, or lost in lazy discussion.

For a moment Yacat watched the children play and said nothing, locking the moment in his mind. He found his wife sitting with the other primary wives of his brothers, and as ever his heart warmed to see her. She was a princess of high birth from Tlanopan, both attractive and intelligent, from a line renowned for its fertility. She had, in other words, been a prize fit for a king, secured for Yacat by his father after his first major victory in war. He had met her once at a festival for noble youth, and when the king asked what he wanted, he asked only for her. No man could ask for a better wife. She had given him three children and many days and nights of joy, and he had not asked for any other wives or concubines. Now he would tell her their son would die.

She recognized his look and excused herself without being called, turned towards her chamber, and dismissed the servants that followed. Once inside, they stood alone on the carpet, surrounded by the many honors and trophies Yacat had earned in war. She bowed in respect. "You honor me, husband. I didn't expect to see you until this evening." He took a deep breath and said nothing, and her expression transformed. "What's wrong, husband? Is everything alright?"

"No," he managed, *things will never be alright again.* Yacat was not a man prone to small talk and his wife did not expect it. In any case, it would not help what he had to say. "I have spoken with the king. He and my brother intend to make their claim for a newly made position of emperor of the three cities." Maretzi knew Yacat well enough to know this news alone would not please him, for it would surely mean more wars for him to fight. But she said nothing, perhaps recognizing there was more. Yacat forced the words. "To win the support of the priests of Centnaz, a great sacrifice will be required."

Maretzi had not understood, and nearly collapsed when he told her. He took her to her bed and held her until she was ready to speak.

"Why? Why our son, husband?"

He felt his jaw clench as he tried to explain. He could have told her about the priest who had wanted her, who had insulted them both and challenged Yacat, forcing a duel to the death. He could have explained his own lack of piety and respect for the religion of blood. But it didn't matter. So he said only: "It had to be someone's son."

"But why yours?" her eyes were wide and she clawed at the bedding. "How many battles have you won for them? What trouble have you ever caused? Your brother Itzil drank all day and night until you and the others stopped him. Patlee wouldn't know his duties if you dragged his whoring face through them like mud!

You are the best of your brothers!"

For a woman from another noble family to speak of Yacat's brothers in this way was almost unthinkable, even if it was true, but he understood and merely held her. "Perhaps that is why, my wife. All will know this is not convenient, not easy, but a true act of piety."

She wept then, with shaking sobs of agony. When it was over she had a look Yacat didn't understand. She wiped the tears from her eyes and nose as if renewed, smiling through the sadness. "I'm supposed to wait another month, and for the priests and physicians to bless it, but I must tell you, it must *mean* something. It must be a sign. I am two month's pregnant, husband, or so they think. I dreamt it would be a son."

Yacat stared into her eyes, so confounded by the lows and highs, and the strange reaction from his wife. Before he could even think of what to say Maretzi took his hands.

"Don't you see, husband? It's the will of Centnaz. He is welcoming you into his grace. He is showing us that with sacrifice comes reward—he takes the life of one son," she choked back the gasping sob, "but replaces it with another."

He pulled her face to his chest to hide his expression. He touched her hair, and tried to comfort her, to agree. He had known he would have to be strong. She held his chest and wept, and when he left her he saw her going to her personal shrine to pray and burn incense. Yacat knew he himself would not pray.

He walked through the harem smiling at the children because his misery was not their fault, but was glad he didn't see his son. He nodded in respect to the wives and concubines and then to Cuexta at the door, feeling as if he'd been dipped in the icy waters of the sea.

He had lied to himself, he realized. For a moment he

had found comfort in a path of destruction, imagining a war against a god, cutting as much rot as he could before his demise. But he knew if he betrayed the priests, it would not just be him who was destroyed. It would be Maretzi and all her children. He had thought perhaps she would feel as he had—that the betrayal of their son was not the comings and goings of divinity, but the shattering of their world. But Yacat knew he was like flint—sharp, and brittle, where his beautiful Maretzi would bend like copper, and so she would survive. His other children were young and they too would recover, until perhaps one day they'd forget even the memory of their older brother. For them he understood he must live a lie, betraying himself as he would betray his son.

Perhaps for some sin in a past life it was his punishment to live without honor. In a way, he envied his son in that moment. He alone would be given the mercy of death.

Still, there was work ahead. First Yacat had a duty to his king, only then to his family. He was a prince and general of Copanoch, and soon a brother to an emperor. Perhaps the toil would save him. Perhaps if he fought the wars to come, if he dealt with these strange barbarians and smiled through his teeth at the priests, keeping order and serving the law as he gave those who deserved it dignity, and those who deserved it death—perhaps if he spent every waking moment of his miserable life helping others in all the small ways he could, it would redeem him.

He left the harem resolved, knowing that was his only path. But as he crossed the halls and the terrace, out from the palace and into the light of the sun god, whose light revealed all darkness, he knew, too, that was another terrible lie.

* * *

Zaya's night dreams still lingered when her jailers came. It wasn't the guards, who had largely been polite, but rather three men in white cloth and feathered headresses, their limbs circled with rings of gold and silver. They lifted her up, and when the shaman rose with his quiet menace they panicked and barked for the guards, who came forward with spears and swords and nets, gesturing to withdraw.

"I'll be alright," Zaya told him, trying to feign confidence, though she was terrified. The shaman took a deep breath and stepped away, then the guards motioned for him to come with them.

"If death awaits us. I am sorry."

"You warned me", she said. "It was I who insisted."

A strange relief came with the words, for she was reminded of the unlikely chance of their meeting, and that the gods watched over all.

The feathered men dragged her roughly back to the streets. The city seemed all but asleep, the bustling roads she had seen in the day now dark and lifeless. The men pushed her onwards, though she didn't fight them, and once or twice she nearly lost her feet on the slippery cobblestones.

They walked along the buildings, only one or two of which glowed with dim light and murmured with happy voices. But the men did not go into one of these.

Instead they took her to a vast stone building much like a palace, save that it seemed composed almost entirely of steps leading to three layers of flat, square platforms. It didn't seem like a place people lived. They marched her to the first platform, where other robed men and a gathering of mostly naked men and women were waiting. The robed men dabbed these others with paints or doused them in incense. Her escorts brought her to this line, and began tearing at her clothes.

She fought them, which earned her a hard slap across the face as four men seized her and pulled her to her knees. Her heart hammered now, and still she fought, even as the men cut the sailor's shirt from her body. Near the hard stone of the platform, she began to smell the blood. It was old and rancid and stained everything. Before the line of painted captives she saw an altar, a cauldron, and a table set with knives.

Her mind blanked, resistant to what seemed the only conclusion, and she stared at the fine, white robes of the men. She clung to this, thinking men who killed would never wear such things, that the blood would stain them and never come out. As if they had read her thoughts, most of these robed men stripped their clean, white robes and placed them together in a pile. Beneath they were painted with images of wild beasts in reds and blues. Their bodies were often scarred in neat rows, as if the damage had been self-inflicted and controlled.

Zaya roared as she fought to her feet, thrashing at the men who held her. None of the others resisted. Her captors seemed almost confused, enraged, and began calling up the steps for men in armor, who descended towards Zaya with spears. There were so many. They were above, below, all around her. She couldn't escape.

They bound her hands roughly and pushed her towards the altar, one of the robed men sneering and hissing harsh sounding words in her ear. She couldn't stop them. At least five men held her arms and legs, bracing her forward as one yanked her head back by her long hair. She stared up at the sky and sang the song of Haki the brave, forcing her breath and will to hold the sounds, and so show the gods she would die without fear.

More angry words echoed around the square, but in a

voice Zaya recognized. At their sound several of the hands released her instantly, and she was able to turn to see the sad warrior from her cell at the bottom of the square, panting with a handful of men at his side.

For a long moment the men stared and said nothing. Then the maybe prince came forward and Zaya could see veins bulged in his neck, his eyes wild with a rage she could hardly believe. The robed men panicked and took up their knives, yelling at their warriors as the men came to blows.

The prince moved like a hunting cat. He pushed aside a spear as if he swept a branch, crushing the wielder's face with a brutal strike of some wooden club.

Men were shouting "mahala!" on both sides, as if both in encouragement or terror, and Zaya wondered if this were the name of their god. The prince struck down another guard, and soon both sets of warriors were together and wrestling over spears and swords. In heartbeats it was over, and the prince held the man who had escorted Zaya with his hands around the man's neck. His eyes were bulged, his lips curled in a terrible sneer of pure hatred. His men seemed to be calling to him, trying to pull him away. He whispered words Zaya couldn't understand, and released his grip.

He gestured to Zaya with a hand, almost in dismissive afterthought. She reached for the torn rags of her shirt and the prince barked in a language-crossing order of haste. She abandoned the efforts and crossed an arm over her breasts, following her savior and his warriors down the steps and back to the streets without a glance back at the strange temple.

In something of a daze, she was lead back to the palace, far away from the cell she had been in before, down corridors and up stairwells past intricate carvings and murals of men and beasts.

At last she entered a room fit for a queen. A huge

washing basin that looked like bronze or gold stood in its center; animal furs covered the floor, leading to a wide-framed bed, and walls cluttered with wardrobes and tables. It smelled of pine and spice, and a young, flat-faced girl waited beside the bed on her knees, almost in supplication. The prince gestured inside, then turned away and closed the heavy door without a word.

Zaya stood with her arms crossed over her chest, still trembling as the girl rose and managed to lead her to the basin, gesturing inside. An image of the steaming cauldron at the temple flashed before her, but she forced it away, disrobing what remained of her clothes to sit in the tepid water.

She still saw the look in the men's eyes that had held her—the fanatical gaze of zealots locked in the throes of religious fervor, immune to and perhaps even relishing her screams. She had no idea why they had taken her at all, never mind why her *specifically* and not the shaman, or why she'd then been saved. Terror clung to her mind from being trapped in an unknowable prison. The shaman's words came again, ringing like prophecy in her ears. '*To be without words will make us animals to them.*'

She wondered then how a sheep must feel, ripped from the herd though it understood nothing—led blindly to the slaughter without knowing why it had been trapped or chosen or killed. Men, after all, did not explain themselves to sheep.

The girl washed the paint from Zaya's skin, humming as she picked dried blood from her hair, while Zaya stared blankly at the stone.

Chapter 16

On the third day since their landing, Chang found an armory in Ruka's quarters. Along with several stacks of papers—usually detailed drawings of sea animals, or star patterns—there was a collection of iron weapons and armor hung neatly on the walls. At first Chang simply goggled, running his hands over the spears, swords and long daggers, all of which were smooth metal from end to handle, rather than wooden shafts with metallic tips. He had never seen such a thing, nor metal with an almost blue tinge to the finish. Beside these, there were ten sets of fine chain links almost like 'shirts', too small for the shaman, or indeed any man of ash. Chang could only conclude they had been made for islanders.

He informed the captain, who insisted on seeing the items for himself. When he arrived he stared and shook his head, muttering, 'god cursed savage' beneath his breath.

The crew were promptly equipped, with their thickest cloth worn beneath the iron rings for another layer of protection. They complained of the heat and the weight, but after testing each other's armor with playful—and utterly ineffective—thrusts and stabs with their weapons, they soon quieted.

On the fourth day, the captain ordered landfall. This time they went North, choosing a series of high cliffs to make their approach, hoping it would obscure the sight of their ship. They left Old Mata with the Pitman to ready the ship in case of problems, and the others boarded their scouting catamaran, armed and carrying barrels and other containers to re-supply. Only the captain wore no armor, preferring instead his thin black silks and a collection of knives. No man considered him unprepared.

Only a few steps from their landing they found more signs of human life. Nets hung on the closest trees used as make-shift warehousing, rope strung between these and several wooden pillars to form a kind of hanging shelves.

"Keep your eyes open," said the captain. "Not all the natives may be of the same group, and we aren't here to kill. If we run into much trouble, we head back to the ship and move."

This suited Chang and his men fine, and they nodded without complaint. They followed along the beach at first, but everywhere inland seemed covered in the same dense jungle they had found before. Sooner or later, it seemed, they would be forced to move deeper.

The captain seemed as reluctant as the men. At last with a quiet sigh he marched into the trees, leading them on for half the morning before they came upon a fast-moving stream and decided to re-fill their water. This they did, though they needn't have bothered, for by afternoon the sky had clouded over and begun to rain in a manner rarely seen even in the isles. The downpour was so thick, their two shipguards later told them they'd begun to panic and bail with buckets before they realized the shaman's ship was designed to funnel most rain through the scuppers.

They at least had roofs over their heads. The landing crew waited rather miserably in the trees, exchanging three flasks of rum in a sodden circle, huddled beneath the thick, wide leaves of the largest tree they could find. When it was over, the clouds passing as quickly as they'd arrived, the jungle sprang to life.

Wide red flowers opened like sentient creatures seeking the sun; birds sang in a chaotic choir, and ants marched up trees like writhing carpets, an endless army invading the world. Other, winged insects filled the air with buzzing and clicks, and soon the men were swatting at mosquitoes, or some kind of stinging fly.

"Let's get the bloody hell out of here, Lucky," complained the Steerman, slapping himself in the cheek. Chang's instinct was to ignore the man, but this time he tended to agree. His sweaty skin felt as if it crawled, and no amount of itching or rubbing ended the agony. Every piece of his body was either slick with sweat or red with stings, and all he wanted was to board his ship and never touch land again.

A low growl brought Chang to his senses, and he turned to see bright eyes staring from the gloom of shaded trees. For a moment he stared, unable to comprehend, then barked a warning to the others. Only the captain stood his ground.

The rest cried out and drew spears or knives as they huddled together and withdrew. For a moment Chang thought the eyes might belong to the monstrous pilot, and he forced himself to inspect before he reacted. Before he could, a huge cat-like beast emerged, its night-black fur slick with rain, two fangs the size of Chang's knives jutting from its jaw. It stood at least his height at the shoulders.

A long knife was in the captain's hand, and his gaze never wavered from the creature.

"See the men back to the ship," he said calmly. When Chang didn't move, he almost shouted. *"Run."*

* * *

After several long strides, Chang turned to Basko and slapped his back, already regretting his choice. "Lead them! *Go!*"

135

With that he turned back and grit his teeth, his compulsion to leave no man behind infuriating. He re-entered the edge of the clearing, and saw the beast's eyes and teeth, first. It growled, raking its claws through the air, but touched nothing. The captain didn't attack, instead springing away at inhuman speed, stopping each time as if only curious. The huge cat followed, eyes squinting as it slowed and pursued, for all the world as if the two were *playing*, or in some kind of dance.

The scene was too much for Chang—another living nightmare that almost leaked his bladder down his leg. He turned and fled. He caught the others in a rhythm of stumbles and ragged breaths, until they stood in a ring panting, eyes roaming each other to perhaps confirm the thing they'd seen.

"We have to get the captain." Chang almost groaned at his own words.

"Like hell we do," said the Steerman, to a few grunts of approval.

"He's dead," said an oarsman. "So it's our bloody boat now. I say we take her and sail."

"Sail where," Chang hissed, smearing a hand over the stubble of his hair.

"Home," the oarman insisted. "We know the way well enough, neh? Keep the sun to port, and keep 'er steady. We'll make it."

"And the pilot? The girl?" Chang spoke as if only curious. A few men at least showed signs of guilt, but not much.

"Wit' respect, Lucky, we all know they're dead. And even if.."

"We don't know shit," Chang said with a bit more force.

"Even *if*, they ain't our concern. We're bloody sailors,

not landsmen soldiers, neh?"

"Aye."

"Right."

These and many sounds of agreement sounded from the men. Chang met their eyes one by one, ending with Basko.

"You all agree? We leave the man who freed us. We take all his...gifts," he gestured to their armor, and nodded in the direction of the ship. "We leave the pilot, who saved you. We leave Zaya, who danced and sang with us. Leaving mine to die, is that how I'm known?"

"There's nought bloody all we can do for them, Lucky!" The Steerman's cowardice was growing wild in his eyes and frothing on his lip. "Look at this place." He gestured hopelessly at the trees.

"Gentlemen." The calm voice of the captain entered their little grove, and the men spun with weapons drawn. "Calm." The captain stepped from the shade with his hands upturned. He looked entirely whole, and unharmed, his black silks without a single shred. Chang felt himself relax—until he saw the cat's giant eyes.

"Shit! There!" The Steerman pointed into the trees, where the creature's bright pupils shone like firelight.

"Calm, gentlemen!" The captain stood between them, his hands still raised. "This will be difficult to accept...but," he shrugged. "I believe the beast is tamed. It seems, well, I think it wants me to *follow* it."

Chang blinked as he processed the words, glancing at the open mouths of his comrades. He suspected he spoke for all of them.

"Captain, are you out of your bloody mind?"

The assassin shrugged and tilted his head with a kind of concession.

"Well, it stopped trying to eat me. And it kept trying to go North until it noticed I didn't follow, then it circled back and…I don't now, *gestured*. You tell me what that means."

"It means we run back to the ship as fast as we fucking can," Chang said, a growing concern in his gut.

The captain frowned, and looked to the creature, which for all the world seemed to point North with a tilt of its giant head. The men withdrew and groaned near in unison at the sight.

"Enlightened preserve us," Chang fingered Roa's charm in his pocket, and heard the men muttering their own divine pleas.

"Well that settles it," the captain smiled, as if this were all some grand adventure. "We go with the cat."

He extended a hand North to the animal, which licked its lips and turned as if it understood. Chang feared even to look at the reaction of his men. He couldn't begin to imagine what words of comfort would make their situation reasonable. They were across the entire world, beyond an endless sea in a damned jungle filled with murderers, being guided deeper by a huge, intelligent cat.

But then, he supposed, living on a floating piece of wood on the open sea was not what most men considered reasonable—a good pirate had to have perspective.

He grinned a little as inspiration struck, sheathing his knife as he followed.

"The cat scares me right enough," he said without looking at the others. "But that man is worse."

He slapped at an insect as he walked on, grinning as he heard the men trudge behind.

* * *

Chang began to hate the jungle. He and his men were

by no means soft city island folk—they could work for days and maybe weeks with little rest if required, but they weren't used to marching in armor. They weren't used to bending their backs with supplies and weapons under a dark canopy that smothered light and the open sky, suffocating them on all sides with heat and clutter and pestering life.

"We can't march forever," the Steerman complained for the fourth or fifth time as the day wore on.

"Tell the damn jungle beast we need to camp," said an oarman without a note of jest.

Chang snorted and tried to pretend he too wasn't exhausted and miserable. His feet felt swollen to twice their size, squeezed in his sandals like prisoners bound with rope. They had crossed a near stagnant river and been covered in some kind of leech for their trouble. Now the ground ascended endlessly, as if they climbed the widest, most infuriatingly gradual mountain known to man, and would never reach its peak. Every muscle in his legs had moved past burning to a dull, pitiful ache, replaced only by bouts of trembling weakness. The third time he felt he couldn't take another step, the captain raised a hand for the men to stop.

"We've arrived," he said, though it seemed to Chang as if the jungle looked no different than the rest.

He was about to ask how the man knew they'd arrived anyplace when the first piece of foliage moved, clinging to the tanned flesh of a man.

A curved, green bow moved with it, and all around the sailors men stained with camouflage rose from the bush or from behind trees with bows and arrows ready.

"Ah." Chang found he was too tired to be afraid. He slumped his pack to the ground and sat, groaning as the weight eased from his legs. "Tell them we followed their cat, Captain. I'm sure that will explain everything."

Now that he mentioned it, Chang realized he didn't see the cat at all. This struck him as rather funny, and while it seemed beyond unwise, he very nearly lost himself in a fit of laughter.

The ambushers were coming closer, some now holding wooden spears and other primitive weapons, until a growl sounded from the trees. The golden eyes emerged, then the beast turned and continued North, until the jungle dwellers gestured for the sailors to keep moving.

Chang rose with an audible groan, not sure if he'd have preferred death. Every step was agony, but not far from their ambush the trees began to thin, and then clear, until they were replaced by huts and proper houses built in lines and rings.

All around them, foreigners worked or sat in clusters. Half-naked women busied themselves with a thousand tasks, preparing food or fussing over fabrics, pots and rope while their children played and hollered without concern. Chang could see only the handful of men who had ambushed them, and one or two older men in the camp. The rest were boys, no more than ten years old.

"Impa tahaya man?"

An older woman blocked their path and spoke nonsense. She was half-naked, her sagging breasts mostly covered by beads hanging from her neck. Her hair was long and greying black, her skin pock marked and weathered. But her sharp eyes held the fire of command. She inspected the sailors, gesturing at the men and speaking in long strings of incomprehensible words until one of the warriors ran off into the trees. The rest stayed and pointed at the ground, and Chang sat without a second thought.

"I bet they feed us to the cat," the Steerman muttered, tired enough he'd moved from cowardice to pouting.

The crew of *The Prince* sat in silence, huddled together with bows and spears pointed somewhat lazily in their direction. Now that Chang could see all the foreigners, he decided he and his men could almost certainly destroy the poorly armed warriors with little trouble, unless there were more hiding in the trees. He was nearly ready to suggest it to the captain, when the warrior returned.

An old man limped beside him, leaning heavily on a gnarled stick as he squinted up at the crew. The huge cat strolled beside him, yawning as it leapt and settled on a cart, and stared. The tribesmen kept their distance from the old man. Chang noticed most averting even their eyes as he passed. He sat on the edge of the same cart as the animal, and sighed.

"Forgive my people's distrust." His words almost echoed, fading to a whisper in Chang's ears. "We are used to outsiders being our enemies."

Chang blinked and turned to see his men were wide-eyed.

"You speak *Batonian*?" whispered the captain, even his stern face slack with awe. The old man smiled, and Chang shook his head, having clearly heard the words in his native tongue—a language spoken by very few people left on the continent.

"Didn't speak Batonian, Captain. Not to me."

Again the old man smiled, revealing only a few red teeth. His strange voice echoed again as if next to Chang's ears.

"The mountain's gift has many uses. The first is Tongues. You will understand my words for a time, and I yours. I know you are strangers here, and that you came from the sea. My name is Pacal, and I have many questions. In return I will answer yours as best I can." He gestured to the trees, and perhaps the sky.

141

"Welcome, guests of the High Mountain Tribe, to the valley of the gods."

Chapter 17

"Stop staring at the women." Chang barked at Basko, then promptly ignored his own order. This time it was two girls carrying water from a nearby river, their skin exposed save for a thin covering over their waists. The girls noticed their admirers and smiled, and Chang took a deep, calming breath, trying not to think of Zaya living in endless misery amongst her captors. "But I bet you've charmed them, haven't you Macha?" he whispered. "Yes, with your siren song. I hope you have."

"What's that, Chiefy?"

"Nothing." Chang ran his knife over another foreign root, grimacing at the sloppy cut. "What shall we do today, Captain?" he muttered. "Oh I don't know, Chang. Maybe skin more red root? A fine idea, Captain." He flicked the last piece of the hated skin into his pail, and lifted another. Beside him, Basko growled as he skinned a knuckle for the dozenth time. He'd been too worried of his own incompetence to use the flint knives of the natives, instead resorting to his bronze, but it was too dull and took three times the effort. Brave Basko was always stubborn.

"Do you think they eat anything besides this damn root?" the big man said glumly.

"No." Chang flicked another piece. "I think they sleep on beds of red root. I think they drink red root and fuck red root."

"In that order, Chiefy?" said Basko, and Chang at least managed a grin.

Three days now they'd lived amongst the natives, swatting at mosquitoes, shivering in turns from some spreading cough, and eating red roots for what felt like three times a day. It became clear that at least three quarters of the tribe were women, girls, and old men, though whether the men were dead, out hunting, or at war, Chang didn't know. Regardless, he and his crew were watched and doted on by a host of half-naked beauties with dark hair and skin like Chang's, who brought food and water and blankets as they giggled and tried to communicate then ran away.

Every night the captain sat with their elder, or chief, or whatever the hell he was. They spoke over a campfire too far away to overhear or see, then he'd come back and sleep in the huts they'd been given, stinking like firesmoke and—Chang was *certain*—some kind of proper drink.

"Well, it beats prison," Basko sucked a finger. "Barely. But by god I could use some rum."

"In prison there was a chance to escape." Chang sighed, then stared again at the captain's fire. "What the hell are they tonguing about, do you think?"

"Don't wanna know. The captain," Basko looked around, as if the man might be near. "He didn't run from that cat, neh? Didn't even look afraid. Might be the old sorcerer king bastard gave him magic, way he just appears and you never see 'em. Somethin' ain't right."

Chang nodded but said nothing. When he'd boarded the *Prince* he'd been worried about the complex sails and the big ashman warlord, which were strange enough. Now there were foreigners who could speak any language using magic rocks; a new land beyond the sea; giant, thinking cats. Who the hell knew what was next.

"Chang."

He stood to attention, annoyed at his own response.

"Aye, Captain?"

"Join us at the fire, Chief. You should hear this. And

wear your armor."

The captain walked back to his meetings and Chang turned to Basko, who raised a thick brow. "Leave that knife, Chiefy. These buggers are touchy. They'll grab it up there near their betters."

Chang nodded, but left it on his belt. "If they find nothing they might search my arse to be sure."

Basko shrugged, then his eyes widened in hope. "Think he'll tell us when we go back to the ship? Maybe we'll do some trade, then sail off, aye? Come back with soldiers?"

"I know as much as you do, Basko."

"Aye, course. But I want your oath." The big man rose and his face turned serious. "If there's drink, *proper* drink, or food, something other than red root, you'll bring some back. Swear it, Chiefy. Swear it by your damned evil god."

Chang fought his grin, putting a hand to his heart. "May Roa claim me, brother, I swear."

Basko's eyelids drooped and his chest fell in relief. He sat back on his log and lifted another root, sticking out his tongue in concentration as he peeled.

* * *

Chang put on his armor as ordered, then made his way to the chief's fire, doing his best to ignore the warriors who eyed him. It was soon clear he had crossed some invisible line that marked the normal tribesmen from the warriors, and though they were few in number, these bow and spear armed men were athletic and sharp-eyed hunters. Chang rather preferred not to offend them.

He met the eyes of the closest, nodding in what he hoped passed for respect. Two approached and searched him, their rough hands checking him with a practiced thoroughness. He gave no reaction as they took the obvious bronze knife at his belt. Since they could fill him full of arrows anytime they wished, he thought the blade a rather useless gesture anyway.

"Go now?" he tapped his chest, then pointed towards the fire. The man nodded and Chang walked on. As he did he realized there were far more men than he'd seen before. Hundreds of warriors in different dress and with different weapons, painted symbols and jewelry had gathered amongst the closest trees. The elder, Pacal, was there with the captain, but so too were five others who looked like shamans or chiefs.

Their host waited until Chang sat, then took something from a pouch on his hip and clutched it hard in his palm. He chanted and shook, then dropped it into the fire, sending a hiss of green flame from what looked like a small piece of metal. The scent was familiar—like the thing Chang had thought was a strong drink clinging to the captain.

"You will know each other's words," he spoke in the same disjointed, echoing voice he had first greeted them with. The other men too seemed amazed by the feat and sound before Pacal gestured to them. "These men are chiefs of large tribes who hate the men of the great lakes. They have come at my request." He turned and gestured to the captain and Chang, his eyes and those of the others now roaming the iron mail and plates on Chang's forearms and shins. "These are the foreigners I spoke of, who say they have crossed the Eastern ocean."

The chiefs exchanged neutral glances as the captain bowed in respect.

"The wise Pacal asks, and so we come," answered one of the chiefs in the same echoing words. "Now tell us why."

"The city of Copanoch prepares their holy festival," said Pacal. "I assume it is not just the mistmen who have lost kin, dragged from river or coast by valleymen for their devourer god." No one spoke, and it was clear the answer was 'yes'. "You will all know the myths." He pointed to the East. "Yacotal foretold long ago the valley of the gods was not meant to last as it is. He said men would come from the sea, men who followed no laws, nor feared any wounds." Eyes flicked again to Chang's iron armor, and many of the chiefs shifted in clear discomfort, or whispered amongst themselves. "I believe they have come."

"There are many myths, Pacal," spoke an older man, his voice humming with the strange power. "I would risk the lives of my tribe on very few of them."

"And yet," Pacal pointed at Chang. "Have you ever seen such men? Such armor? The mist tribes have seen their ships, moored now off the Eastern coast. They say they have come from far-away lands, beyond our world. And the mountain would tell me if they were lying."

"Even if they speak the truth," said the same older man. "How many men do they have? How many warriors?"

Here Pacal's confidence dimmed, but he still spoke plainly.

"Ten."

The old chief just managed to hide his scoff, many others seeming close to rising from their seats to leave.

"There are more," the captain's voice rippled through the air like a rock in water with the same power. "My king rules many islands, and men beyond count. More of us will come. We will need allies, we will need friends."

The men looked unconvinced but at least stopped

rising to leave. The old chief shrugged. "What do you want from us?"

"For now, little enough. These…valleymen have taken two of ours. One is a holy man, much like Pacal, the other a woman. All I wish is their return."

"I'm sorry," the old man shook his head with contempt. "But if they are taken, then like my wife and father, your friends are dead, sacrificed to the Devourer."

"That may be. But I will see for myself."

"I have spies trying to bring me word of their comrades," said Pacal. "That isn't why I brought you here. My friends, we have a rare opportunity." The old shaman nodded and stared into the fire before he looked to the gathering. "Do you not tire of the *great* city? I do. I feel its existence like a sickness in my blood, as if some snake bit me as a young man, and every day I die slowly of its venom, wishing only it would speed its journey to my heart. I feel I cannot wait much longer, cannot *survive* much longer." He looked at the men. "Our tribes share many things. Gods. Rituals. Kin. All know of the legend of the travelers from the East. Their coming is a symbol." He raised his voice. "Chief Janab, all know of your history of war, and your great knowledge. How many thousands of enemies do the valleymen have if those enemies were to band together?

"Countless," the old chief answered, his voice tinged with hate.

"In Copanoch, they soon celebrate a festival of the stars, coinciding with the ancient devotions. They will be consumed with their own rituals for weeks, even their armies brought back to celebrate with their kin, and demonstrate their piety."

"How do you know this?" a young chief asked, and

Pacal smiled.

"The mountain whispers a great many things." He whistled, and several nearby animals growled from the trees. "The world itself demands the death of Centnaz and his horrors." He looked again to the fire. "In a few months time, the city of Copanoch will bring her warriors inside her walls, and wash its altars in blood. Their people, from peasant to prince, will soak their throats and minds with drink and plant-smoke. That gives us time to prepare. And a day and a long night to attack."

The older man seemed lost in thought but said nothing, but the younger snorted. "Copanoch has a wall as high as these trees. It is known that evil spirits guard the stone-that they throw men back who try to climb, that any who pass it are doomed. And, they have an army of many thousands. We could never rally enough of the tribes. If you've forgotten, they hate each other almost as much as they hate Copanoch."

"Our new friends have promised to help us with the wall." Pacal gestured to Eka, who nodded. "Once inside, the wood buildings will burn. We will light fires and loose them for the winds, letting the fire kill as many as we can. With their armies unassembled and scattered, we will make them pay for their deeds, and not on the battlefield as they wish. We will burn the unholy Copanoch to the ground, and destroy the House of Mar."

"And their allies," asked the older man, still lost in reverie, no trace of contempt now in his voice. "What of the other cities? Will they not come for revenge?"

"No, Chief Janab. With Copanoch destroyed, they will turn on each other. It is the balance of the three that keeps them at peace, and nothing more. When the great city falls, the faithful of the devourer won't care about revenge, only grasping power for themselves."

The men sat in silence now, many lost in thought.

"Help us rescue our man," Eka spoke again. "And he can help you. He made this armor." He gestured to Chang. "He can make more, as well as weapons from the same metal, strong enough to stop anything your enemies would wield."

"How much more?" The shaman asked, clearly as surprised as the others to hear this.

"Enough to arm your greatest warriors. He can use the gifts of the mountain, like you, Pacal. Perhaps you can learn from each other."

The shaman's smile was no longer that of a spiritual man who desired wisdom, but a greedy king who wanted to own all the world. He smothered it quickly, and looked to the chiefs.

"I will not ask my people to live in fear any longer. I will not watch them suffer the corruption of the valleymen's tax collectors, soldiers, and gods. I will not sit and wait while the venom in my veins does its work and kills what life I have left. I will fight, and ask them to fight, for the memory of their kin."

The old chief, Janab, blinked and rose, looking at the gathering as his face and eyes hardened. "Pacal is right, and his words honorable. I will go to my brothers and sons with his message, and before their festival, a hundred tribes will gather. We will show these murderers and thieves the price of their tyranny. What you do is your own business."

Without waiting, the old warrior turned and his men followed. Others came and offered respect to Pacal and made their own assurances before departing. Chang met Eka's eyes, wondering what the hell exactly they were doing and if it was all just to save two crew, or if there was some other game at play. Nothing the assassin-turned-captain did would surprise him, and frankly he didn't care. It was all the tiring games of landsmen, and all he knew is he wanted to be safely back on his ship, far out to sea. But a good pirate had to be realistic.

When no one was looking, he swiped a bottle of the red-root alcohol from a stone table, and turned back to his men.

Chapter 18

"General!"

Yacat winced and stopped in the narrow corridor. He had been avoiding the court scholars for weeks now but they seemed to have trapped him on two sides. The man and his assistants huffed from catching Yacat's stride, their ridiculous hats nearly falling as they bowed. "General. War-Prince...Yacat, I'm glad I found you. We have been...instructing the prisoners, as ordered, and truly, *truly*, with the male in particular, the progress is... simply, remarkable. *Unnatural*, it is clear. You must see the results for yourself."

Yacat did not care about the results. He had been summoned before the king and expected both chastisement and fresh orders. Not only had he yet again fought with the Devourer's priests, there were reports of fresh rebellion in the riverlands, and several bandit raids on merchants on the Eastern roads. As a rule, Yacat also had no patience with scholars and their tedious arrogance, an opinion he'd developed before they'd finished teaching him to write.

"My apologies, Scholar Tonac, I don't have time. Perhaps when I've returned from my meeting with the king..."

"Young prince." The older man tried his tutor's voice, reddening only slightly as Yacat quirked a brow at his boldness. "Please. Your father...your father and High Priest Nahua have already agreed the prisoners are spirits trapped in human flesh. The female therefore would have been *best* sacrificed on the half moon according to..." the man must have caught sight of Yacat's eyes, and stopped to lick his lips. "Since that was...undesirable, to your lordship, and now considerable time has been lost, we have only three more days to decide if she will again be conserved for a more auspicious date, or if…"

"The prisoners are *mine*, not High Priest Nahua's. I merely haven't had the time…my father…" Yacat stopped and put a hand to his forehead. It would be better to see for himself before facing Etzil. "Just take me to the damn prisoner."

"Of course, my prince. Thank you. Your valuable time is most appreciated. Please follow me."

Yacat obeyed, clenching a hand to smother his restlessness. Scholars were of course learned men with much to teach, but Yacat had no respect for those who did nothing but talk, immune to the consequences of their words. Over the years, Yacat had seen a great many scholars and priests offer terrible advice, even on practical matters like tax collection, land use, irrigation and weather patterns. Not once had he seen one starve.

Men of words alone also grew cowardly, treacherous hearts. Whatever way the wind blew they flit upon the breeze, no values save to spare their hides. After the god-cursed servants of Centnaz had tried to sneak the female prisoner to their altar like thieves in the night, Yacat knew he could not rely on the scholars to protect her. He had moved her to the harem's servant's quarters where he controlled the guards. By all accounts she was doing well enough, but it wasn't her that interested and concerned the palace elite. Yacat had already heard the whispers.

Palace guard said the golden-eyed giant was terrifying everyone. They said he was an evil spirit trapped in human skin, a demon of Kisinc—the reeking god of bad death—sent to the world to eat men's souls. It would be nonsense, of course, but if not the prospect didn't much frighten Yacat. With a soul like his, it was best some demon ate it before he went on for judgment.

The scholars led him down into the dungeons, past the cells currently packed with criminals and slaves to be sacrificed, beyond to the well-kept rooms reserved for noble prisoners. Yacat slowed when he saw the entrance had no door.

"The creature…smashed it, my prince, when he was locked in without food as punishment." The scholar shrugged. "He has several times removed his shackles or any ropes as well, but he never tries to escape. He says he does not wish to be bound, but has nowhere to go."

"You've *spoken* to him?" Yacat said, surprised.

The scholar snorted. "Oh yes. He already reads *books*, my prince, and seems to remember everything. Please." He gestured inside, and Yacat checked to make sure his sword was free and ready.

The two guards in attendance nodded in respect. The barbarian sat at a table covered in old tomes, their pages crumbling and yellowed. He had a quill in one hand and traced letters idly, even as he flipped through sheafs of ancient papyrus with the other. His room was in disarray—the bedding, cushions, and wall decorations pulled apart as if inspected. Scholar Tonac gestured at him and shook his head as if to say, 'do you see?'

"We thought it best not to waste anything of worth," he explained. "We've given him interpretations of old religions, records from kings of centuries past. Nothing of particular value."

Yacat ignored this, though he thought *the past is more valuable than you think.*

"Good afternoon, slave." He stepped forward and the man or spirit turned, golden eyes assessing, judging, in cold silence. Yacat inspected his writing and saw the scripts were traced with impressive detail. Copanoch had several spoken languages used by the different classes, but only one official written system based on image sets, typically simple shapes arranged in patterns. It took many years to learn them all, and only the most educated achieved it.

"So, you speak our language now?"

"I speak enough." The man's voice was deep and powerful, filling the room with ease. "Your scholarship is flawed but thorough. My people used a system of writing much the same."

Yacat blinked, staring. The accent was strange and thick but the words were perfectly understandable and correct. Again Scholar Tonac shrugged as if to say 'I told you'.

"My priests believe you are an evil spirit," Yacat said, trying to stay composed. "How else could a man learn a language so quickly? Unless, of course, you are a liar."

"I am a man, if different than you. I do not speak lies."

"Then you are a spirit, for all men lie." Yacat paced across the room, inspecting the view of the great lake from the single, barred window. "Where are you from, spirit-man? Where are your people?"

"You do not know them. They live far across the sea to the East, and call themselves the men of ash."

Yacat exchanged a look with Tonac. There were many myths in the valley of the gods. Some came from ancient religions, others from stories passed down from parent to child in evening tales from sources and eras none knew. One that had lingered and spread from Copanoch to the many coasts was that one day men would come from the Eastern ocean, and change the world.

"There are no lands in the Eastern ocean," Yacat said

with a disinterested tone. The giant just stared, as if he expected nothing, and did not care if he was believed.

"Why are you here?" Yacat tried. "What do you want?"

"We are explorers, nothing more. My companion, the woman named Zaya—let her return to the Eastern coast and re-join our ship. That is all I ask. Do this and I will answer any question, do anything you wish. I am no threat to you, and certainly an asset."

Your existence is a threat to me, Yacat thought, but without great concern. Whoever these people were made little difference. He had his own problems and no time to bargain with nor chase down legends and spirits. And his father would never free them.

"Your companion is under my protection," he said. "She is perfectly safe, so long as you behave. We will speak more, you and I. But not now."

With that Yacat left the padded prison and took Tonac aside. "Ensure he is cared for. He might be useful to the king." Here Yacat stopped and stared Tonac in the eye, stepping forward until they stood uncomfortably close in the narrow corridor. "And scholar, do not assume that because you were my boyhood tutor, I will show you mercy. I know the priests have their hands in your order's pockets. If High Priest Nahua or any of his creatures comes claiming this prisoner, you and all your brothers will prevent it, or I will bury you in an unmarked grave. Is that understood?"

The old man paled and nodded, and Yacat hoped he wasn't forced to demonstrate his sincerity. He strode back through the dungeons hardly noticing the doomed men in their crowded misery. It was just one more horror in a long list, and instead he prepared his patience for an afternoon of verbal punishment with the king.

156

* * *

Not for the first time, Zaya sang for her jailers.

Once every four or five days it had become a kind of custom for the palace women to demand Zaya's presence. They would provide water with some kind of citrus, or trays of sweets Zaya couldn't begin to identify. Thus plied with favor she would sit and sing her foreign words while they smiled, and their children laughed and played.

Today was the fourth such 'invitation'. Zaya now sat freshly bathed and dressed in fine blue cloth in her appointed chair, the foreigner's version of a lyre in her lap. It had more strings than she was used to, but over the past month she had gained at least an adequate skill. Zaya quieted her audience of women and children with a long, dramatic look to the sun, which peeked from the wide opening in the room. She took on a playing pose and sung softly of Galdra—the Prophet of Nanot, Goddess of law—mixing in her growing list of new-world words. This was difficult while singing, but the women loved it, clapping along as the children danced. Zaya had discovered these people were very musical, with nearly all women trained to sing, and that they favored such talents. That an exotic prisoner had been capable of learning their words and engaging in a favorite pastime amused them endlessly.

A male voice broke the spell, barking from the entrance and warping the expression on every woman in the room. Happy smiles replaced with anxious scowls as the women fled to their rooms, dragging children and carrying bits of their lunch. Zaya stood and stopped playing, unsure what else to do.

Several armed warriors entered at the flanks of a trio

of noblemen. Zaya could already tell most of her captors apart from their dress, and knew by their feather armbands these were warriors. Slaves had rings dangling from pierced ears, lips or noses; nobles —like the three men that entered now surrounded by guards—wore fine dyed cloths, as much jewelry as a rich woman of ash, and carried wooden swords at all times.

Zaya only recognized one of them—Ya-cat, the man who had rescued her on the street. As ever his sharp eyes seemed to scan the room, settling on Zaya with something like a frown. At his side the younger man smiled, the older surveying the room much like Yacat, but utterly without concern—like everything and everyone he saw belonged to him. Zaya understood then this was their king.

"Good morning, slave," Zaya understood Yacat to say. She had learned that at some point in nearly every exchange these people referred to each other as what they were—whether wife, brother, slave, or friend. It was not meant as honor or offense, but marked their strict belief in hierarchy and class. It was to Zaya a constant reminder of the order of things, and what they thought of her. Yacat spoke more words after this, but much too quickly and in any case Zaya understood almost nothing.

The king grunted. He addressed Yacat as 'son', and spoke harsh words that seemed rebuke or command. Yacat gestured in what Zaya had decided was a kind of military salute, then both the king and the other young man turned to leave. The guards went with them, and soon Yacat and Zaya were alone in the courtyard.

"Follow. Now. Understand?"

Zaya nodded, and put her instrument on the chair. She followed the soft clicks of Yacat's sandals from the beautiful women's quarters to unfurnished corridors of rough stone. The slaves, and even the warriors they passed, seemed to sense a dark mood in their leader. They saluted or withdrew from Yacat with considerable haste, and Zaya's heart began to pound. This dangerous warrior-prince seemed to Zaya a tempestuous man, capable of violence or melancholy, moving from one to the other at a moment's notice. When she had first seem him in the prison he seemed a defeated creature. She would not have thought much of him had she not seen him at the temple, where he transformed into a killer and dominator of men. He seemed now to her capable of anything, for good or ill, and in a way, reminded her of the shaman.

"Where go?" she tried asking when she could stand it no longer. Yacat didn't so much as grunt in response. He took her down, ever lower, until the dreary dark of the prison she'd first arrived in became familiar. The slaves disappeared, replaced by warriors guarding every open portal, until Yacat entered one and guards Zaya hadn't seen blocked the hall until she followed.

Ruka sat inside at a stone table. His hands were bound in rope, but he looked otherwise comfortably rested. He sat tall and straight, like a great chief, undaunted by his imprisonment. He smiled as Zaya entered.

Yacat spoke, but Zaya caught only maybe 'punish', and 'slave'. Ruka nodded as if he understood.

"I am being given this one moment to explain. I am to translate his words to you exactly. If he suspects I do otherwise, we will both be tortured. Make your answers brief and easy to translate. I do not speak all their words yet."

Zaya took a deep breath, her heart still racing. "I will try. It's good to see you, shaman."

Ruka said nothing, and Yacat barked harsh words for several moments before they were translated. "Yacat, prince of House Mar, asks where you come from."

"The same land as Ruka," Zaya answered, giving herself a moment to think. Would the shaman have told them accurately? She didn't see why not. "The Ascom," she continued. "A land far to the East, across the ocean."

Ruka translated, then answered almost at the same time as the prince: "There is no land across the ocean." The speed of the translation seemed to surprise the prince as much as Zaya, but not enough to stop him from carrying on. "Are all your men like this one?"

Zaya withheld the foolish smile that threatened her lips. Still, she couldn't help herself. "What do you mean, 'like this one'?"

She watched Yacat's eyes just slightly narrow and refrained from laughing in his face.

"So large," Ruka translated the other's words without expression. "So monstrous and cunning. So quick to learn."

"No," Zaya said, with a brief smile for Ruka. "He is exceptional. Most of our men are much like yours."

The prince seemed to take some comfort in that. He leaned in his chair. "The men you came with—the ones who fled to the sea. Are they responsible for the rebellions?"

Here Yacat watched her very carefully, and she must have made a face because he seemed annoyed. "No. They don't speak your language. Like us they don't even know where they are, or anything about you or your people. They wish only to go home. Like us, they're no threat to you."

Yacat watched her eyes, then took a breath, seeming to believe her. He stood and spoke to the guards, and after a brief exchange, Zaya heard the sounds of their sandals as they walked away. Yacat waited before he returned to the table, his face now reverted to the sad warrior she had first met. He took a deep breath as if resigning himself before he spoke. The translated words were strange to hear in Ruka's voice.

"No one is ever a threat until they are. You are to be given to me as concubine. One of many *gifts* from my father. You will live comfortably in the palace with my wife and children, and live a life of luxury few of my people will ever know." Here he paused, and took another breath. "Ruka was to be sacrificed to Centnaz at the festival of stars, as you were to be sacrificed on a holy day of duality. I have asked for his life. His presence here…unnerves my family, so he will serve me as a slave on the battlefield."

If Ruka felt anything about these pronouncements he hid it well, his deformed face as expressionless as his tone. Zaya had no understanding of why she was to be sacrificed and didn't expect to. She understood 'concubine' vaguely from her time with the women—it meant a wife with less honor.

"Women of my culture choose the men they lie with," Zaya managed to say without emotion. "I will not be your concubine willingly."

Ruka paused for the first time before he translated. When he did, Yacat merely shrugged without any sign of emotion save for his perpetual gloom. "It makes no difference. Here you are a slave, and like the rest of us, you will do what is required."

Zaya felt heat rise to her face. The guards were far away, and both she and Ruka were unbound. Though Yacat was armed, she had little doubt they could seize and kill him before he could use his weapons.

"You are a brave man," she said with the growing menace she felt. "I have killed men in battle. And they were ready with knives, not lying in a bed, with only their own meager flesh in their hands."

When Ruka translated, Yacat smiled, though it faded quickly as he rose. "Bravery requires fear of death. I'm going to leave you now. Speak, if you wish, but be brief, for the men outside will come for you soon." Here he paused at the door, and before the translation, his tone to Zaya did not seem at all to relish the words, merely to state them. "You will not see each other for some time. Perhaps ever again."

With that he left Zaya alone with the shaman, and she found she wasn't sure what to say. This was not her destiny—that much she knew. The gods had not led her here to be a bed slave for a foreign prince, just as they had not led the Godtongue to die on some nameless battlefield. She wanted to encourage him, but even the notion felt silly. Mostly she wanted him to know she was not afraid.

"I have made you a book of words."

She almost jumped as the shaman removed a leather satchel from beneath the table. Where exactly he'd been keeping such a thing, or indeed how he'd created it, Zaya had no idea. But then with the shaman anything was possible. "It is a rough translation of as many as their words as I have deciphered, along with some few conjugated verbs, all written in the island alphabet." He shrugged. "It is likely I will escape or die, for I will not be made to kill, for this man or any other. You must learn their language, and…"

"Then let us escape together," Zaya interrupted. "There are few guards here, and many ways from the palace. Perhaps we could take Yacat prisoner, and bargain our way free."

The shaman shook his head. "To try here would mean more death."

"They have *enslaved* us." Zaya shifted in her chair. "As they do many others. They are not worthy of your mercy, shaman."

He shrugged as if it didn't matter, and Zaya tried to meet his eyes. "Surely, the gods would not have spared you through all your deeds, just to watch you die without at least trying to fight, to..."

"*You saw me on that ship.*" His voice darkened, his face contorting with anger that she now realized was barely suppressed. His golden eyes were rimmed with dark bruise, the whites a spiderweb of vein. He took two long, deep breaths. "There is something wrong, Zaya. A darkness claws at my mind, something I found in the isles..." his eyes drifted as if he looked far away. "I thought I'd killed it. Perhaps it cannot die." He tapped his temple, staring off into nothing. "I am a cup filled to the brim with black waters, Zaya, each new sin a drop that must spill to the earth. I cannot kill. I *must* not."

For the first time, Zaya saw a thing in the shaman's eyes she had not expected—a familiar thing, common and unsurprising in normal men, but something she had hardly believed him capable of. The Godtongue was *afraid*.

She nodded, and took the book. "Then I will endure. When the time is right, we'll escape, and unravel this mystery together. That is my vow."

Ruka sat back and smiled faintly, his eyes regaining some focus before he spoke. "Your parents too were very strong. Yacat will give you a room, and privacy. Hide the book, and learn quickly. I'll try and get you a message. I don't know why, but I think we have little time."

With that they stood, and Zaya strode to the greatest living hero of her people, and held out her arm. He took it, and squeezed. "Until the gods bring us together again, Ruka, son of Beyla."

He nodded. And perhaps it was only her imagination—a desperate wish from a childhood hero, but she thought perhaps as he answered, she saw a hint of pride.

Chapter 19

The guards no longer touched Zaya at all. They led her back to the women's quarters with something approaching deference, eyes downcast and gesturing her on more like the men of her homeland. It seemed 'royal concubine' was something rather more complicated and useful than 'slave', but this brought her little comfort.

The other women welcomed her with words she didn't understand. They perfumed her with incense and offered her a sweet alcohol much like the islander's rum. The kindness and pageantry surprised her, but their smiles were different than before. When Zaya had been just a slave singing for their amusement, they had laughed and embraced her without reservation. Their smiles were full and unguarded, their joy in her singing much like that of the children. Now, though, their eyes were cautious. One in particular stayed at the edge of the gathering, and the others quieted when she finally approached.

"Sister," she said, leaning forward so close their cheeks touched. When she withdrew, Zaya bowed and repeated it as best she could, and the woman turned and walked away without another word. The others followed, and Zaya was left alone as if she had gained some disease that might spread to any too close, her mere presence a corruption to their beautiful home. She understood then that she had just met Yacat's wife.

The servants settled her into her own room, complete with a wardrobe of mostly too-small clothes, a copper tub for washing, several instruments with strings or tubes, a plush raised bed draped with sheets and blankets, and many boxes filled with jewelry and fabrics. She was given her own personal servant, and understood she could roam the palace more or less freely—with an armed escort, of course.

As soon as she was able, she dismissed her servant, hid her book of words beneath her bed, and knelt with her head down.

"Hear my vow," she whispered to Edda, Goddess of words, her hands at her lips, "I will be free of this place. I will make the name Zaya, daughter of Juchi, worthy of remembrance, or I will burn in the mountain forever." She prayed too to the Mother, to watch over her parents and siblings in the Ascom, and over Chang and the crew of the *Prince*; she prayed to Nanot, Goddess of law, to bring her justice for the misdeeds against her. And before she rose, with a final thought to the god of the mountain, the god of chaos and sire to men like the shaman, in case all else failed, she prayed to Noss.

When she was finished she opened the book, and practiced. Ruka had spelled the words as they sounded with the islander's alphabet, because their own people used symbols, or runes, to represent words, and it was almost useless just for sounds. She had learned the island tongue as a girl and knew it well, so she whispered the sounds over and over, trying to learn most of the words in basic questions or answers she expected to need. When the sun had risen high enough she knew the afternoon meal would be served, she again hid her book.

She went out and ate with the women, who at first were awkward but soon ignored her and returned to their talk and laughter. She listened carefully, trying to pick out individual words she knew and which words came before or after. She realized she needed some kind of ink to add to the shaman's book, which no doubt had many missing words. When she felt enough time had passed she rose and returned to her room, allowing her servant to brush her hair, bathe her in the tub, oil, perfume, trim, massage, and finally help settle her into her bed.

"What is name?" she asked as evening came, and the girl jerked as if she'd slapped.

"Temolata, honored concubine," she answered, or close enough.

"Thank you, Temolata. Please. Zaya." She gestured to herself.

The girl shrugged or maybe nodded, mumbling something about 'being ready', or 'prepared' in several different ways before giving up and leaving the room as swiftly as she was able. When Zaya felt it was safe she again took her book of words and practiced, knowing if the shaman thought it important, than almost nothing else mattered.

She lay in her fine bed of cotton blankets, staring up at a darkened ceiling covered in painted scenes of gods and men, marveling at life and fate and all the twists that had brought her here. Her belly was full, at least, her body warm and comfortable from Temolata's attentions. And though she was a slave and things could change again in an instant, she decided, the day had not been so bad.

* * *

Yacat finished his long day of marching in another pool of blood. His feet were as cracked as his lips, and the violence of a few moments of deadly work still tingled in his limbs.

"Is it more rebellion, lord? I thought the Acolca had been pacified."

Mictlan, one of his senior officers, panted and

167

scanned the trees with wary eyes. Between them they had killed two scouts and chased away a third before Yacat's red-faced bodyguard and attendants caught up.

Yacat almost snorted, but hid his expression. *Pacified. Rebellion.* Such fine words men used for ugly things. No people were truly *pacified* unless you killed all their men and enslaved their children. And was it *rebellion* to resist a foreign boot on your neck?

"It's just boys playing warriors," he said without emotion, "a few fools hoping for glory."

Yacat kept the concern from his face, and inspected the corpses of the young men at his feet. They were dressed like his lesser wolf-warriors, with markings that meant at least one kill or capture to their name. On closer examination, though, he could see the ruse. Their weapons were shoddy, their bodies too lean and without the refined muscle of his well-trained army. He had been walking ahead with Mictlan when they attacked.

When the young men approached he had assumed them new recruits sent to find him with a message. Then they had cried out and drawn flint blades, nearly killing him without a fight. But old instincts died hard. Yacat had caught the first and opened his throat with his own knife, while Mictlan tackled the second. *Tahana,* Yacat thought, *the great and legendary warrior-prince, nearly dead at the hands of a boy.*

He felt only mild disappointment they hadn't succeeded.

With a glance towards his warriors, he saw the lesser officers and noblemen standing nearby pretending not to watch him. The Acolca tribe of the West forest were considered both loyal and cowardly, and not in any way expected to cause trouble. Yet here they were, two of their sons dead at Yacat's feet. It was possible the would-be assassins had just been ambitious youth, as he said. Perhaps they didn't even know who he was, and simply attacked what looked like a high-ranking warrior. But he didn't think so.

"We'll go West," he told Mictlan, and anyone else listening. "Bring the corpses. I'll give them to their chief."

The men smirked at that, and Yacat readied to move on as if equally amused. His gaze swept his thousand troops, catching on the tall, unnatural appearance of the new, foreign slave, standing erect and proud like a wild oak amongst the lesser rabble of the warslaves. He had been armed with nothing more than a wooden club, but seemed unconcerned and unashamed. His golden eyes were locked on Yacat.

"Lord?" Mictlan waited at Yacat's side, accustomed to an official order.

"Standard march, commander. North-West to the Acolca."

Mictlan nodded and gestured to his standard bearer, who waved the image of a bloody fox to signal caution and possible battle ahead.

They walked in relative silence save for the sound of sandaled feet on sandy rock. Yacat began to notice there were no fishermen on the banks of the great lake. He saw no travelers on the road to Copanoch, nor heard any villagers gathering wood or fruits in the nearby woods. By the time they arrived at the outskirts of the Acolca, he was not surprised to find the town abandoned.

Mictlan eyed him with a questioning glance, but Yacat did not stop to explore. Instead he walked on, past several locked barns that made no sound, past the large temple to Awonotza, god of the sun, and the twenty odd fine houses of the tribal leaders. He walked right to the high cliffs that overlooked the lake, rising steeply to several mountains beyond in a beautiful, if perilous path. He knew that is where the chief and his warriors would be, because that too is how Yacat would defend this town. He looked to Mictlan, who just now seemed to understand. Like a wave the same understanding swept the officers and then the warriors in a mixture of rage and anxiousness.

"They will all die," hissed Mictlan. "Chief Tomoa would still be a slave if we hadn't given him his title. I'll tear out his heart and feed it to his children."

Yacat waved a hand for calm. He pinched the narrow bone of his nose and walked closer to the cliffs, then called up in a loud voice.

"People of Acolca. I am Yacat, son of House Mar, and prince of Copanoch. Why do you hide from us? Are we not your allies?"

Only the sound of the birds could be heard, and Yacat feared there would be no answer, and that his hand would be forced. Instead, what appeared to be a large rock flew from the cliffs, landing not far from Yacat's feet. Along with his warriors, he stared at the 'rock' until he realized it was the bloody, wrapped head of a king's servant.

"There is your kinsman!" called a strong voice from the cliffs. "Take him, and leave our land."

Yacat quirked his brow as he examined the bruised, pale head. A representative of King Etzil Mar was left in every village as diplomat and tax-collector, and Yacat had little doubt this was him, though he'd never met the man. Villages like those who lived in Acolca were ruled by strict hierarchies of kin. They knew everyone in their village, and everyone from nearby villages, so they expected Yacat not only to know this man, but be related to him. Neither was true, of course, and the feeling was no different than the thousands of dead Yacat had seen during a lifetime of war. Still he sighed, and looked away.

"You have broken the king's law, Chief Tomoa. Tell me why."

He heard a scoff, and spitting fury.

"Law? What laws does your king respect? His ambassadors force us to pay, or his warriors steal from us, and take our women. What use are your king's law to us?"

Their use is irrelevant, and of course they do, Yacat wanted to snap. *To call a tax collector corrupt is to call rain wet. Men are greedy, lustful knaves and honor is a rare gem amongst a field of salt!*

Instead he gestured to his army, in case someone was watching.

"Those laws bind these warriors to me, and me to my purpose. Come down and surrender yourself, Chief. Don't make us come up and get you."

"Your kings, your cities, and your gods are doomed," yelled the angry voice. "Every town, every chief of the valley hates you. All of you. We'll suffer you no more, son of Mar. Your time has come."

Yacat shook his head and glanced at his men. Some now smiled in anticipation, knowing they would be given the chance at captives and plunder, and that the Acolca were a prosperous tribe who would have considerable jewelry and many daughters. The fact brought Yacat no comfort.

"Come down, chief of Acolca," he called one last time, feeling no different than a slave must feel. "Come down or your houses will be burned, your grain eaten, your people killed, or taken."

There was a pause this time, as perhaps the villagers at least considered the offer. The answer, when it came, was clear and confident—a brave call that earned Yacat's respect, and made him less desirous than ever to do his duty. In a strong, manly voice, their chief called as if he had some chance. "Come and take them."

Chapter 20

"There's only two paths up the cliffs, *Tahana*." Mictlan returned panting and bloody from his first attempt up the mountain. The Acolca warriors were guarding the steep inclines from above, loosing arrows, javelins and rocks onto Yacat's men as they attempted it. Already many had been wounded, some severely enough they would likely die.

"Enough. Call them back." Yacat growled and stared at the thick jungle on both sides of the mountain. "Keep looking for other paths."

"Lord, there's no point. I have a scout who knows this area very well. He was born here and he says…"

"I don't care what he says, keep looking."

With ill-concealed annoyance, Mictlan turned and barked to his scouts to renew their efforts. Yacat stood and watched the mountain, angry at the violence, angry at the rebellion, and at the rife corruption which no doubt created it. It seemed almost impossible to govern so much territory and so many men without greedy opportunists lying and abusing their charges without constant supervision. You could hang a tax collector and stifle it for a time, but it always returned.

"We'll be here awhile," Yacat said to his other officers. "Set up camp. Search the town for food and get water from their well. But figure out if they've poisoned it."

"They won't have poisoned their own well, *Tahana*," said Mazat, Yacat's brother-in-law and a panther warrior with several kills. But when he saw Yacat's eyes he closed his mouth and nodded.

The small army of warriors set about exploring the

town on guard for ambush. Many supplies had been abandoned, many animals left behind, and the crops of maize and amaranth remained in the field. It seemed their decision to climb into the mountains had been done in some haste, and therefore without the intent to stay up there for long. Did they expect reinforcements? Or something else to take their attacker's attention? Yacat explored the chief's house himself, looking over religious icons, children's toys, clothing, still unsure why he'd rebelled. Corrupt tax collectors was nothing new, and he might have complained to the royal family before he took such drastic measures. So why now? What hope did they have?

Evening fell quietly as the crest of Awonotza flagged and fell. The officers would expect Yacat to sit with them around their fire, laughing and gossiping and maybe discussing strategy. Most were good men and Yacat liked them, but he found he had no stomach now for the brotherhood of warriors. Instead he walked a ways from camp, with some difficulty dismissing his bodyguards as he walked along the edge of the great lake that brought so many life. He thought of his wife, and though he knew his feelings were impossible and unreasonable and that she could do nothing else, he felt a kind of hatred at her betrayal of their son.

"What is it in me?" he asked aloud, looking up to the stars. "Why must I suffer when all others say it is right, and divine?"

As ever, the gods did not answer him. Yacat returned to the camp by moonlight, and for a moment froze, thinking he spotted a beast lurking in the night. He realized it was the war-slave, Ruka, his golden eyes staring from the darkness. The king was not foolish to be wary of him, Yacat thought. He saw in those eyes the same monster he'd seen in the prison—an evil spirit, just as the priests had said to Yacat's father—an ill omen released from the god's prison to devour the lives of men. As it turned out, they'd urged Etzil not to sacrifice him lest they anger the gods with the gift. Better to keep him far away, they said, better to let others kill him.

Out of curiosity, perhaps, or just lack of purpose, Yacat sat beside the creature. His huge hands whittled a piece of wood with a bronze knife he must have found in the village, moving with a craftsman's practiced ease.

Yacat sat but found he had nothing to say. 'Are you an evil spirit sent to destroy me?' seemed unlikely to work. 'What have I done to anger the gods?' seemed equally silly. In the end it was the slave who broke the silence, without looking up from his work.

"What happened?"

Yacat's eyes narrowed as he stared. The slave's incredible aptitude for the language was either trickery or magic, and his dropping of all honorifics and niceties in polite speech was certainly intentional. Yacat didn't bother to correct him.

"What do you mean?"

The slave shrugged and lifted his carving to blow off a piece of scrap. "You are powerful and young, a prince amongst your people. So I must wonder, what is it that destroyed your joy?"

Yacat clenched his jaw rather than answer. *Are you mocking me, spirit?* he wanted to shout. *Do you know everything about my life, and yet sit there and pretend ignorance, speaking as if you don't?*

No, Yacat breathed, he didn't believe that. Not truly. No evil spirit would allow itself to be taken so easily, to be imprisoned and enslaved. Whoever this 'Ruka' was, he was just a strange, foreign man, deformed and bizarre, at the very most possessed secretly by a trickster spirit. The thought calmed him.

"What do you know of my joy, or sadness, slave?"

The strange man glanced up from his work. "Nothing. But I know your look. I have seen it many times in mirrored glass, and in clean, clear pools."

Yacat stared, then snorted. In normal times, a quip would form on his lips and he would put such a comment in the fire where it belonged. Instead he looked out into the darkness that reflected his heart, imagining his son as a boy, laughing as he lifted him.

"I've lost men for nothing," he said bitterly. "Tomorrow or the day after I will go up that mountain and lose more men, and kill and enslave those people for nothing. I see no way to stop it." He turned and spit into the dying fire. "There is the use to my titles and power."

"Your men seem eager for it," said the golden-eyed man or maybe spirit, who should not speak the words of Yacat's people so well. "Are you not?"

"I have never wanted to kill," Yacat hissed, then quieted, because he knew it wasn't true. As a younger man he had felt the joy of battle, when he had survived duels and captured his first prisoners and won himself fame and his father's pride and favor. "Glory fades," he heard himself saying, "the faces of the dead remain."

"The dead remain," repeated the foreigner, almost like a prayer. They sat in silence for a time before the giant spoke again. "If you wish, prince of the new world, I can help you take that mountain. Though I am a man, and not a spirit as your people believe—you can use my strangeness. Say it is my will that the townsfolk live. Or make up some other lie. What is true is that I can help you protect the lives of your men. But that is my price. Spare those townsfolk, and I will help you. Many who would die will live, and the great legend of *Tahana* will grow."

Again the perfect words seemed impossible, the understanding inhuman or a trick. Though Yacat's world was now as dark as the night, he had to admit, he was curious about this man, and how he could do as he promised.

"Tell me how."

The giant smiled with angled teeth. He held out a four-fingered hand, and revealed his carving. It looked like a tall, rectangular house with wheels, a thin platform at its peak. The giant gestured towards the town. "We'll need wood. I will start by pulling apart those houses, and I saw wagons that might be useful."

Yacat said nothing and gave no reaction, but as if he meant to start immediately, the giant stood and turned towards Acolca. How a man would work in the dark Yacat had no idea, but he still said nothing as the giant walked away. Instead he stared a long time at the carving in his hand, feeling a strange sense of smallness, even helplessness, as the world changed around him.

* * *

The spirit-man made considerable racket all night, and an equally considerable pile of lumber by morning. Yacat sent his slaves to assist when the sun rose, but let his warriors sit idle because to assist a slave would have shamed them. He sat and watched the frame of the strange device come together, then an ascending staircase surrounded by four rectangular walls resting on long piles. When his officers could stand it no more they sent Mictlan.

"*Tahana*—what…what are the slaves building? And should we not keep looking for paths up the mountain?"

Though it was clear to Yacat now what the spirit

intended, and he suspected it would work, he had to decide now whether or not to back the project. "No path will be necessary, Commander. I know the way up that mountain. Sit and relax. In a day, perhaps two, I will show you."

Yacat took some pleasure in the man's confusion. He clearly had questions but instead saluted and returned to the officers, where he no doubt tried to pretend confidence as he explained.

By the next nightfall Ruka had begun to betray his true nature. Again the slave worked in the dark, almost entirely without rest now for two days and nights, and Yacat knew a moment of fear. Only once or twice did Yacat see him eat with the slaves, drink a bucket of water, or walk to the woods to relieve himself, as if he maintained his flesh only for appearances. By afternoon on the second day, using ropes and wooden ramps, he and the slaves managed to lift the towering structure onto the wheeled frame. It stood taller than several houses stacked one on top of the other, at its peak some kind of opening with a ramp that might extend. It looked almost exactly like the carving.

When it was finished, Ruka walked purposefully from the town, his huge, pale body covered with a sheen of sweat. He sat next to Yacat and inspected his tower from afar. "The townsfolk will be watching, and may guess the tower's purpose. Wait until nightfall, then roll it there," he gestured with his chin towards a low section of the mountain. "Your men can climb and gather, then attack from the East."

Yacat could hardly believe the man's arrogance, or perhaps confidence. That a slave would tell a general of Yacat's stature how to do anything was beyond belief, further proving this was a spirit and not a man. Yacat nodded noncommittally. "If the device is sound, I will do as you suggest."

The spirit's golden eyes narrowed.

"It is sound."

"Good." Yacat smiled. "Then you will be inside it, and the first man up the mountain."

"I told you, I will not kill," the giant's words failed to hide his anger.

"Then wound, and capture. It's all the same to me, slave."

The big foreigner's shoulders flexed like a bow curving under strain. "It is a weak man who risks only the lives of others," he said with the same quiet menace, but Yacat was no longer afraid of him. He snorted and stood, feeling his strength and spirit renew at the prospect of battle, though he wished it wasn't so.

"I agree. That is why I will be the *second* man up the mountain. Now go, rest and eat, if those are things you require. I'll collect you when the sun falls."

Chapter 21

Explaining Ruka's plan to Yacat's officers was harder than expected. They feared the tower would tip, that the enemy would wait for them and attack any man who tried to come out, that it wouldn't get them high enough to matter. Mostly, they just didn't trust Ruka.

"Nor do I," Yacat said with a smile, his mood much improved at the possibility of death. "That's why the giant will go first."

He explained that if the enemy waited for them they'd simply move the tower and try elsewhere, or in the distraction send men up the paths. They still complained, but ultimately, he did not need their approval.

As darkness fell Yacat donned his armor. His slaves painted his skin, scented him with smoked perfumes, and arranged his headdress and feathers. For several years now Yacat had run out of space to wear his trophies in battle. He wore the full markings of the eagle warriors, keeping the rest in his meeting room to remind the officers.

In the history of their people, few were known to have killed or captured so many as Yacat, and all were older men. He was the youngest warrior of Copanoch or any other city in the valley to have earned the final feathers, and beyond. It was why they called him *Tahana*, why they feared and respected him, because in a hundred battles he had killed or captured men personally every time. How many deaths and captured slaves he was responsible for, he no longer knew. He was the victor of the war of two kings, the killer of a dozen chiefs, the destroyer of rebels from one side of the valley to the other.

Now he would put down these latest uprisings, and who knows what else for his ambitious father, and his brother, the soon-to-be emperor. But it made no difference. He was as much a slave as the warriors outside, and the only escape was death.

When he was ready, he banished the slaves and stood alone in the dark tent, staring into nothingness.

"I have never lost a battle," he whispered to the gods. "I did my duty, I was never cruel or weak. Yet all I love is ash. Tell me, mighty stewards of the heavens, how is that justice?"

Without waiting for an answer, he strode from his tent, stood beside the spirit made flesh perhaps sent to destroy him, and pushed the tower in the dark.

* * *

As the spirit-man had expected, the townsfolk of Acolca were watching, and waiting.

Yacat hunched inside the tower with Ruka and a dozen of his warriors, and the slaves wheeled them towards the mountain cliff. The strange construction tilted and creaked, and though Yacat welcomed death he still felt the animal panic of fear. He flinched at the cracks and booms as rocks and arrows struck the tower. A javelin tip pierced the wood and shallowly cut a panther warrior's cheek. The man moved his head from the wall and said nothing. Inspired by the display of courage, Yacat took a breath and called out, his voice echoing down the tower.

"For Copanoch, and the king!"

The men cheered their approval, and the tower struck hard against the stone cliff and stopped. Ruka turned his strange eyes towards Yacat, then with something like a sigh, gripped the rope that released the platform at the top of the tower. It fell open, smashing loudly on the hard rock of the mountain, and the giant raced across.

Yacat followed with his shield raised, eyes straight so as not to see the high drop on either side. An arrow whistled past his arm, another hit his shield and stuck, yet another skimmed the flesh of his shin. He growled at the pain, but could have wept at the joy of battle, as all other things faded to nothing. For this moment there was only the grip of the pommel in his hand, the hot breath filling his lungs, and the men who wanted his death.

He heard the whistle of a javelin and dodged as he spun his shield against another arrow. As Yacat had learned in his first battle, where two thousand men filled a marsh with their corpses, on the battlefield, as in life, there was one rule that almost always worked: attack.

He raced at full speed across loose rocks, complete confidence in his own agility. He felt rather than saw the giant as he passed, hollering another war cry as he swerved from more arrows and found his first man—an archer loosing from a high stone. Without slowing, Yacat slashed his obsidian-edged sword across the man's gut, and felt blood spray against his neck. Yacat had always had one great advantage over other warriors in battle—he despised making men slaves, so he fought only to kill.

Enemies closed behind him now but it made no difference. Two more loomed in the dark ahead, and Yacat lost no time. He crashed shield to shield into the first, then dropped and sliced across the man's legs, ripping a terrible wound. The edge of his obsidian was sharper than any bronze, and cut through even thick wool gambeson with ease. Sometimes it would break on bone or wood, and so a man's blows must be precise. Many warriors carried two or three blades for this reason. Yacat carried only one. He had not broken an edge in five battles.

As his first enemy fell he rose and slashed his blade down the other's face and chest before he could fall away. He turned and found several more, knowing he had run too far too fast, and was nearly surrounded. He felt his joy rise, hoping an honorable death might find him here before they took his son. And perhaps, if he died in battle, the boy would be spared. Despite this, Yacat would not betray his gods or his ancestors and fight without all his effort. He had his pride, and his heritage. He would not go without a battle.

"Come then!" he roared and leapt at another man. "Take your glory, men of Acolca! Come and kill a prince of Mar!"

Together, they tried.

A spear gouged Yacat's shoulder, but bounced away. He'd felt the thrust before he saw it, and dropped his arm, deflecting the speartip from a proper hit. In the same motion he slashed his blade up and half-severed the hand of a bearded warrior armed with a mining pick. He blocked a hurled stone with his shield, then spun away.

There was only one motion in battle, and Yacat knew its rhythm. Ahead. Always ahead.

He raced yet further into the enemy, ignoring the men trying to surround him. Beyond he saw women and boys scattering on the plateau, terrified villagers trying to run down the paths with supplies clutched in their arms.

Another warrior tried to stop him, and Yacat slashed his throat. Still he charged.

Two arrows hit his armor and maybe pierced, but he did not feel them. He found the archers trapped against a stone wall and cut their bows, then their arms, then their backs as they tried to run. He heard more arrows whistling through the air and dropped to a knee behind his shield, but the shots had been wide. He hissed in scorn and chased these men too, cutting down another spearmen who tried to stop him. When the archers were dead, at last he turned to face the group of men he knew had followed.

But there was only the golden eyes of the giant, and behind him, Yacat's warriors. They stood with a group of tribesmen who had risen their arms in surrender, and thrown down their weapons. More knelt with defeated eyes. Yacat looked for enemies, for danger, somewhere, *anywhere*. But there was none.

"Mahala!" cried Yacat's second, his bloody fist raised, his eyes held in reverence. *"Mahala! Mahala! Mahala!"* yelled the warriors.

Yacat stood panting as he glanced at his own body. Arrows stuck from his shield like a porcupine's quills. At least three had failed to pierce his chest, another his shoulder. Blood dripped from him like morning dew, and he had lost track of the men he'd killed.

"Where is your chief," he said with the contempt he felt for the men for failing to kill him, and himself for the love of death.

"He leapt from the cliff," said a young man on his knees. "I am his son. I am chief of the Acolca now."

Yacat rammed his blade into it's scabbard, eyes sweeping the many men and strong boys who could still have fought him, including the chief's son. "No," he said, neither with pleasure nor remorse. "You are a slave of the sons of Mar, along with all your people." He ignored the giant, who alone matched his gaze with eyes that seemed to pierce the world. Yacat gestured to Mictlan with his chin. "Take them."

* * *

"My mighty son returns!"

King Etzil rose from his limestone throne, his attendants bowing at his feet. Once, Yacat would have reveled in the compliments of his father. Now he saluted as required, and smiled as expected.

"I do my duty, lord."

"Your humility bores me, son. If I had five such loyal servants already we would be emperors. Drink! Eat! Sit with me and take your prize."

It was the king's custom to share a meal with victorious generals. He would grill them on the details of the battle as they drank, and before it was over he would give them a gift or even let them choose their reward, within reason. He had always favored military men, or so Yacat thought. Now he wondered how the king flattered and rewarded his priests.

"Thank you, lord." Yacat sat, nodding in respect to the heir, who stood in a corner with men of state pouring over messages. Yacat saw a platter of food lain out, and dipped bread in oil and pepper and ate in silence. Battle always made him hungry.

The king gestured at the fresh, if shallow, wounds on Yacat's neck and head. "You risk yourself too easily. I'm told you were the first into battle, and that you fought like a man possessed by spirits."

Yacat nodded and shrugged with the same gesture, gulping watered wine as he moved on to a flank of pork.

"They say you killed five men, and wounded four more," the king went on. "Nine in a single battle, Yacat! No living warrior in the valley that I know of has ever done such a thing."

The number was vaguely surprising. Yacat hardly

remembered the details of the battle. Once he would have felt pride—even glory at such a deed, but now it put him from his appetite. He left the pork half-eaten on a plate, and said nothing. His father frowned and leaned in his chair.

"There are more rebellions."

"So our captured rebels tell me," Yacat answered.

"They say the Huixly, the river tribes, even the barbaric mistmen from the jungles and Western mountains are gathering—that they've made a peace for the first time in decades."

Yacat nodded, feeling his excitement grow. The might of his city was vast, its vassals stretching from East to West across the valley, with at least twenty thousand warriors at their call. They would gather and quash it, that was inevitable. But fresh rebellion meant more battles—more chances for Yacat to risk himself in combat.

"I will be sending your brothers, Cuali and Patla to deal with it," said the king, and Yacat felt his eyes snap to his father's like a trap.

"*I* am General of the interior," he tried not to raise his voice. "I have never lost a battle. I return now stained with the blood of your enemies, and you replace me? Have I not…"

"Yield, I yield!" The king raised his hands, then laughed and looked to his eldest son across the room. "Our spitting viper strikes. Look how he speaks to a king. Gods preserve me. I do not send them in your *place*, Yacat. I am *promoting* you, to Lord General of all my armies."

Yacat stopped and in his heart heard himself shouting *no, please, no*. He thought of the old general currently in the position, a cousin of the king and more a diplomat than a warrior. He spent most of his time flattering rich noblemen, and very little on the battlefield.

"Your brothers need experience, Yacat," the king was saying. "They need some damn danger and discipline as well. And you, my son, need rest, and reward." Here he gestured, and one of the attendants with the heir arrived with a scroll. "This is an official deed to the rice lands East of the river. From this day on, the sons of Yacat will be landed lords."

Yacat stared at the unfurled scroll bearing the king's mark, and his own name above the royal decree. As the son of a concubine, it was not customary for him to be given land. As a lord he would no longer live in the king's court, only attending him when required, and otherwise ruling over his own people. The specific land being offered had belonged to the crown for centuries. It was rich and close to the city, and giving it was a sign of trust, and respect, and an honor greater than any Yacat could remember his father giving.

"Does my gift please you, my son? Do you see now how I value you?"

Yes, Yacat thought, which only made the sacrifice of his son worse. It meant his father was so blinded by ambition and perhaps belief that still he would do this thing, and cover the guilt and shame with gifts. He looked into the eyes of a man he once thought great, now a fool who tried to win love with bribes.

"I see, father," he whispered. "And I thank you."

The man nodded and beamed, clapping Yacat's arm.

"You may take what officers you wish as aids, and throw out or use whichever of the old general's retinue you like. I leave it all in your capable hands."

Yacat nodded, unable to process the hills and valleys of his life. He thought maybe, just maybe, away from the city he could go on. With enough time, perhaps, he could forgive his family, if not himself. He smiled and thanked his king and father as befit the gift, but failed to bond with him as he might once have done.

"Well." Etzil rose and sighed as he looked at his impatient advisors. "Sometimes I wonder who is truly king. Is it me, or these tiresome drudges with their quills." Yacat smiled politely, and the king waved him away. "Go. Inspect your land, and take your new concubine." Here he waggled his thick brow. "Rest. Recover. And by the fifth day of the new moon, come back and whip your lazy brothers into shape for me, *Lord General*. I do not ask a simple thing for they can hardly piss in the right pot. Go my son, and make them men for me."

Yacat saw the love still in his father's eyes, but it brought him no comfort. He said the only thing he could think of that was true.

"I am yours to command, my king."

Chapter 22

"Mistress! Please!"

Zaya seized Temolata and pushed the much smaller girl stumbling across the room. "I will *not* spread legs," she growled for the second time, and the exasperated girl began to cry. "It is *expected*, Mistress. Your body must be hairless. It isn't painful." After this she tried and failed to explain what was in her mixing bowl, which appeared to be a kind of paste to slather over Zaya's skin.

"If it isn't done, Mistress," the girl managed through her sobs. "I'll be punished. You are a royal concubine, you will not be harmed. But I...they will give me to the Devourer!"

In the past month, Zaya's grasp of the foreign language had increased in leaps and bounds. She had always had a gift with tongues, and already spoke several of the languages of the isles and the continent. Her book of words had made it far easier, and the language of the valleymen was very clever and simple to learn, with clear rules and few exceptions. She didn't know who the 'Devourer' was, exactly, beyond being a god, but she knew being given to him was entirely bad.

With a deep breath she at last accepted this latest indignity, sitting on the table with her legs apart and her dress hiked up to her waist. The girl shook her head, and with some struggle removed the dress altogether. Zaya sat uncomfortably as the girl arranged a tray of tools, which included a vat of oil, several seashells, the white paste, and a series of rough and sharpened rocks. Zaya seized the stone table and forced herself to stillness, but nonetheless prepared mentally to batter the girl away if there was pain.

Her legs were oiled, then the rock scraped carefully in long, sure strokes. The tools were so incredibly sharp the hair sheared away without effort, and the same process repeated on her arms and armpits, and finally the paste was applied between her legs. Zaya squirmed at the strange sensation, but as promised it was not painful, and after a delay Temolata again used the oil and sharp rock. It took much of the morning, and when it was finished her skin was bathed and scented in more oils. Beads, rings and paints were fastened or smeared in her hair and on her face until she could feel the weight of it all. At last she was given a new dress of thin cotton, which seemed to Zaya conspicuously loose and easily donned or removed.

Red-faced, Temolata at last breathed a full, comfortable breath, inspecting her handiwork.

"You are very beautiful, Mistress. The prince will be pleased."

Zaya frowned, but took a similar breath.

"Thank you. I know you only do…" she struggled for the word, "duty."

"Yes," the girl nodded vigorously. "Now you must do yours. And you have learned so many words, and so quickly. The prince will be so pleased." She took Zaya's hands and smiled with encouragement. "Prince Yacat is a handsome man, and very kind to his wife and children. As First Concubine, your sons will be royalty. You are a fortunate woman."

Yes, Zaya thought wryly, *such a fortunate slave.*

She nodded in what passed for respect to a servant, and Temolata told her not to disturb the paints on her face or the set of her hair, and to avoid eating until the prince arrived to collect her.

"Would you like some Ektha spice?" she asked, and Zaya shrugged in confusion.

"It will stop your…" the girl reddened slightly, and threw up her hands. "Stop you from shitting. So you are very clean. For when…"

"No." Zaya felt her own face glowing with heat and hoped it didn't disturb the paint. "I will not." When the girl nodded, but remained, Zaya took another breath to control her frustration. "Where I going? What I doing?"

The girl's gaze danced across the floor, then she glanced out the only window and frowned at the sun as she rose.

"Whatever the prince says, Mistress," she said with a tone that implied the questions were truly foolish. With that she left Zaya alone in the almost sheer, immodest gown, with nothing to do but sit on her bed, and wait.

* * *

The prince's late arrival caused a flurry in the woman's quarter. From listening to bits and pieces of gossip, Zaya understood he was being honored by the king—that he was one of the most important men in this land, and being made more so. This surprised her, considering his relative youth, and his…morose countenance in her presence. But whether he was pauper or demi-god, it made little difference to Zaya, so long as she was his slave.

Several of the women's servants collected supplies and clothing in crates, which were loaded onto wide, flat carts carried by half naked male servants. These all crossed their hands in some kind of supplication in her presence, and she stood awkwardly at the door to her room hoping they didn't find her book of words. Mostly, she watched the other women's faces. All wore carefully guarded expressions of polite contentedness, and did not look at her. She noticed Yacat's wife also

191

stood at her doorway, similarly dressed and ready to leave. Zaya winced at the thought of an outing with her, but realized if she attended, perhaps Zaya would be spared...the difficulties of a private setting.

Prince Yacat at last entered the quarter with a handful of guards. The simply adorned, pale shadow of a man Zaya had seen before was entirely gone. Now the prince's strong chest was painted with reds and blues, bare save for a bronze medallion; his limbs were wrapped in coils of thin rope, spiraling down to the sandals on his feet; feathers jutted from a headdress that looked like the jaws of a wolf, while gold rings hung from his dark hair. Where before his proud face turned with a dour expression, now he smiled and looked on the world as if it was his. He walked first towards his wife, but stooped to a knee and gestured for his children, who ran out to him. The girl he lifted and tossed high in the air, then became more serious with the boys, who he asked several stern questions before wrapping his arms around them with a playful grin.

The women seemed hardly to breathe as he finally approached his wife. They exchanged words Zaya could not hear, though the prince's expression seemed to have cooled. With a snort he turned his back and walked away from her, and a young wife near Zaya gasped softly. His sandals clicked as he approached, and Zaya bowed her head as she'd been taught, and said the words that were expected.

"I am told you learn our words quickly. Is that so, Honored Concubine?"

Zaya prayed she had translated correctly, and met the prince's eyes, though she wasn't sure that was correct.

"Not quick enough, Great Prince."

Yacat's smile was wide and attractive. His eyes roamed Zaya from head to toe in a way that brought heat to her face. "I take my children to see lands that will one day be theirs. Will you come with us?"

Considering Zaya had absolutely no choice in the matter, she thought the question mere formality. But she played her part. "Of course, prince. My honor."

The smile remained, and maybe widened. "You are my official concubine, so now you should call me *Tekit*. It means…" here he shrugged and looked to some of his guards with a wry smile. "Patron? Lover? It doesn't matter. That is the word you should use." Here he waited, rather expectantly, and Zaya felt her skin redden again.

"Yes, *Tekit*."

He nodded, then the servants and the guards and the children all gathered and moved as if they shared some common understanding, and Yacat said his formal goodbyes towards the remaining women. Even Zaya could sense the shame and insult done to his wife, though she had no idea why. Yacat seemed to sense it too, but in response, he moved closer to Zaya, and put his hand on the small of her back to direct her onwards.

"There is a large estate," he said, much louder than necessary for her to hear. "The children will play for hours on their own."

Zaya said nothing, focused entirely on showing no sign of her anxiety or anger. What she would do, exactly, if the prince tried to seduce her, she wasn't certain. But she fought the urge to slap the hand from her back, or touch the knife she'd tied to her thigh.

* * *

They traveled on foot from the palace, surrounded by guards and servants. Yacat walked, but offered for Zaya to 'ride' on one of the flat platforms carried by the men. She refused, but he insisted, and so she found herself carried on the shoulders of ten slaves, painted and dressed like a noblewoman, escorted through a foreign city.

The townsfolk stared, often with mouths agape, as she passed. Many made gestures that could only be called religious, and some sprayed a kind of dusted perfume in her direction, which by now she understood to be a kind of respect.

The city swarmed with activity. Merchants called from every corner at the procession, sometimes rudely ignoring their custom to do so. Young boys were sent scampering from nearby stalls to hold up jewelry or clothing for her, others sweet treats or pottery, only leaving if Zaya shook her head.

Yacat seemed at first tolerant, and then annoyed. In fact all his charm and interest vanished once they'd left the palace, save for the occasional smile for his children. He guided the party through cluttered streets with impatience, hand constantly on the hilt of his sword.

Zaya well understood strong, quiet men. The men of ash, her people, were illiterate warriors who bore hardship in silence, whose only answer to suffering or dishonor or almost anything was violence. As she looked at the man she had first thought weak, she now saw something both greater and more tragic—a caged animal, a deformed spirit, his strength trapped with invisible chains.

"Did you bring my...instrument?" she did her best to look at the crates from her platform, but the men carrying them paid no attention. Finally she reached from her seat and lifted the lid, shifting her weight to one side and causing the men carrying her to grunt in surprise. They gestured for her to be still and mumbled polite words in rude tones, but she ignored them. "Ah ha!" Zaya found the handle of the foreign lyre and pulled it out before she obeyed.

She strummed softly for a time, the tale of a shackled prince forming in her mind. It did nothing to diminish the stares and constant attention of the foreigners, but Zaya was accustomed to attention. By the time they reached the edge of the city, she felt some of her paints running in the heat, but with a half-formed song in her mind cared little for the world around her.

The prince led them on a well-trodden road through fields of crops Zaya didn't recognize. The children were allowed to wander freely now, and soon the boys were chasing each other with kernel husks, leaping and hacking like warriors. The prince was watching them, and she saw his emotions mix and warp across his face, both joy and sadness mixed to some bittersweet potion.

She didn't understand it, and looked away. She had seen only the dense jungle and the city, but as she looked out across the countryside here she saw far-away mountains ringing the horizon. Crops rose and fell across the hills in unified squares, a patchwork of yellows and greens like a quilt from her homeland. Well-made roads criss-crossed the land, with small towns along their edges. It was, in a word, beautiful.

"Does it now please you to be a concubine?"

Zaya blinked and saw the prince was staring, his expression impossible to read. Zaya decided not to take offense.

"My fate in hands of gods," she said, and believed. "I do only…as I can."

The prince watched her, perhaps for mockery, but finally looked away. "That seems a useless distinction. How can you know what to do, and what you cannot?"

Zaya smiled, and waited for the man to again meet her eyes.

"I try."

He snorted and walked on, putting his daughter on his shoulders for a time. The worn roads and long villages thinned and all but disappeared, ending in a fortress of stone. Here the men challenged Yacat but soon saluted and led him onwards, along a narrow road through marshy fields and at last an estate. The children ran towards it with excitement, but Yacat had stopped and stared with a guarded expression.

"I have seen enough stone buildings in my life," he announced. "Would you rather play along the beach?"

The children shrieked in approval, and Yacat ordered his guards to find an appropriate spot and bring food and toys for the water.

"My lord," said the chief bodyguard, clearing his throat. "Should we not follow the king's instruction? I was told to take you to the house."

"Do as you like, soldier." Yacat stretched his arms and turned to the water. "But my children and I are going to the beach."

The guard frowned but soon followed, and the servants walked on in silence, at last placing Zaya gently alongside a sparkling blue lake that seemed to go on forever. Along its coast, thousands of reeds sprouted in verdant patches, whistling with the breeze. Further in, Zaya could see fishing boats and merchants crossing from one side of the lake to the other. The banks were smooth sand like the island coast, and the children ran into the water without hesitation.

"Your lands are paradise," Zaya said, looking out at the sky reflected in the water.

Yacat smiled and lay beside her, eating grapes from a bowl. He took off his headdress and lay back on the sand.

"Tell me of your lands, Zaya. This mythical place across the sea."

As was often true Zaya couldn't tell if the man mocked her or not. She looked at the children playing amongst the reeds and imagined the rocky coast of the Ascom, the dark water so cold you could freeze in summer.

"Have you seen snow, prince? *Tekit*." she asked.

He yawned and ignored the slip. "Yes. In the mountains. And at the Northern edge of the valley, it can snow."

"Imagine it as lake. Covering world like blanket. So thick, sometimes until end of summer, too much for sun to melt."

She felt awkward trying to explain with her limited words, and hoped she'd used them correctly. She blinked and found the prince staring, a slight smile on his lips. His eyes wandered along her face and hair, down the thin garment to her legs. While Zaya was not unused to the attention of men, to be so boldly inspected was both insulting and uncomfortable. She looked away to cover her embarrassment, focusing on the children at their play.

Yacat had two boys and a girl, the oldest perhaps ten. The boys fought and splashed as the girl stood on her own picking reeds, and Zaya felt the prince's hand touch her brow, pushing a strand of hair behind her ear. She blinked, but ignored it, focusing on the little girl so happily at her task. The prince's finger slid down her cheek to her chin.

With her eyes focused on the water, Zaya noticed a patch of reeds near the princess moved, and not from the wind. Hair on her skin prickled and her heart suddenly pounded without clear understanding of why.

Were there predators in this place, she wondered? Something like a shark that might be lurking in the lake?

As was so often true in life, she felt a moment of decision. She could sit and do nothing and risk nothing, or act on intuition alone, and perhaps be a fool. She rose and waved her arms, shouting at the girl.

"Atzi!" she yelled the girl's name. "Come back to beach!"

Little Atzicoya frowned as she saw Zaya, but perhaps out of habit from obeying adults, carried her handful of reeds towards the water's edge. As she did, the patch of reeds shook and scattered. It wasn't a creature that emerged, as Zaya had feared, it was a man.

Three naked warriors rose up from the water carrying knives and spears that had looked like reeds. The first splashed his way towards the boys in the water. The other two charged Yacat.

The prince sprung like a wild animal, on his feet growling in the blink of an eye, sword drawn and racing towards the water as he yelled at his sons and his guards. Zaya saw the panic in his eyes. He was too far away from the man in the water. There was nothing he could do.

Zaya was calm, her resolve warmer than the bright sun that prickled and likely burned her fair skin already. Destiny was never made for mortal hands. As a skald she knew there was only the choices given with the time and power you had, and as the two warriors charged Yacat, Zaya made hers.

She reached a hand under her dress, ripping the knife from her thigh. That she had hidden one at all might mean her death, but there was no time to worry on that now. The assassins were young, strong, and athletic, their legs pumping as they crossed the wet sand. They ran almost right past Zaya without a glance.

She grabbed one by the throat and plunged her knife for his shoulder. Her hand slipped on the wet flesh, and her blade raked down his back instead. He cried out in surprise and slashed at her leg, the blade biting but too shallow to matter. Zaya kept stabbing, seizing the young man's knife-arm and plunging her own blade to his chest. They went down to the sand but Zaya was on top and just as strong as her opponent. When the assassin stopped resisting she stood covered in blood, looking up to see Yacat kill his man with a slice across the throat.

Guards were pouring down the beach now from the house and caravan. When they saw Zaya armed and covered in blood they charged, but there was still time. Yacat's sons were throwing rocks at their attacker and running through the shallow water. He would catch them soon, just as the guards would reach Zaya. But there was still a little time.

She lifted the assassin's spear, blinking away a tingling light-headedness as she focused on the weight of the weapon. The wood was sturdier than it looked—not made for throwing, perhaps, but it would do. She took a final breath and held it, ignoring the shouts all around her, both from the guards and the children. There was only the target.

Yacat was at the edge of the water, charging into the lake, but he was too slow. Zaya released her breath as she summoned all her strength and focus, lunging into the throw with a lifetime of training.

The guards shouted to their prince in warning, though he did not turn or slow. The spear sailed past him, close enough Zaya nearly gasped, and found its mark. The assassin clubbed Yacat's eldest boy with a fumbling blow as the spear pierced his back. He cried out and slumped, then Yacat was on him, hacking him into the shallow water until blood pooled at his feet.

The guards struck Zaya and threw her roughly to the sand. She looked up to the sky and couldn't understand why it seemed so round and blurred. She blinked and looked at the cut on her leg, gasping as she saw blood pouring from her thigh. She had never seen so much of her own blood, and her head lolled at its own weight as her gut clenched.

"Don't harm her!" The prince was shoving men away, then on his knees at her side. "She saved my son," he growled with something between rage and grief. She tried to thank him but couldn't seem to do more than smile. He was shouting for physicians and wrapping a cloth so tight around her leg it hurt. Something struck her face hard, and she blinked in surprise as Yacat yanked her hair and looked into her eyes. "Stay awake, Zaya. Look at me. Help is coming."

She looked up into his dark, foreign eyes, and decided they were beautiful. She tried to do as he asked, but it was too hard.

She lay back feeling a clammy sweat on her brow, still smiling at Yacat's words. "She saved my son," he'd said, and she knew it was true. She had made her choice, and did not regret it. Though she heard no music as she might have hoped, as she looked out at the clear, blue sky reflected in the water, she thought, at least, it was a very good place to die.

Chapter 23

Yacat decided not to wash off the blood. After seeing Zaya to his physicians and being assured she would live, he returned to the fortress. There he recruited a hundred soldiers and arrested the entirety of his guard. "You men," he gestured to a host of older Panther warriors. "With me. The rest of you, keep them here." He would torture at least their officer, and let the rest of the men hear before they were questioned.

For now, his father must be told. He marched down the corridors with his bloody sword in hand, wishing only for more men to kill.

He couldn't believe assassins had reached his children, nor could he believe his foreign concubine had saved them. That he did not know if the men had been after them, or him, plagued his mind with every step.

The march back to his father's palace was silent. Yacat's soldiers followed him with spears in hand, no doubt uncertain what threats to watch for, or what they'd be ordered to do on arrival. Sweat dripped from their faces but Yacat did not care. He roared his way through the city streets, citizens sometimes shrieking at the sight of him before they scattered. He was stopped only briefly at the palace until the men realized it was him beneath the blood.

"Are you alright, *Mahala*?" Even the royal guardsmen at the entrance paled at the sight of him, and Yacat paused. The man's markings showed him as an Eagle warrior, a blooded soldier with heroism rewarded clearly on his armbands. Yacat released a long breath and clapped his arm.

"I'm fine. Take me to my father, soldier."

"My lord." The man saluted and obeyed, and together they crossed the courtyard and entered the keep, where Yacat was nonetheless forced to wait until his father was ready. He was offered a basin and cloths to wash himself, but refused. He thought it best to let the man see the results of his gifts.

It was Uncle Anatzi who came to retrieve him, his eyes revealing the false confidence of his practiced smile. "By the gods, Yacat, are you alright?"

"I'm well enough. Take me to him."

Anatzi frowned as his eyes roamed Yacat's weapons. "Your blood is up, Young Yack. Will you keep your temper?"

"*Yes I'll keep my fucking temper*," Yacat shouted in his face, then paced across the waiting room.

"I see." Anatzi poured a deep glass of agave and set it on the serving table. "Drink this. And take deep breaths."

Yacat snapped his gaze to the old warrior's eyes with a jerking sneer before he breathed and took the drink. "Alright, I am calm," he promised when finished, throwing his sword to the tiles. "I'm feeling *murderous*, but I am calm."

Anatzi took the empty cup and quirked his brow. "In your case, nephew, perhaps that is the best we can hope for. Come with me."

They entered the throneroom together, where Yacat was somewhat glad to find the king attended by a collection of his brothers. Yacat had indeed calmed somewhat by the time they surrounded him and sat him down at a table with more food and drink and asked for an explanation. He expected at least one spy or soldier had already told his father the broad strokes, but he gave the details anyway.

King Etzil listened in silence until his many sons

looked to him for opinion. He met Yacat's eyes, raising his hands as he shrugged. "A family like ours has only enemies, and subjects, and one can become the other with the rising of a single sun. What would you like me to do?"

"Nothing," Yacat realized as he said it. "Just don't interfere. I'm going to look for traitors, and deal with the guards. In the meantime, I want the foreign slave, Ruka, back at the palace."

The king frowned. "Is that wise, my son? He's an evil spirit made flesh. All the priests agree."

"Not only is it *wise*, father, he may be one of the few men I can trust to guard my children. He will be armed, and placed in the harem."

Saying it out loud was strange, and yet somehow Yacat knew it was true. Whatever gifts he had in life, knowing the measure of a man was one, and somehow he knew this spirit made flesh was one to be trusted to keep his word beyond all reason.

"Outside this room," said the king with a flat voice. When Yacat frowned in confusion the king repeated himself. "One of the few men *outside this room*, you can trust, surely."

Yacat bowed his head then looked at his king in frustration, wondering how he could be so blind. "There were three men on that beach, Father. Only two of them came for me. I was alone, it was perfect. So why would they attack my children, who have no claim to any throne?"

The king said nothing, his expression unchanged, and Yacat decided he was not so foolish after all.

"It is *your* priests, Father. Only they know my son will be sacrificed. They mean to kill my children so they can't be sacrificed. They have betrayed you and told your enemies, who mean to interfere."

203

"Perhaps," the king agreed.

"Perhaps? Must they kill one of them before you see it?"

"We cannot know," the king raised his voice and his younger sons looked to the floor. "This, my son, is why you make an excellent general but would make a poor king. You wish to know at all times who are your friends and who are your enemies. A king understands there is little difference, that a man can be both and each and neither in an afternoon."

"And what are the priests today, father? Friends or enemies?"

"Enemies!" The king spit as he blew air. "Until they are subjects. Their attack failed. We go on as before."

Yacat clenched his jaw, looking over his family, all of whom refused to meet his eyes.

"Are you so eager to kill your grandson?"

"I am eager to bring my family greatness!" the king rose and stepped forward.

Yacat felt his own rage building, but held it back when he found Uncle Anatzi shaking his head. Still, he tasted bile on his tongue and it leaked into his words.

"I've enjoyed our talk as much as my reward, Father. May I go now and ensure the safety of my children? Until you *need* them, of course."

The king's jaw flexed several times before he spoke. "You're angry. I understand. Go to your family, and when you've calmed yourself we can speak again of these rebellions and what we're going to do about them."

"As you say." Yacat nodded in required respect to the king and his heir, then turned from the room.

* * *

The head guard admitted his guilt after a long night of

blood.

"They took my children!" he screamed to the torturers. "I had no choice!"

Yacat memorized the names of the men who'd approached him, but had little hope of finding them. He kept his family at the palace rather then his new estate, because at least in the palace only assassins could threaten them. This had the unfortunate consequence of placing him at his father's disposal, and so he accepted his new duties as Lord General of the armies, and tried to advise his brothers with the rebellions.

"The mist tribes are deep in the jungles, who even cares about them?" Cuali whined as he looked longingly at the alcohol stored in the war room. Yacat shifted and tried not to think of all the better men who should be generals, and would be, were it not for his brother's royal blood.

"Rebellion is like wildfire," he explained. "It must not be allowed to spread. One of you will take a thousand men and deal with them. Make a lesson of their warriors. Take their heads to their allies on your way back to Copanoch."

Neither man volunteered. Instead they whined and offered foolish suggestions until Yacat lost his patience and ordered Patla into the jungle, and Cuali to patrol the coast. On another day he'd have been red with contempt for their sniveling, but all he could think about were his children.

His habit became a visit twice daily, and he made a kind of peace with his wife. His cold distance had wounded her, and she didn't understand. She thought his new concubine had captured his heart, temporarily bewitching him, and he thought this fiction a kindness. Surely it was easier to believe your spouse loved another more, than to know they no longer loved you at all.

Yacat made good on his promise to return Ruka to the palace, and placed him at the harem doors. His presence disturbed both the guards and the family, but the king could not deny the request so soon on the back of the attack.

Ten days had passed since the attack, thirty more now before the festival of stars. Yacat dealt with his morning obligations, then walked to the harem for the first of his visits. He found the giant staring like a statue at the side of the other bodyguards. His eyes seemed relaxed, but active, his manner always as a hunter close to violence. He had only been allowed to carry a club, which he in any case left sitting on the tiles. Yacat stopped at the guarded corridor and frowned as he considered his family in the rooms beyond. He spoke more to himself than the men.

"There are windows in the harem rooms. The walls are high, but still, skilled men might scale them."

Ruka's deep voice answered instantly.

"I barred the windows with hard metal. They would not get in."

Yacat felt his mouth work as he considered asking where the man had gotten the bars and how he'd placed them, but shook his head. You did not ask a spirit how it worked its magic.

"Thank you, Ruka."

He nodded to the other guards and walked past. He knew their pride was stung at the giant's presence, and that they despised standing next to him all day, but he did not care. The women and their children gestured in respect as he passed them, and when he'd spotted Maretzi and all their children he felt the same small moment of relief that always came. Seeing them, he knew this time why he had truly come, and walked on.

"How is she feeling, physician?"

"Well enough, Lord General." The old priest of the god of the dead stuffed bloodstained bandage into his satchel along with an ointment used to prevent corruption. "She will recover fully, but should stay in bed for at least two more days to align her health with the stars that portend recovery."

Yacat was aware of the many feminine eyes on his back, but ignored them. "Thank you. You may go."

Without waiting for a reaction, Yacat opened his concubine's door and walked inside. He found Zaya relaxed on her bed, hands fiddling with an instrument. Yacat's people loved music as much as sport, and even princes were expected to learn, but Yacat had only ever had a single talent.

Zaya had not been done up as was customary for a prince's visit. Her hair was greasy, her dress pulled up around her strong, pale legs, her face without paints or jewelry. Her plain beauty struck him, and he found he much preferred her this way.

"Your large friend now guards the harem," he explained as he closed the door. "The gods may move him, but I fear for any man who tries."

Zaya smiled with her teeth, and Yacat found this appealing, too.

"I'm pleased. Though, not afraid," she answered, her voice strong.

"Are you ever?"

Here she squirmed and adjusted her leg, and the injury brought Yacat back to the beach. They had not spoken since that afternoon of blood, and he wasn't sure what to say.

"Not if…faithful." She frowned. "But, I was afraid on sea. I cannot swim. I thought I'd die in endless water, and my gods felt…far away."

"I should like to hear of your adventures." Yacat

walked to the bed and sat in the nearby chair. "And of the world you come from."

One of her eyebrows raised, and she gestured at her leg. "Well, I am your slave, *Tekit*. I must do as you ask."

Yacat smiled, though he felt a strange kind of embarrassment. He had treated the girl as little more than a pawn in his games, yet she had risked her life, and saved his children. With rebellion and the awful fate that awaited him, he had not given these strangers the attention they deserved. He met her eyes.

"For your actions near my estate, I owe you a debt. I cannot offer you and your companion freedom today, if that is your wish. But one day I can, and will. That is my oath."

The girl watched him, her foreign green eyes moving back and forth across his before she seemed to make a decision. "Then, I glad I used knife on your enemies, instead of your throat."

Yacat had decided to let the matter of the hidden blade pass, but whether it was the surprise of the brazen threat, or the pleasing sound of her accent, he couldn't help but laugh.

"Well," she settled back on her cushions and closed her eyes. "You ask of my world. What would you like to know?"

Yacat still wasn't sure he believed she was from across the sea. But he had to admit he couldn't explain either of the extraordinary captives, or the ship that fled the royal fleet at a speed that sounded impossible. If it were true, Yacat knew he should care a great deal more about these foreigners and their people. Yet he found he couldn't. The foundation of his own house was rotting, and unless he could fix that, it made little difference what happened in the outside world. Every threat, great or small, could destroy the weak.

"If we were in your homeland now, what would we be doing?"

Zaya laughed but kept her eyes closed. "Nothing, *Tekit*. Your warm, noble blood would freeze in veins."

Now it was Yacat's turn to smile. It faded though, as his pleasure at the girl's presence dissolved beneath the weight of his future. His isolation, his otherness, felt like iron chains around his chest.

"You've learned so many of our words, and so quickly," he almost whispered. "Do you know too of the Devourer, Zaya? The god my people call Centnaz?"

He knew he shouldn't speak of it—that he should hide away his fears and weakness or else risk allowing it to destroy him. But he had to let it out.

"Yes," Zaya said after a delay. Her eyes opened, alert now as they watched him. "My serving girl speaks of him. He sounds…unpleasant."

Yacat snorted, and took a long breath before he spoke.

"My son is to be…given to him. There is nothing I can do." When she said nothing he again met her eyes. "Do your people do such things?"

The girl swallowed but did not look away. "I'm sorry. No. My people do not do this thing. But our gods can be cruel also. Those like Ruka, born…wrong? Often abandoned. There are laws, but, often broken."

Yacat stood, forcing the thoughts from his mind. He smiled for the brave, mysterious woman who he owed for the children that would survive, and therefore what remained of his happiness. He knelt and took her hands in his.

"Thank you, Zaya, for the lives of my children." He kissed her knuckles, and though she tugged slightly to pull away, at least did not look horrified. "Though I cannot free you yet, to me you are a free woman, not a concubine. You will not need that knife strapped to your chest." He smiled. "Perhaps you should wear it anyway." She stopped resisting, and so he let go. "I have enjoyed our conversation. If it pleases you, we will have another soon."

She smiled. "It would. It does."

Yacat rose and left her to rest, his mind drifting far away as he ignored the women and servants of the harem. Twenty days to go. Twenty days before the festival of stars, and a new life without honor. He knew he had to make use of the time he had, he only wished he knew how.

Chapter 24

The giant's chest blocked Yacat's path halfway through the harem.

"Oh." Yacat stopped a finger's width from hitting breastbone and stepped back. He looked down to see neat, dark rows of freshly planted seeds, dug into a square of the flower gardens. Ruka's huge hands were stained with dirt, his forehead ruddy with sun.

"I thought you stood at the gate all day." Yacat said to cover his moment of surprise. "You've been busy."

The giant stared as if smalltalk were beneath his efforts.

"Well." Yacat cleared his throat, lacking the attention or strength to engage with the strange spirit-man and his discomforting presence. "You needn't worry. Your companion will be alright."

"Yes," Ruka's deep voice answered. "Despite the arrogant incompetence of your physicians."

Yacat cleared his throat, preparing to walk past the man when he spoke again.

"I am told Zaya nearly died to protect your children."

Yacat stopped. "She did."

"I wondered why she should do that." The giant's tone implied he knew, but Yacat could only think *good question.*

"To earn my favor, perhaps," he said without belief.

"Perhaps." The spirit sneered. "Or she is a brave warrior, incapable of idleness in the face of evil."

At this Yacat's mind emerged briefly from the fog, his eyes narrowing as he met the giant's gaze. He was growing tired of the spirit-man's barbs and contempt, of feeling judged by those bright, animal eyes.

"What do you know of anything, slave?" he snapped, expecting at least caution but instead seeing only amusement in the thing's eyes.

"I know you walk this place like a phantom in a man's skin. I know you destroyed that tribe without pleasure or desire. "

"You aren't wise to speak of spirits living in flesh, slave. My father's priests would have your blood on an altar were it not for me."

"My eternal gratitude," said the giant, displaying none. "And I have told you, your priests are ignorant fools. I am as much a spirit as you are, *Mahala*."

Yacat grit his teeth and a clenched a fist, angry to be lectured by anyone, never mind a foreign slave. What did he know of Yacat's troubles save as an outsider looking in? Who was he to speak so casually of impossible things? No matter what Yacat did, he knew his family would pay the price. There was no resistance he could offer that would make any difference. He was one man. He couldn't stop an entire religion from spreading.

"There's nothing I can do," he snarled, mostly angry that the thing had provoked him so easily.

When he at last looked up to spirit's face he found both the contempt and judgment gone, but also not a trace of pity.

"I am but a slave, as you say, great prince, and not a spirit filled with wisdom. But, before a man accepts a life of joylessness and resentment, telling himself at all times there is nothing he could do—perhaps first, he should *try*."

With that the giant stooped to his garden as if the conversation was over. Yacat stood with balled fists and no words, then growled as he strode down the brick pathway, uncertain where to direct his anger.

He found his wife playing with their children at the fountain. She was laughing and smiling and for a moment she looked exactly as she had those years ago, and his breath caught. He knew he could not play with Zolya, that he could never hide his pain and was therefore useless now to the child for months. Yet here he was, laughing and splashing with Maretzi, being loved. Yacat watched them and felt his anger cool. He knew the god-cursed, evil spirit was not entirely wrong. Yacat might at least try to influence his family, to speak what was in his heart, before he accepted the doom.

When Maretzi noticed him, he smiled and gestured to her bedroom. She sent a servant to play with the children, then went in, red-faced and wet from the spray, as beautiful as ever. He hadn't been with her for a long time. She noticed his eyes as he closed the door, and started taking off her dress. "No," he stopped her, coming to his senses. "I just wanted to speak with you."

"We can speak after, husband. The pregnancy will not be harmed. When I was carrying the other children we still…"

"It isn't that. I didn't come here to." He closed his eyes, fighting for calm and to remind himself what the hell he was even trying to do. What could he say? 'Do you and your whole family buy into this nonsense? *Truly*? Can you not see how foolish it makes us? How it creates hate and despair and makes us think so little of life?'

His wife's expression changed as he delayed, her pleasure draining and twisting into something he'd never imagined on her face.

"Is it this concubine? Zaya?" He blinked and saw the rage behind his wife's eyes. "First you leave me here while you take her to see your land, land that will belong to *our* sons. Is her pale skin and hair so beautiful? Do you forget me so quickly?"

"No." Yacat stepped closer, feeling his temper flare at his own ineptitude at anything but war.

"Now, you won't even lie with me," she looked away.

Yacat took her arms until she met his eyes. "You are as beautiful to me now as the day we met. I haven't lain with Zaya, nor did I choose her—it's another 'reward' from father as so many things. I'm sorry I've been so distant. I am still angry but not at you." He saw the hope grow in her eyes, and felt almost shame for it. There was still a distance between them he feared he couldn't gulf—the broken bridge between one who had chosen life and lies, and another who'd chosen truth and death.

"Why are you angry, husband? Every day I realize more and more how blessed you are. You have been chosen, as our son has been chosen. Oh if only you could see your future as clearly as I do, Yacat."

Yacat felt his hands tightening on her arms and forced them open. How was it possible to both love and hate the same person? What could he say to her? "*Perhaps you should try*," the shaman's words echoed in his ears, his mocking arrogance, his righteous eyes.

"You're hurting me, husband."

Yacat blinked and loosened his grip. "I'm sorry, Maretzi. I cannot stop thinking of our son...he is so young, he doesn't understand..."

"I have told him, husband." Wetness formed in Maretzi's eyes. "He understands. He wants only to make you proud. He's so strong and brave, husband, just like his father."

The words sounded far away as Yacat backed to the door. He could have killed her, then, he knew, just as he knew it would have been a monstrous injustice and after he would have plunged a knife through his own heart.

"Please, husband." Maretzi was coming forward to embrace him, panic now in her eyes. "I wish only to serve you. I love you. I have loved you from the day we met."

"I know," he mumbled, holding up a hand to warn her away. He turned and left her room, closing the door as he cut her away from his heart, feeling more trapped and alone than before. He left the harem without looking at his children or the guards, foot following foot into corridors swarming with life that felt so far away.

Later, Yacat found Uncle Anatzi where he always was when not serving the king—watching the city guard train. Today they played courtball in a hundred teams in the palace grounds, laughing and shouting as they raced across the grass in a thousand displays of skill. Yacat had never much cared for such games. He played with his brothers and enjoyed sharing the bond of competition, but that was all. Who was best had never mattered to him, and when he was young he had at first disappointed his father and uncles when they thought him lazy, and unambitious—until they'd put a sword in his hand.

"Old Goat," Yacat called as he crossed the grass with a bottle of balque—an expensive drink of special bark soaked in honey and fermented.

"Ah, the lord of war graces us with his presence." Anatzi gestured to his closest aid, and the young man's eyes widened when he saw Yacat. Others waiting nearby noticed him and clustered around Anatzi, standing like fools as warriors awaiting command on the battlefield. "See how they kiss your feet, Mahala?" Anatzi snorted. "Once it was I who commanded such respect. Once it was the mighty Anatzi who loosened young bowels with a word."

"They would respect you more, uncle, if they didn't see you sit on your arse eating sweet meats every day."

"Ha!" Anatzi stood and waved away the men. "He's not here to see untrained boys. Off with you, sycophants! That means arse-licker, fool boys, *go*! He clearly needs a great man's wisdom."

Yacat smiled, despite everything. "It amazes me to say, uncle—but you are right. I thought we'd drink in the old barracks." He lifted the bottle, and the old warrior grinned as he glanced around—as if the king's favored brother might be caught and punished for getting drunk.

"You young soldiers," he rolled his eyes. "In my day a man could drink and walk at the same time. Why wait for the barracks?"

They took turns doing just that, strolling along the well-kept fields of trampled grass as the older man made conversation. Anatzi was the sort who could speak all afternoon without saying anything of consequence, so Yacat mostly listened to stories of plain things made interesting. They reached the old barracks, which were used now for palace storage, and had been a place for secret talks or young lovers for years.

Still, Yacat struggled to speak his mind. They drank and spoke of old battles and wounds. Anatzi had been the general of the interior for two decades, and put down as many rebellions for more years than Yacat had been alive. In a rare moment of silence, Yacat at last held the bottle in his hands and looked at the floor.

"What do you think of my father's plans, Uncle? With the priests, and my brother. On the…matter of main concern."

Anatzi snorted. "Your father always was so damned superstitious. *Emperor*." He seized the bottle and swigged. "*Emperor, emperor, emperor.* There I said it!

And whose to hear or care, and what could they do in any case." He sighed. "There's little to say. Etzil never understood why the three cities should be ruled separately. Your grandfather would tell him because every family had its own gods and ways, with seventeen gods we didn't share and family religions even here amongst the noble families. Etzil didn't care. He said it was foolish and unstable and sooner or later there would be war, and he was right. But then Centnaz's priests spread from town to town, family to family, and soon became the path to unity. It was they who made it possible with a shared belief, nephew. You must give them that."

"Even if that belief is monstrous, Uncle?"

Yacat managed to meet the man's eyes, but didn't find the judgment, concern or even false jest he might have thought. Anatzi just shrugged. "I'm not a pious man, and too simple for theology. But life is sacrifice, is it not? Every choice destroys the rest you might have made. A man gives his life one way or another."

"But we *force* men and women to give their lives, Uncle. And not in a lifetime, but on an *altar*, in a moment's work."

Anatzi's eyebrows raised. "And we don't in war, *general*? In childbirth? In construction and in the fields? For the valley to thrive, some must die. It is no different whether they are sacrificed to protect us from our enemies, or to protect us from the gods."

Yacat felt his hope slipping away. He wanted to shout *but it isn't true, they are liars and thieves and destroyers*! But who was he to say otherwise? Who was he to refute the priests and the gods? "And children, Uncle? Children like my Zolya?"

The old warrior pursed his lips and drank. "I lost two children before they were five, Yacat. If I could have given one to protect the other, I would have." After a long silence between them, he slapped Yacat's thigh and grinned. "If a belief in dick-eating piranhas made your father emperor, he would feed all our cocks to his pond, and sleep soundly."

Yacat managed to produce a smile. He loved this man, as he loved his wife, but it made things no easier. Perhaps it made it worse.

"Just think what we might do!" Anatzi's eyes sparkled a little as he looked to the pitted stone of the crumbling barracks. "My brother is a man of vision, and your brother is his father's son. They'll do great things, with our help, and the blessing of their god. We'll connect the cities with new roads, increase trade and allow travel until our nobles are all so mixed they'll have forgotten what it was to live without emperors."

All built on a lie, Yacat thought, but could not say. Yet how could such a thing ever last? Why build a house on sand, when one day it must surely fall?

Uncle Anatzi was still talking. "We'll make the House of Mar live for eternity," he said. "We'll guide them, us old soldiers, we'll keep 'em practical and remind 'em where they come from. Guide your brother, Yacat, as I've guided mine. We're the same, you and me."

Yacat smiled numbly, struck by the thought. Anatzi had been the hand of King Etzil for decades, training the army, destroying rebels, protecting the border. Though he had spent a lifetime serving his family and his city, all the while it had become more rotten, more corrupt, the lands outside its borders more bitter, repressed, and enraged. *Yes, Uncle*, Yacat thought sadly, *we are exactly the same.*

He finished his drink and let Anatzi talk, alone again despite the man's company. He had tried as the spirit suggested, as perhaps he should have done long ago. But his regrets made no difference now.

Anatzi was right—Yacat's brother, the heir, was his father's son. Whatever tool gave him power would be used without a second thought. What gave that tool its power made no difference—what the price would be he would pay without care. Telling him not to use that power would be like arguing with the sun.

And so Yacat had spoken with the most practical, loyal man in his family, who could at least bend the king's ear if he wished. But it seemed he too had been captured by the great dreams of power, blinded from the dark by a light too bright and close for the open eye. Yacat had tried, and he had failed.

Chapter 25

On the second sunrise, Zaya rose groaning from her bed. Her leg ached with a dull pain, and her vision swam worse than at sea, but she kept her feet. She dressed on her own, and when Temolata found her she fussed and panicked and fetched the physician, who inspected the wound and at last grunted his approval.

"Walking only," he explained with a tsk. "Your elements are still imbalanced, and will now take *another* three days to align."

Zaya nodded that she understood, no intention of obeying. Ruka had been treating the wound in secret, applying some tincture of herbs Zaya couldn't understand how he'd even managed to make, and been more confident in the recovery.

"You are healing quickly," he explained the night before. "The danger is passed, ignore the priests. Avoid knives in the future."

She'd blinked and looked to his strange eyes for a trace of humor, and perhaps found the slightest twinkle.

"Thank you, Ruka, I will try."

For the next several days she made it her habit to walk the walls of the harem, humming the songs that battered her mind half-formed and haunting, never leaving her alone since childhood. As before the women seemed content to ignore her, but now only looked with concealed eyes and wary faces, as if she were some kind of tamed predator. The guards, on the other hand, treated her like a queen.

"My lady," one had stopped her at the entrance on a walk, some kind of jewelry in his hands. "This is for you, left by Mahala...by Prince Yacat. If you wish, you can wear it here," he gestured to his own arm, which was wrapped in a similar bracelet.

"Thank you." Zaya took it, unsure exactly why she was receiving it, or how to put it on. When he noticed her hesitation the young warrior put down his spear and clasped it just above her bicep, sticking the feather out behind. He stepped back and swept his eyes over the fit.

"You killed two of the prince's enemies," he explained with a grin. "So you are a wolf warrior. I am also to tell you, you are no longer confined to the harem. As a warrior, you may roam the palace where you wish, unless told otherwise."

Zaya returned the grin and made the gesture of respect she had seen the warriors give. The young man returned it.

"We have heard you killed a man from forty paces with a spear," he said loudly enough for the other guards. "When you are recovered, we should like to see you throw."

Zaya looked for mockery in the mens' eyes but found none. These people were very athletic, she knew. Their children played endless games with weapons and toys that had them racing, wrestling and kicking rubber balls all day. No doubt things changed little when the boys grew to men. She nodded, and carried on her walk.

"Bring spears, targets, to courtyard," she called to them. "Tomorrow."

They laughed in pleasure and a few banged their spears on the ground. Zaya walked back to her room, seeing an almost open-mouthed shock from the other women when they saw her armband. She did her best to conceal her pride.

That evening she made use of her newfound freedom,

wandering the palace at first with a limp, then with the help of a walking stick. The palace writhed with activity. At first she had been concerned she'd be stared at and questioned in every hall, but the busy servants and guards hardly noticed her. Artists painted every flat surface with bright colors or images of half-man, half-animal gods, and Zaya soon recognized the single eye of the Devourer, Centnaz, staring down from the heavens beyond even the sun. Others carried multi-colored cloth from room to room, packs of seamstresses and their apprentices carrying bundles and trying not to drip their sweat to stain the fabric. Zaya assumed it was all in preparation for the festival to come.

With her small window of anonymity, she searched the palace, going down and down and following the view from windows until she found at least three ways out of the fortress. Two were guarded by many warriors and perhaps even barracks outside, but one seemed to have no more than five, and she suspected there would be other entries. The next day, she decided, she would go outside, and see if she could find a path to escape.

Though she wondered now, was it necessary? Maybe the best thing for both her and the shaman was to wait until Yacat could free them as he promised to do. The truth was, she trusted him.

When the night grew dark she went back to her room to rest. There she found the shaman waiting outside, his back to the stone and his eyes through the open section of roof to the stars.

"I've explored the palace," she whispered. "There are many exits. They're all guarded, but we might escape at night if we chose the weakest."

The shaman nodded but said nothing, and Zaya shifted her weight from one sore leg to the other.

"Do you think the others…have waited for us? Will

they have sailed home and trapped us here?"

The shaman blinked, his expression forming more awareness, as if he'd almost been sleeping with his eyes open.

"No," he said. "Eka will not leave me here."

Zaya had no desire to disagree with the Godtongue, but while the captain of the *Prince* seemed a most competent man, loyal was not the word she'd have used.

"We've been gone a long time," she tried. "The sailors are in hostile lands with no way to know we're alive."

"Even so. Eka will find me, alive or dead."

"Eka, perhaps," Zaya frowned. "But the others…" She shifted her weight. "They might…overrule him. It would be one man against ten."

Surprisingly, Ruka smiled. "Few alive can *overrule* a master of the Ching. None are aboard the *Prince*."

Zaya had never heard of a 'master of the ching', and was too tired to be much interested. She understood the captain had been a kind of priest from a small monastery in the isles before he became the king's assassin, but that was all. She left it alone.

"If we escape," she asked. "If we get home, back to the Ascom, what will we tell them of this place?"

The shaman looked away, his eyes glazing again, as if overwhelmed by memory.

"Nothing."

Zaya felt her mouth open and she shook it closed. "Then why come?" she managed to say respectfully. "Why if not to find new people and change the world again?" The shaman took a breath and met her eyes.

"Without my ships neither people can cross. Who knows how long it will take." Zaya stared, unmollified, and the shaman's eyes narrowed. "Knowledge is its own reward. All my life I have dreamt of the edges of the world." He rose slightly, looking angrier by the moment, though Zaya said nothing. "I have already taken one people across an endless sea. Once in a lifetime is enough."

Zaya shrugged, and broke the stare. She wasn't sure what else to say. She thought of Chang and the others and their talk of mutiny, and wasn't so sure of Ruka's words. She suspected Eka was dead, and the sailors on a desperate attempt to sail home.

But what point in saying so? She bid the shaman good night and returned to her room, contemplating her future. Later, lying on a thick bed filled with cushions, she decided life here would not be so terrible. It was beautiful and rich. Copanoch was powerful and mostly safe, despite its enemies and flaws, built on land her own people couldn't imagine in their wildest dreams. To be Yacat's warrior-concubine would not be so terrible a fate.

The thought of it made sleeping more difficult. She tried to occupy her mind with thoughts of home, and she knew she would miss the cold, crisp air that seemed to fill your lungs to bursting. The isles, and even this new land, sweltered with a wet heat that made breathing difficult and left a constant sheen of sweat. She would miss her parents, her brothers and sisters. She already did.

But no matter what, she saw no way home now without her benefactor, and the shaman. Though she suspected the *Prince* was lost with all her crew, perhaps with Yacat's help, Ruka could build a new ship. With a new crew, and his knowledge of the sea, he could still take them home. It was her last thought before sleep.

* * *

Zaya woke to men's voices and laughter. For a moment she forgot where she was and panicked, rolling out of bed with her hidden knife gripped firmly in hand.

"Mistress—you shouldn't...are you alright?"

Zaya's heart pounded and her leg ached as she blinked herself awake. Temolita was halfway in the door across the room, dressed and ready for the day. "Prince Yacat and some of his warriors are in the harem, mistress. They are preparing the garden for a... I'm sorry, I don't even know. Some kind of game, I think?"

The harem. Copanoch. Yes, Zaya had forgotten her dreams but remembered the sea and landfall and a hundred things that somehow were real and now her life. She recalled agreeing to the spear throw, though she hadn't realized the prince would come, and she sweat at the thought.

"Thank you, Temolita, I alright. I dress self and out shortly."

"Yes, Mistress." The girl disappeared, and Zaya limped back to her bed. Most of her 'official' clothes were so bulky they'd interfere, or so immodest she wouldn't wear them. She settled on a loose shirt she could tie around her waist with rope, grinning slightly as her fingers expertly wove a half knot and slipped it tight. She did the same with the matching loose skirt, tying it around her good thigh, leaving the other mostly exposed. She wore sandals that at least vaguely matched the rope, tied up her hair, and at last put on her armband, before taking a long, steadying breath.

It didn't make much difference, after all. It wasn't life or death as it had been on the beach. So why did she feel so nervous? Surely it was more than pride—surely her standing mattered, and she merely recognized that.

And perhaps, yes, she knew, she wanted to impress the prince.

She stepped out smiling but only slightly hiding her limp. It was always best, in a performance, to have witnesses concerned at the outcome, and for their expectations to be low.

"Good morning, Tekit," Zaya bowed her head in respect and approached the group of men in the garden. Their conversation ended, their eyes sweeping her in a now familiar, if still uncomfortable assessment, far too bold for her own people.

"You look like a warrior queen." Yacat stepped forward with a hand on his chest. He smiled as he looked at her feathered armband, then gestured at the men. "The men here tell me you've agreed to a martial contest. Well, obviously I could not miss such a spectacle."

Zaya felt heat rise to her cheeks. "I said I would throw spear. I hope he hasn't…overpromised."

"No, he wouldn't dream of it," Yacat said with maybe sarcasm, and the other men laughed. He stepped forward and put his hands on Zaya's arms as he looked at her leg. "Are you certain you're healthy enough? Perhaps this was foolish. There's no hurry, and it's quite understandable…"

"I'm well. Is that target? Let me see spears."

Yacat smiled and it spread to the men. "No matter how the contest ends, brothers, I tell you I saw it with my own eyes. She speared a man like a fish at forty paces, and saved a prince of Mar."

The men seemed almost to swell with respect as they nodded in her direction, and she couldn't help but feel the warm spread of pride in her chest. Yacat gestured towards a stand filled with spears, then led her forward.

"Young Cuali here will throw with you. He's a fine arm, and what's a contest without some competition, yes?"

The warriors stomped their feet in approval and Zaya didn't mind. She walked to the rack and lifted a wooden spear, the shaft too short and the tip too long. But it was no worse for throwing than the weapon she'd used on the beach, and perhaps slightly better. She lifted it and was surprised at the light weight, especially at the tip, and realized it was a kind of rock rather than metal.

"Will it not break?" she frowned. The prince shrugged and drew another, tossing it to the young warrior.

"Quite likely. But you needn't worry. Be careful, though, the flint is very sharp. These are proper weapons used for war."

She nodded and rolled her shoulders, stepping to a colored marker the men had lain on the grass. As she did she saw Ruka watching from the entrance, and she nearly groaned. The Godtongue's favored weapon was a javelin, and legends of his throws were told all over the Ascom. It was one of the reasons she had learned all her life.

"I hope Cuali has eat breakfast," Zaya said as she breathed. Her nerves steadied now as the thing drew close. She heard the men's laughter faintly as if from another room, the sound of her breathing clouding the world. The weight of the spear replaced all, then the square shape of the target across the clearing. An image of the young man she'd killed by the lake flashed before her eyes, but she blinked it away. With a two step lunge, she spun her whole body into the throw, smoothly releasing just as she intended.

The spear soared fast and straight, cutting through the square to pierce the ground behind, shaft plunged firmly into the dirt.

Her ears rung with the howls of approval from the men. Women and children were coming sleepily from their rooms, blinking up at the dim light from the breaking dawn, then gaping at the men in the harem clapping in Zaya's direction.

"It's your throw, Cuali," Yacat laughed with the others. The young man put a fist to his chest and bowed his head low.

"No need, Mahala. A wise man knows when he stands before a master. I accept defeat."

The others howled and clapped him playfully on the back as they collected the spears and the target, and all the while Yacat watched her with his lopsided smile. "Indeed he does," he said quietly, loud enough only for Zaya to hear.

She released a breath and tried not to be bothered by the endless stares from the women, especially Yacat's wife, who stood by her children with tired eyes. Zaya forced herself to look only briefly towards the shaman, not daring to hope for approval. He was already turning back towards his post, but before he did she saw his face, and though it was stern as ever, she thought yes, he too, in his way, was proud of the throw. It was a strange feeling, the accomplished dream of a little girl, to impress the great hero of Noss.

"Will you walk with me, Zaya?" Yacat motioned towards the harem entrance. "There's been a fine rain, and on such days I like to walk in the gardens outside the temple of the dead with bare feet."

Zaya matched his smile. "I would like, Tekit." And it was true, she would.

He took her hand, and walked away from the harem.

Chapter 26

Eighteen days before the end of the world, Yacat thought, then tried to put it from his mind. Zaya's hand was warm and strong in his, and he let her use it for support to keep pressure off her wounded leg. Together they walked through mostly empty corridors of painted stone, still too early for the palace to be awake save for a small portion of guards and servants.

He wasn't sure why he'd brought her save that he didn't want to be alone with his thoughts, nor in the company of anyone else he could think of. He wasn't sure what that feeling might be called, but it was at least affection.

"You are alright to walk? Your leg isn't too painful?"

"Shall I kick you with it?"

Yacat grinned and pulled her onward, out the rear of the palace towards the old temple grounds. The differences between his new 'concubine' and every other woman he'd known were stark, and most refreshing. Royal women were not raised to match words with princes. No doubt they could be as annoyed or frustrated as any other, but they did not voice it. Like his wife they held their tongues, guarded their words, and obeyed their husbands. The gulf was uncrossable. You might watch love bloom in their eyes, or disappear, but you would never hear why, or how. He couldn't blame them, he supposed. Courtly life was dangerous and filled with rules. The sons and daughters of nobility were privileged in ways the common folk could barely dream, but so too were they imprisoned in ways they couldn't understand.

But Zaya was different. Yacat stepped from the cold

stone of the palace to the perfectly trimmed grass of the temple grounds, and slipped off his sandals. He was about to tell her to do the same when she did it on her own accord, and he smiled. Even in that simple thing the difference was pronounced. She had not waited for instruction as his wife would have done. She had seen and chosen, as she had seen his son in danger and chosen. He met her eyes and she returned his smile, her pale toes spreading in the grass.

"Mmm." She sighed. "You were right. Feeling is very pleasant."

They walked on, hand in hand, the cool dew of the night rain leaving slick trails in their wake. Beyond them the high pyramids of the old gods loomed like small mountains, built in a perfect circle, matched to the constellation of the star-ring.

"I come here when I need peace," Yacat explained, as ever in this place both sad and alive, a heightened sense of the ancient, and his own mortality. "The old gods are out of fashion now. My family does not come to them for guidance. The priests do not keep the flame of Tamate lit, nor the pool of tears filled and cleaned. Only the servants come to clean and trim the grass. They are more like tombs than temples."

"Yet you worship? You honor them still?"

"In my way," he said, then thought on it more deeply as he had many times, still unsure of the answer. "I am not a pious man," he said. "But I feel the loss of our... traditions, replaced by beliefs and rituals far more cruel." He shook his head. "I have long seen corruption and incompetence in the administration in my family's kingdom. I've done what I can, and for a time thought any change would be welcome. I was wrong."

Zaya squeezed his hand, and he smiled and walked on. He knew it wasn't right to speak to her of such things. It was weakness and he should be silent, yet it helped.

He took her past rows of lychee trees, their fruit ripe and some already dropped to the grass. He plucked one and ripped it open, handing it to her. Without hesitation she smiled and took a bite, eyes widening, almost teary. Yacat was surprised at the reaction and annoyed to have upset her. "What is it? Is it too sour?"

"No. Is nothing. It's…just. In my homeland, fruit does not grow. There's…nothing like this."

He nodded, unable to imagine a place that didn't grow fruit. He pulled her onward, to the gateway of the gods, built so intentionally low it made them both bow to enter, and beyond to the temple plaza made from pink marble to glow red in the sun. "Dawn will come soon." He took her to wide benches covered with thatched reeds, the strands built tight and smooth, layered until it softened. The fountain of life lay to their left, gurgling with clean water piped from the lakes, the pyramid temples to their right.

"It so beautiful," Zaya stared with open mouthed awe, and Yacat smiled. "Did your father build?"

"No, they were here long before the fortress. It was built around them." He pointed to the temple of the dead, and the symbols written on the gate. "What you are now, we once were. What we are now, you shall be," he read, and Zaya smiled. "This place has stood for a thousand years, perhaps more. Do you understand this? Thousand?"

Her eyes widened in disbelief, and Yacat laughed.

"Do your people not have such things?"

She shook her head. "My people…great warriors, not builders of temples. We make statues of gods and heroes." Here she reddened slightly, which Yacat found most appealing on such a brave woman. "When first saw you," she looked away. "You remind me of one."

231

Yacat grinned and sat closer, pleased at the thought. "A god, or a hero?"

She took a breath and again met his eyes, forcing a smile. "I shouldn't have said. Tale is tragic, great man whose life was sadness."

"I see." Yacat kept his expression light, but felt the truth of the assessment in his chest. He looked to the top of the pyramid, which glowed slightly now as the sun's rays broke softly over the horizon.

"But I was wrong." Zaya had lifted her hand, and touched Yacat's face. "Now I see strong, good man, too good, he tries to carry whole world. Need you carry so much weight?"

He covered her hand with his, no idea how to answer.

"Is this place not proof?" She gestured with her head. "World goes on, long after you, and me. You have only little time, and few choices. Then gone."

Yacat blinked and watched the green of Zaya's eyes, lit and glowing now from the sun as the world glowed red around them, and he thought if there was a more beautiful sight in all the world, he need not bother seeing it. He noticed raised bumps on Zaya's skin and frowned, realizing he should have thought of the cool, damp air.

"There are blankets in the temples, I think. I can fetch some."

Zaya's smile matched her eyes, indulgent, and something else. "I daughter of ash, prince of paradise. I not cold."

She ran a thumb across his lips, and he kissed it, and came forward until she was in his arms and his lips on hers. He felt his body tremble with desire as he lowered her to the bench, a feeling now so long withheld he had wondered if it died. He stopped and held her hands, closing his eyes with a shudder.

"My son...I should take no comfort with his fate so close, so terrible. What sort of man and father would I be."

Zaya sat up, her long, pale legs on either side of him, their faces so close their noses almost touched. "You not listening," she said, running her hands through his hair. "My people...live with tragedy. Always hunger, war and cold. They learn long ago to take comfort. To live, when it is summer."

The wisdom of these words required no answer. Yacat pulled her to his chest and wrapped her legs around him as he opened her lips with his tongue. Then they were tearing at each other's clothes, groping and exploring. The world froze as Yacat moved inside her, bathed in the red dawn built both by gods and men. It went on forever, it was over too soon, and he lay in her arms with his mouth buried in her neck, breathing in the scent of her.

It did not last, as such things never did, but in that moment at least Yacat felt he might survive the loss of his honor. And even if he didn't, before the world lost all meaning and color, at least he had known beauty, and happiness, and what it was to be alive. It was all the ancient gods had ever offered, before the Devourer and his endless promises. Perhaps it would be enough.

* * *

Zaya clung to Yacat so he wouldn't move, still trembling from the lovemaking. When they could stay still no longer he rose with a sigh, and grinned. "That was satisfactory, honored concubine. Thank you."

She laughed and pushed him back with a knee. "I about to say same."

He would assume, no doubt, she was more

experienced in such things, and she did not wish to let on otherwise. His smiled widened and his eyes roamed her near nakedness until she rose. But like the pleasure and brief moment of oblivion, the lightness faded. They dressed and linked hands as they left the temple grounds in the morning light, the cool dew a welcome relief from the heat still lingering in Zaya's body. When the moment felt right she asked, very quietly:

"Can you not ask king? About your son?"

He did not answer right away, and when he did his face had drooped from the earlier joy. "I can only stand at his side, and help him die with dignity. If I am strong enough perhaps he will know himself a hero through my eyes."

The words touched her, and broke her heart, but she knew to speak no more. They walked in silence to the palace entrance, and though there were servants and priests moving to their tasks Yacat stopped her here and kissed her with as much passion as at the temple.

"I may not see you much...before the festival. There are rebellions and much to do. I'll have little time."

Zaya understood and wasn't bothered. She still wondered if she had lain with him for herself or for him, and hoped it could be both.

"Thank you," she said. "For showing me temple, Tekit."

The spirit of a smile returned to his eyes, and he nodded in respect. "If I can spare the time, I will see you."

Zaya let her fingers touch his strong arms and chest and she met his eyes, more certain by the moment her decision had not just been to comfort the man. "You know where room is. Does not need much time."

He grinned and kissed her and left her at the entrance, knowing she wore the feathered band of a warrior and that he needn't escort her back to the harem. She went more slowly, memory flush with the images and sensations of the morning, feeling expanded and changed, as if a new window had opened in her mind. When at last she reached the women's quarters she felt the eyes of Yacat's wife and kin but had never been less bothered. She found the Godtongue tending a small garden on the grounds, and she leaned against a nearby pillar.

"Do you have a moment, Ruka?"

He nodded and rose, eyes squinted as he inspected the row of shrubs he'd apparently planted. Zaya took a breath, trying to collect her wits and shake off the ever-present anxiousness in the man's presence. She kept her voice low.

"There is little time before the festival of stars. When it's over, I think Yacat will help us. We could ask him for supplies, labor, even the crew needed for a new ship, if you can build it. I thought you should know."

The golden eyes met hers but only for a moment. Then the shaman looked away, gaze as ever almost far into the distance.

"I have told you, Zaya. Eka will come."

"Yes, I know, shaman, but..."

"No, you do not, nor have you listened since the day I warned you not to sail with me." His brow twitched and his hands opened and closed, as if he struggled with emotion. "Captain Eka and I are killers of men, old monsters who goad the other further into chaos. Our doomed crew is as worthy of the noose as the sea, and none will mourn any of our passing. But you, Zaya, are a different creature. *You* are yet worthy of life and love, and might find both here at this prince's side, as you would in the Ascom or anywhere. Your fate is not bound with mine. It never was."

She found her jaw open and clenched it, her heart falling cruelly from the soft mists of the morning. Before she could speak, Yacat stepped from the gardens with a bundle of cloth in his arms. "Good morning, Ruka," he stepped towards her, eyes soft as they landed on Zaya. "A gift, so you don't get cold again." Here he smiled. "And you forgot your knife." He handed her the weapon with his hand on the blade. "I wouldn't have you unprotected."

"Thank you." Zaya took both in awkward silence, until Yacat looked from her to the shaman and raised a brow.

"Have I interrupted?"

There were servants nearby and maybe women of the harem, and their attention only increased Zaya's feeling of sudden embarrassment. She searched and failed for something to say.

"Yes, prince, but perhaps you belong." The shaman stepped forward, his huge presence suddenly so noticeable and dangerous, eyes boring down like the glare from some ancient lighthouse, revealing all with a pale, sickly light. Yacat's hand went to the hilt of his sword, mouth opened to respond but the shaman ignored him, deep voice commanding attention. "Still I watch you walk this place diminished, as if you are weak and helpless and have no choices. But that is a lie as pathetic as your gloom."

The prince's surprise darkened, his expression hardening. "How dare you, slave. You think you know my troubles but you know nothing. You think I haven't tried? Nor did I ask..."

"Like Zaya you speak when you should listen. You are not weak, *Mahala*, you are filled with pride. It is that pride that makes you fear mere *words*—the words of men who will say 'he betrayed his king! He betrayed his people!' Yet in your heart you know instead you choose to betray your son, another sacred duty, a loyalty so deep it rested in the bones of mothers and fathers before there were kings, before there were *words*. You have chosen, Yacat, which is your right. But do not act as if it's otherwise."

With that the men stared, Yacat's eyes bulging in rage, his hand clenched on his sword. The moment lingered dangerously, then the prince turned away from the garden without a word, and again the shaman stooped to his garden, huge hands so wrongly gentle in the dark soil.

"That was foolish," Zaya hissed, angry at the man's treatment of both her and the prince, noting the women were near enough they might have overheard. "He is our only supporter here, without him…"

"I thought your life was in the hands of the gods," Ruka interrupted, planting another tiny root firmly in the soil. "Is Yacat now a god?"

Zaya clenched her jaw and found any response dried on her tongue. Not wishing to hear another word, she turned to her room, and closed the door.

* * *

Days passed after the temple visit in almost tedious routine. Zaya played her instrument and composed songs, but they never lingered in her mind nor seemed more than cleverness and skill without a shred of meaning. She ate what Temolata brought her, and walked the palace grounds, re-visiting the temple of the dead at least once every day to see the sun rise or fall. The festival of stars loomed closer every moment, but Zaya avoided the shaman. He seemed disinterested and occupied, as if he had no time to think of anything that mattered.

On the third night Yacat came to her door. She took him to her bed without a word and undressed him, straddling him on the huge, foreign cushions until she shivered and collapsed, rising and falling through a fog of lust that matched their breathing and brought a sleep so deep she remembered only her dreams until morning. They did not speak of the shaman's words, or much of anything, instead making love again in the morning more gently, and quietly, until the prince was forced to the tasks of the day.

The palace and harem transformed for the festival. What began as largely plain grey or brown walls of stone or clay were now covered without exception with various paints or dyes. The faces of the valley men's gods stared from every corridor and doorway, welcome mat and ceiling. The nobility, and even the servants, wore special clothing and carried new tattoos or jewelry on their skin or around their necks or arms.

Every night after the third, Yacat came to Zaya's bed. Some nights were tender, but most became urgent ruts, as if they both tried to break down their fears and angers with the other's body. After, they would lie in each other's arms with little to say except tender nothings, an unspoken sense of dread for the future.

Zaya liked to think of herself as brave, but each day she didn't or couldn't face the shaman came as stark and unavoidable proof she had less control over herself than she believed. At first she blamed him, or told herself there was no purpose. She thought again and again on what he'd said—that she could make a life with Yacat, that her fate was her own. At length she agreed that yes, she could—this place was beautiful, she respected him and lusted for him, and surely that was enough clay to build a future. That he had a wife did not sit so easily. To have more than one matron was unheard of in her culture, and only women in the Ascom might ever take more than one mate at a time.

Regardless, she had nothing to do but wait. Days of learning words and boredom passed until the nights with Yacat that turned all to color and reshaped her knowledge of the world. Then it was the last night before the festival, and when Zaya wanted him most Yacat didn't come. She expected he was drowning his pain with drink, buried in some dark room with his demons. She slept little, and woke to the day of the ceremony. The royal women rose before dawn to prepare, painting and dressing themselves and their children with the help of a small army of servants. Temolata prepared Zaya with paints and jewelry and a dress of sheer cloth wrapped with more fabric for her modesty.

"As a childless concubine, you will go to the great square almost last, Mistress—after the royal family and honored guests, but before the servants."

Zaya nodded but said nothing, anxious and distracted. When she was finally ready she stepped outside to watch the others and just to stand without being fussed over. The wives and concubines of the House of Mar looked like birds of paradise, their shawls raised like plumage above their hair, bright clothes wrapped in delicate layers from neck to shin. Some twitched as if they couldn't still, their pupils large and shifting from side to side. Others spoke and laughed too loudly, their movements pronounced in the familiar sway of the drunk. Zaya saw some still drinking from clay cups.

"Sister." The voice of Yacat's wife, Maretzi, came from across the grass without a drop of the warmth the title might imply. Yacat's wife crossed the small distance from her room to Zaya's, and for a moment she wondered if she had heard her husband lying with another woman for the past several nights. From the venom leaking from the woman's eyes, she thought yes. "Love is fleeting, is it not?"

Zaya took a deep breath and nodded in respect. She could see her pupils were large and dark with some drug, and didn't want to antagonize the woman. "Yes, sister, for us all."

The hint of a polite smile vanished. "Tomorrow the House of Mar will be emperors, and my son will be the deliverance. Enjoy your time as my husband's whore. When it's over, you'll be nothing." She turned away, as if her victory were complete. Zaya spoke softly to her back.

"I'm sorry for your son, Maretzi. I wish he not die. With or without Prince Yacat, I am still warrior, still Zaya. And I wish you no ill will."

The woman slowed but said nothing, and walked away. Soon the royal family left in a procession of colors and chatter, all the children save Yacat's doomed son in an orderly line along their mothers.

Then there were only a few servants, Zaya and Ruka, and as she stared at his stony calm she took a breath and crossed the garden. She had almost reached him when she heard loud footsteps, then watched at least ten warriors emerge from the harem gate. She recognized none of them, and knew they were not harem guard.

"Your prince's protection has ended for me, I think," said the shaman, his lip curled as if he'd expected some treachery. "Do not interfere."

"Why?" Zaya's heart began pounding in her chest. "What do they want with you?"

The warriors ignored her, four moving to Ruka with rope and shackles while the others stayed back with spears. Their leader looked up at the much larger man, but stayed far out of reach.

"Slave, you come with us. Do not resist. Understand?"

Ruka smiled without pleasure, showing his jagged teeth. "You needn't bother with those, little things," he almost whispered, his voice strange, less articulate.

"Where you taking him?" Zaya demanded, stepping forward to push away the shackles. "He belong to Prince Yacat. Lord General. *Mahala*. Who are you to take anywhere?"

The soldier's eyes narrowed with contempt, his eyes on Zaya's armband as he gripped his spear. *"I am a servant of the King. And by order of my lord, I will take this slave and put him on the altar of Centnaz, so that his evil spirit is cleansed before the coming of the stars. Do you understand now, concubine, I am a servant of the king!"*

The four men seized Ruka's hands and bound them in the bronze chains, wrapping rope around his waist. As in the jungle he did not fight them, extending his arms to help them along.

"Shaman..." Zaya said in her native tongue. "You must fight. They're going to kill you. Even if Eka...even if he is coming..."

The godtongue shivered as if with acceptance as he met her eyes—the greatest living hero of a culture of warriors, his shoulders hunched, his gaze subdued. "Goodbye, Zaya," he said, almost absently, and the men dragged him onwards. He turned back at the gate, bringing the procession stumbling to a halt with even this mild resistance. "Promise me, daughter of Juchi..." he seemed suddenly worn, and exhausted. "If you see your father again, tell him," he smiled. "I'm glad I saved him. He has raised strong children."

With that, he vanished around the corner, heavy steps sounding off the painted stone long after he'd vanished from sight. Zaya stood listening, feeling helpless, and never in her life more alone.

Chapter 27

Chang's latest new-world lover helped him don the pilot's armor. The linked shirt of fine chain slipped over his head easily enough, but the vambraces and chest plate were difficult to manage alone. He showed her what to do, and she ran her fingers over the metal with wide, almost reverent eyes.

"Good, Teotel?"

Chang smiled and pat her hand on the fastened metal. The girl knew a few words and phrases in the island tongue now as he knew a few of hers. 'Teotel' meant something like 'spirit man', for many of the locals thought he and his crew were some kind of prophetic warriors from the rising sun. Chang did nothing to dispel this notion.

He slapped the girl's rump and with a final sigh stepped from his guest house. Basko and the others were already out and waiting at the edge of the town's clearing, many of their own women nearby and wishing them tearful farewells.

The few local men left in the same way—walking from houses with spears, bows, and wooden swords strapped to their bodies, parting with wives and children with a courage they likely didn't feel.

Chang found he had begun to like these tribesmen; they laughed loudly and easily; their women went to whatever men they liked unless they were married, any children raised and seen to by any member of the tribe as if each were their own. They had domesticated every kind of animal you pleased, from wild turkey to monkeys and dogs, all the way to the great and dangerous hunting cat they called 'Wanchoo'.

Chang almost smiled at the sound of a low growl and put a hand in his pocket. Without looking he removed one of his last chunks of salted pork as the huge cat emerged from the shadows behind the houses. He had been feeding it now for weeks—at least once a day as he settled into tribal life—helping prepare their feasts, patrol the edges of the town, or keep the lonely young women company. The tribesmen of 'the Northern mists' helped the sailors journey back to check on their ship, to make rope, fill water-barrels, and re-fill their stores with salted meats from their hunting or their own butchered animals.

"Good boy." Chang forced himself to be calm and unafraid as the dangerous creature approached. It licked its chops and rammed its head against Chang's arm before taking the meat directly from his hand, then produced what might be called a purr in a smaller creature, but what for him was really more like a rumble. Then it turned and disappeared into the trees.

"Waste of good meat," Basko said as he joined his watching men, a few others grunting. Chang ignored them and took his last, still-sealed drought of rum from his pocket, wiggling his brow at the men.

"Nevermind that." He shook the bottle and sniffed, closing his eyes.

"Dear gods in heaven." The Steerman's eyes followed as if he'd found an exposed woman's breasts, many of the others mouths hanging and no doubt salivating at the thought. Not a man had drunk a proper drop of anything so strong since landfall, nevermind a proper island rum. Chang pulled it back with a loud tsk.

"Captain says we march till the tribesman say stop. Men who keep up share the rum. Ka?"

"Ka. Aye, ka." The Steerman licked his lips. "Should we take a sip now, and the rest later, Chiefy?"

Chang stuffed the bottle in his bag, and turned to the jungle, the crew lining up behind.

Dozens of other tribes waited in the trees, or already marched towards 'Cope-a-noke', though with the dense foliage it was impossible to tell their numbers. In the many days since the meeting of the chiefs, Captain Eka said the new worlders had gathered thousands of warriors from many different peoples, some from far-away mountains or coasts, often speaking different languages entirely. They shared few gods and customs, often with different skin, hair and eyes as well as dress. But they were united with a single, communal fact: hatred of the three valley cities and their alliance.

That day they marched in an almost eerie quiet, surrounded only by the constant shuffling and scraping of unseen feet and branches, or the occasional call of some curious bird. Chang wished early on he'd never heard of freedom, or ashmen, or armor—and that he'd never risked the dark sea or wondered what lay beyond. The sounds of feet crushing leaves or stumbling over fallen trees became the sounds of waves, and the creaking of wood buried deep in his own ship's hull. The sweat dripping down his face was a soft rain on a dark night, his watch almost over on the rail.

Then men were chirping and whistling and the tribesmen stopped to sit or lay where they'd stood, yet others moving off into the trees. They ate fruit-crusted meat, they drank good water from water-skins—and the few men of the mist tribes sat near them with Captain Eka and the shaman Pacal. They lit no campfires, but then none were needed in the sweaty heat of the jungle, and Chang just thanked all good spirits it didn't rain.

In the morning, they marched again. By afternoon the dense jungle faded, until lone patches of trees broke otherwise uniform layers of farmland. As the horizon opened, finally Chang could see the foreigner's numbers. A true army emerged from the trees.

In ragged waves, thousands of these new worlders left their camouflage armed as a motley militia of good spears and bows, wooden swords and flint knives. Their faces were painted, their bodies smeared with mud or covered in heavy cloth. He watched more and more leave the jungle before his neck had tired from craning, and he turned back to trudge behind the captain.

The few towns they met were seemingly abandoned. Here and there they'd find old men caring for a penned up herd of animals, and the tribal scouts would leave their corpses along the road. The city of Copanoch soon loomed in the distance—a huge capital of rust-colored walls, clay and brick stacked row upon row, houses and towers with windows open like ten thousand eyes.

"There lie the temples of Centnaz," Pacal pointed at a dozen pyramids in the center of the city. "There is where the House of Mar will have spilled the blood of my family, and the blood of your comrades."

That morning the shaman had gathered most of the crew and bathed them in smoke from his 'holy rock', and their voices hummed with the now familiar magic.

"Will it be protected?" asked the captain. "Many warriors?

"Oh yes. It is a holy place to them. A circle of stands will rest on a stone square beyond the steps. There will be warriors, and noble families, but our warriors will help you. We will kill everyone we find."

"Everyone," Chang agreed, "except the large, pale-skinned man and woman."

For a time the shaman said nothing, and Chang almost repeated himself until the old man spoke.

"If they live. When it is over, we will meet here at

dawn.

"If we live," Chang answered, expecting a grin that never came.

With every word Chang had detected the pure venom in the man's voice, the hatred in his eyes. It seemed wrong on a shaman or priest, as surely a man of gods and spirits should be beyond such things. The look was echoed on every warrior around them, but only on the holy man did Chang find it disturbing. For the first time since they had landed on the coast, he felt the very real desire to turn back for his ship, leave Zaya and the pilot to their fate with a prayer and his apologies, and never touch this land again.

Instead, he marched. With the others he passed five more ghost towns and a dozen more corpses along the road. He marched over fields of the hated red root, then over rice, corn, and agave, knowing ten thousand feet trampled it behind him. For a surreal moment he wondered how it was possible so many people and so much land existed all his life without his knowledge. But here it was, and so was he, so he banished this thought along with his fears and the disturbing hatred in the other men's eyes. He would save Zaya, and the pilot. He would get his men from this place. And in the greatest ship in the world, *his* ship, he would take them all home.

"When we reach the city it will be nightfall," said Pacal, "the moon and stars will be bright tonight, as bright as any night of the year, or any year for a hundred or more. That is why the tyrants call it holy. Once we're inside, stay with the mist tribes, and they will guide you to the temple grounds. Most of this army has their business in the city with oil and fire. Hurry to your friends, and escape, or you will surely burn."

Chang's heart raced at the look in the man's eye, but Captain Eka only nodded.

"Do they have no sentries? Have they kept none of their armies from celebration?"

The old shaman snorted. "Are we not whipped, spineless dogs? They have no fear of the tribes. But tonight, my friends, they will learn. Oh yes, they will learn."

Later, with the sun falling and the city's walls rising before them, Eka moved to Chang's side. He pointed at the temples, his eyes gaining the same look they'd had when *The Prince* left her first shore, or sailed into a storm—as if only in that moment of chaos and danger was the man truly alive.

"We'd best hurry," his usually monotone voice held a tinge of excitement, and he slipped his black mask over his face. "Whatever the shaman says, there will be guards on the wall who've seen the army and run to tell their masters. These people have no rams, no siege weapons. And you heard them at the meeting—the walls frighten them."

Chang blinked, and glanced at the high stone, no concept of how the men would even get inside.

Eka had removed a pouch from his hip, and now rubbed his fingers with white powder from inside before handing it to Chang. "If I were you, I'd take off that armor until we've dealt with this."

For a moment Chang stared, not understanding. He had marched for a day and a half, and he was tired and hot. Before he asked why he should do that or anything he began to understand, and the captain's frozen face cracked with a smile.

"We are sailors, not monkeys," Chang hissed.

The captain inspected the walls, then started walking. "Today you are both, Master Chief. The tribesmen are not capable. None of their people have ever climbed such a thing. Straighten your spine, Chang, few are as able climbers as sailors, and the stone is pitted and old. I assure you, I have climbed much worse."

* * *

Chang swore a sacred oath not to look down. He heard Basko grunt and almost slip but he had no attention to give his men, his every trembling effort focused on handholds barely observable in the moonlight. Then he was at the top, and the shadow who called himself a captain was pulling the crew to the lip of the wall. Chang mumbled a thanks as he breathed away the fear, then flinched as he noticed two corpses lay near his feet.

"There are more coming," Eka whispered, gesturing down the wall. "I think there's a barracks just North of us. We must hurry."

The night split with a man's dying scream, and the sailors all turned as more of the city's defenders rushed from the main street with spears and bows, loosing missiles at the climbers as they reached the top. "Quickly," Eka growled, turning for the gate.

Chang grit his teeth and clutched his knife, desperately wishing for the first time since he entered the jungle he wore the pilot's armor. His men behind him, he followed along the thin rampart, lifting a rock from one of the many piles clearly left out for a defence of the walls that hadn't happened. But whether he was caught and killed *during* his climb, or inside the damn city, made little difference to Chang.

"There's the winches." Eka pointed at the interior of the gate, which were guarded by at least five men huddled against it and scanning the dark. "No time to wait for the tribesmen. Charge them."

Without waiting to hear what his men thought of that,

the captain leapt the last few steps from the wall and sprinted with his head down and knives readied like claws.

"To hell with all kingsmen," Chang spit and followed, making sure Basko was at his side. They descended the ramparts with nothing but knives and a few rocks, breaking into a sprint behind Eka. The gate guard saw them coming and shouted a warning, some looking down the street for relief that hadn't yet come. Then Eka was on them, a wolf in a chicken coop. A spear sailed past him and sprays of blood followed his knives.

Chang roared and faked a lunge at another man, then sidestepped the spear thrust and seized the shaft before leaning in to stab the warrior's throat. The Steerman bounced a rock off the closest guard's cheek, and Basko grappled him to the ground. An Oarsman seized another, and the crew swarmed them stabbing. For the first time since they'd landed, at least things felt a little familiar.

"Grab that winch." Eka pointed at a huge, spoked wheel wrapped with rope. There were four to move the gate, catches wrapped in layers of rope and tied in knots. The crew of *The Prince* could hear shouting now from down the road and towards the Northern barracks —men gathering in angry confusion as they rushed towards the gates. They had little time. But then, they didn't need much.

With the almost inhuman competence of a lifetime at sea, the sailors pulled apart the knots and loops and freed the winches in moments, heaving in unison without pause as the heavy gate groaned.

Guards were coming now in half-formed clusters, a few dozen and then a hundred racing towards the wall. They were too late.

Tribesmen charged through the crack of the opening gate, loosing arrows and javelins and racing North and

South along the wall. The city guard tried to stop them, to charge the gate and make their way to Eka and the crew. But the invaders didn't stop coming. The tribesmen poured through screaming with wild hate, throwing themselves without caution at their enemy and overwhelming the insufficient guard. The crack of the gate became an open wound, then the door slammed into the stone as they fully opened. The 'siege' of Copanoch was over in minutes. The sacking was about to begin.

* * *

Zaya walked with the other slaves to the ceremony of stars. She heard drums, dancing and singing, with high pitched screams ranging from horror to ecstasy. As she came closer to the temple grounds, the sound pulsed from windows and doors, lights flashing in the distance from many fires. Her feet seemed to fight leaving the palace, and she had the strongest urge to flee.

"This way, mistress," Temolata said with a face that implied this was obvious, not understanding Zaya's hesitation.

Still, Zaya resisted. Already she could smell the sweat and perfume, incense and cooking meat. But none of it hid the scent of blood.

Soon the others swept her along in a flowing procession of bodies. She walked out into the cooler night air, looking up to the night sky only to realize the stars were all but shrouded in smoke. People stood everywhere. Wooden stands had been built all around the temple grounds, row upon row of rising seats leading to the pyramids, a patterned criss-crossing of wood and stone.

The large column of palace servants moved out into the celebrations, clustering together as if for protection. The elite of Copanoch drank a dozen kinds of alcohol and smoked a heady weed that blurred Zaya's vision even from a distance. Some already lay all but comatose, others leaping in frantic mania, yet others making love in the open for all to see. Zaya found she couldn't tear her eyes away from these, her mouth hanging in the baffled shock of cultural anathema.

"They sacrifice their shame, their privacy," said Temolata, on seeing Zaya's expression. "It is a holy thing, mistress."

They walked on, every step still growing Zaya's feeling of anxiousness. Somewhere ahead, Yacat would be with his family, speaking for the last time with his son. The shaman had almost mocked him for his part in this, for his helplessness, which seemed to Zaya both cruel and unfair, for what could the man do? And for all his talk, the shaman was now also somewhere in the temples ahead, trapped in a cage, perhaps to die with the hundreds or maybe even thousands of other sacrifices. Zaya wasn't sure which fact brought her more sadness.

Yet the song of Haki the Brave played in her mind—the words of a great hero, sung so many times by her father, echoed in her mind.

"A man fails in two ways," went the legend's words to his men as their ending loomed. "He quits, or he dies. Are you dead?"

Zaya knew a thing wasn't over until the very end—that life might change in a moment's work, that the tales that lasted generations could come from a single act of courage and fortune. Zaya was not resigned to any fate but the one she had yet to choose; Yacat was a good man, a prince and warrior, and no matter how things seemed, the shaman was still the greatest hero of ash.

As they came closer to the platform square of a temple landing, the people were covered in more paint than cloth. The same wooden stands had been raised all around it, in the center a huge bonfire and tables surrounded by priests and royals. It was all arranged to be seen from many directions, with gaps in the stands for crowds to see past to the center. Beneath the stands, their wooden bars flickering in the firelight, endless cages filled with slaves.

"Our place is there, mistress," Temolata pointed to a spot in the stands. "All have their places assigned."

In the center of the temple grounds, beside the fire and the priests, there was also an altar, and a cauldron. Already old men stood with their arms wide, speaking to the crowd. All the faces Zaya could see flickered strangely with fire and moonlight, and she realized half their faces were painted dark with color. She climbed up to her seat feeling suffocated with sweaty, sweltering life. The impending misery of her future returned, drowning the words of heroic tales as quickly as the drums and shouts silenced the music almost always in her mind. She found she couldn't sit still, and scanned the cages for the shaman, unable to see much in the gloom beyond the fire. When a man was brought to the cauldron and dumped in to boil alive, and the other servants were distracted, Zaya went down to the cages. She walked along peering in at the mix of men and women, from elders to children, until she found the gap of bodies—the wide berth given to the pale skinned giant sitting alone on a bench, staring into the night.

"Shaman!" The Godtongue blinked from his corner but did not respond, or even seem to see her. "We must try to escape," she hissed. "You can break the bars, and we can run. It seems the whole city is drunk with revelry, now is the time."

The golden pupils flicked towards her, as if surprised

to be disturbed. "Some things cannot be escaped, young skald. I am sorry, but I will watch."

Zaya curled her hands around the bars, knowing she could pry them with a good spear, and that the shaman could surely break them with his bare hands. The man seemed so resigned, yet watching in judgment—so calm, yet his jaw clenched as if every moment were a struggle. She wanted to scream, to run away, to fight, anything but sit and wait for whatever would happen to happen.

"We cannot stay here. *Now* is the time to act. I won't watch this madness!"

Ruka's intense gaze broke for a moment as he smiled. "A single choice of courage can change everything, Zaya, daughter of Juchi. But today is not your day."

Zaya realized the crowd was cheering, the priests and royals had their arms and voices raised. At last Yacat emerged from the temple in his ritual clothes, painted, and armed, his son at his side.

Chapter 28

Yacat walked through the holy square as if in a dream. As a boy he had played ballcourt here with his brothers, running up and down the temple stairs if they kicked it off the edge. There had not been a festival of stars in fifteen years, and his memory of it was through a child's eyes, filled with sights and sounds made even blurrier by the alcohol he'd been allowed to drink. A feeling of utter change now consumed him—the cages and slaves that had in his youth been a small sideshow were now the main event.

Unlike most of his family, Yacat was stone sober, hot and sweating, and the people around him seemed mad and monstrous. He saw his wife in the stands with the other women swaying to the music, lost to the poloat plant. He didn't blame her for this, but still he sensed the beginnings of hatred, and looked away.

For his son he knew he must be strong. He put a hand on the boy's shoulder and lead him forward, allowing no concern on his face. The boy was breathing hard but walked on bravely, and Yacat was proud of him, which only made the agony worse. When they reached the square he met the eyes of his brothers one by one, then Uncle Anatzi, and finally his father. The great king of Copanoch stood next to the altar, just as he said he would. Many vile things could be said of King Etzil Mar, but coward was not amongst them.

The priests of Centnaz were chanting their nonsense. Yacat looked at the cages and the slaves, their hands trembling on wooden bars, eyes wide in terror. He blinked, and wiped water from his smoke-filled eyes, because he thought he saw the golden light of Ruka's stare deep in one of the cages, and on inspection realized it was so.

With a snort, he understood. The king believed the strange man was an evil spirit and wanted him gone, and while killing an evil spirit on the day of the gods didn't seem wise, Yacat's father had always been more practical than pious. Yacat considered what he might do, if it mattered. If *anything* mattered. The strange eyes seemed to be watching him in the chaos, passive, calm, still in judgment.

"The time has come." The king was gesturing to the circle of blue and green paint already stained with blood. Nearby listeners shrieked and cheered, the sacrifice of a prince's son unheard of. No one in Copanoch had ever done it, and perhaps no one in the whole of the valley. As if the ramifications had not yet dawned on them, the lesser nobility cheered at the spilling of royal blood, ecstatic and proud of their king, and no doubt Yacat, for their great display of piety.

Yacat felt the urge to vomit. He looked at the corpses already piled behind the altar, wondering how any sane man could destroy the lives of others so casually and call it righteous, whatever their sins. Why the gods would let these priests push such lies without punishment he had no idea, yet they did. The men of the Devourer were the heralds of Copanoch's doom. Long ago they had planted their seed of evil into the people, their dark ambitions ignored, their contradictions and awful deeds masked behind a cloak of fine sentiment. Now the city would reap its rotten harvest.

The noise of the revelers made speaking difficult. Yacat looked to Anatzi, begging for him to see the horror, to understand, to help, knowing he wouldn't. He knew any impassioned speech he made now would change nothing, accomplish nothing—that it was too late when faced with a mob to appeal to their reason.

There must be blood. He called over the din. "Take me, my king. I, Yacat, general and prince of Mar, called Mahala, I offer my life freely. Let it appease your god. Not the boy."

Enough people heard. A grin spread across the cheeks of High Priest Nahua, even as the others sneered and Uncle Anatzi's face reddened. Only Etzil did not flinch, or balk. Only the king.

"Come to the altar, Zolya," he said as if he hadn't heard. Yacat's blood pounded in his veins, pulsing like lightning in his vision. The crowd began to blur. Sound became far away, and again Yacat looked to the cages, to Ruka's golden eyes burn like tower fires guiding him home. Yacat swayed, and held the boy's shoulders.

"I'm ready, Father," said Zolya, pushing forward against his hands. Still Yacat did not release him. He felt the weight of the sword on his belt, allowed even here in this holy place because of his rank and past glories. The priests saw his hesitation. High Priest Nahua stepped forward, cruel triumph in his eyes, spittle on his lips.

"Wisdom requires sacrifice, my lords." He called, as if educating a sinful child. "Do not let your faith waver in the decisive moment."

Yacat shivered, warmth spreading down his spine. That such darkness could hide behind empty words galled him, and struck him with fire. That it should be ignored or accepted as wisdom by otherwise brave men broke his heart. Strange, that a lecture by fools should be the thing that finally saved him.

"There we agree," he shouted, feeling a strange confidence build. "And if you and my father were to cut off your own flesh, I would serve you faithfully. But to sacrifice others for your own gain is not holy, *priest*, it is cowardice." He looked to the king. "This is *wrong*, father, and always has been. I will not let you kill my son."

Etzil's calm vanished, anger coiling like smoke around his face. "I am *king*! You are all mine to sacrifice, here or in battle, *in any way I wish*!"

"Please, father." Zolya tugged at Yacat's hands. "Let me go! It's my duty. I am *honored*."

Still Yacat held the boy fast. "You are king," he said, recognizing he ignored the boy as his father ignored him. "He is my son, and the bond of fathers and mothers to their children existed long before kings. I will not break an ancient vow for your *politics*." He looked to his child. "One day you will be a man, my son, free then to give your flesh to any cause you wish. Until then, you will obey me. Step back."

The boy looked from Yacat to his grandfather, pale and trembling as he did as commanded. The king's honor guard sensed conflict now and moved a step closer to their king—Uncle Anatzi amongst them.

"Bring him, Yacat." The king's voice had lost all trace of a man arguing with his kin. "The time for talk is over. If you are too weak, stand aside."

Yacat shook his head, and did not move. The king turned his face away, and Uncle Anatzi stepped forward, sweat dripping down his temples.

"Little Yack, please…" he said softly, crossing the square until he was but a few steps away.

Yacat met his eyes and loved him no less now then he had as a child. "I'm sorry, Uncle. But reach for my son, and I'll cut your arm off."

The moment froze at the threat of violence, and three more of the king's guard came forward. Anatzi's eyes flickered upwards, ever so slightly, and Yacat drew his sword as he spun. In an arc of violence practiced ten thousand times, he spun the flint-edged blade at a soldier reaching from the stands, and cut through half his neck. Unable to scream, the man fell face first and curled grotesquely on the stone.

Onlookers cried out in confusion now. A mixture of drunk and sober guards stepped from the stands or the prison or stairways as the king stared, his men surrounding Yacat on three sides.

"Nephew…" The pain and fear was obvious now on Anatzi's face.

Yacat felt the blood dripping down his sword. "I'm sorry, Uncle. But good man or bad, it matters only what you do. Stand aside."

The priests were spitting in rage, assuring the Devourer's wrath and shouting obscenities. The king's face was puffed with rage, his eyes deadly.

"Throw yourself at my feet and beg for your life!" he roared. "*Do it now.*"

Yacat's breathing had calmed, the decision made. He would fight and die now, and be at peace. It would not save his son, but he would go to whatever gods existed with a lighter spirit. He had failed in the past, but in the end, they would know he had risen, and honored them.

"When I am gone, Father," he met the man's eyes. "Ask if these priests bring your people goodness, or evilness. Ask what has become of your city, and your house. Ask what killed your most loyal son, who serves you even now. That is all I wish."

Etzil's jaw trembled until at last he looked away. "Kill him," he said, voice low and torn with fury. "Kill him and take the boy."

Warriors who had known Yacat for years stepped forward, but did not charge. The strangeness of such a moment was too much for them to act quickly, and they looked to Anatzi and each other, unwilling to be the first to strike.

Anatzi came first. Yacat had sparred with him a thousand times as a child, grown under his tutelage as a warrior even after his first battles. But that was long ago. The big man came with sweating hands, his grip too loose and unpracticed. Yacat did not meet it. He swerved with all the speed and strength earned in a decade of war, twisting past the razor edge of his uncle's sword. In a moment's work it was over. Anatzi stumbled back, his chest opened from waist to shoulder, eyes wide as he stared.

Another guard forced Yacat back with a thrust of his spear, yet another from the stairs swung a club for Yacat's head in a downward arc with great speed. Yacat barely ducked in time, the air whipping past his face. He heard his son cry out but he could not look away.

There was only battle now. All thoughts of regret, past or future fell away. Guards attacked from Yacat's other flank but he was ready now, and there would be no mercy. Twisting his wrist, Yacat swung his sword upwards and nearly cut the closest man's arm at the elbow. Blood sprayed as the warrior cried out, and Yacat pointed at the closest temple wall. "Keep your back to the stone." He commanded his son, pointing at the rise beneath the stairs, then turned back to face his attackers.

More guards were ascending the steps, yet more using the paths from the stands. Half the army was likely in the temple grounds. The king looked on, his eyes first on his brother lying on the stone, then again locked on his son.

Yacat almost laughed. The great and powerful lord of Copanoch, furious, and helpless, just as he was against the madness of his priests. Though Yacat knew he was going to die, he felt for the first time in many years and perhaps all his life, truly free. All his life he had held his tongue. All his life he had warped his life to accept a thing he found monstrous, losing bits and pieces of himself along the way. But not anymore. That truth made him more powerful than a king, or the priests, or the crowd. His soul had called, and he had answered. There was no greater victory.

Yacat touched the four feathers of his armband, earned over a lifetime of blood. There was so much pride and shame and regret in the simple touch, all the deeds that had made him who he was. He knew then it was an illusion, meaningless save for the strength it gave him now. There was only one truth, one reality that required no words or gods or advocates—Yacat's son stood behind him, and those who would harm him ahead. Yacat gripped his sword, and charged.

* * *

Zaya watched the prince's exchange as long as she could stand, then gripped the prison bars.

"Shaman!" she cried over the noise of the crowd, and the musicians, and the men arguing in the square. The great hero sat still and calm, staring out at the royal family. Zaya didn't spend the time to look to see if she was noticed by the other slaves and servants. "They are distracted, shaman, and the night is dark enough. Now is the time. Let's *leave*."

"And where would we go," the shaman almost whispered.

"Anywhere, Godtongue! The jungle. The sea."

"We came from the sea, and I have told you to call me Ruka." Here the shaman shifted and clenched one hand to a fist. "I sought paradise once. Now I know life is the same wherever it is found. The strong rule, the weak obey. There is no escaping it."

"Please." Zaya felt a kind of panic she couldn't explain. She felt as if time itself was hunting her, that she had mere moments to avoid disaster. She searched for the bar that held the cage doors, but felt her hope drain as she realized there was a thick bronze lock. She turned as a man cried out in terror, and Zaya saw Yacat had severed a priest's arm in the square. Many in the crowd gasped or yelled in anger, and the king's men moved from every direction towards the prince. "Please, Ruka," she said, her eyes impossible to close as emotions warred in her heart. "I don't want to see him die."

At last the shaman stood. "Death comes to all things. But I will help your lover, for all courage must be rewarded." The man's huge hands wrapped around the bars, and he closed his eyes, breaths quickening as he spoke with strained calm. "Some things cannot be escaped, Zaya, only faced. Let us both learn from the prince's example."

Zaya felt a hum on the air as if before a storm. She wanted a knife, or a spear, to be out of her long, foolish dress and wrapped in leather and mail rings. She ripped at the seams to free her thighs and shoulders. "You are still one man, shaman. You cannot save him from so many guards."

Ruka smiled. "You wish to know the truth of legends, skald, then here it is: to the great heroes of your book, if the cause is righteous, the odds make no difference." He swallowed, then all but whispered, his voice husky. "If they can stop me, they deserve to. Come, brother. You are needed."

The bars shook in the shaman's hands. His lips curled in a snarl, revealing his angled, jagged teeth. When he opened his eyes, it was as if he'd forgotten where he was. He squinted away from the square's firelight, golden eyes drifting over Zaya as if he didn't know her. The exhaustion that had haunted him for weeks seemed to vanish, his shoulders straightening as he breathed deep, long breaths.

"Imprisoned again, brother, and everywhere the scent of blood and terror. How familiar." The smile vanished just as fast, the eyes dulling as even the voice changed.

"We save the warrior, and the boy." Ruka pointed, and clenched his jaw. "The others in that square are yours. I will need your strength."

The sounds of fighting had increased, and Zaya tore her eyes away to look at Yacat sparring with a dozen warriors. He raced across the ground hacking at any who followed, using the cluttered square and confusion to keep them from surrounding him, his son forgotten against the temple.

Ruka laughed, and though the sound was rare enough, it was not even his. The tone was harsh and cruel. "My dreams are dark and crowded, and I missed your weakness, brother. Your *rules*."

"Just swear it," said the other shaman's face, then transformed and smiled again.

"As you wish. Let the sons of Beyla unite again. It would make our mother so proud."

With that he stepped away from the bars, until only his golden eyes shone in the gloom of the cage. He spoke again with his own voice. "Run, Zaya. Escape as you wished in the chaos. They won't notice you soon."

"I won't leave you," she answered, also stepping away from the bars. "My fate is bound to yours."

The eyes crinkled as the cruel laugh again sounded in the dark. "There, brother, is a *proper* servant."

Sparks flared in the gloom as if a torch had struck. Embers sizzled and lit the shaman's body from nothing as the air shimmered, and Zaya blinked from the sudden light. Ruka stood impossibly garbed in iron armor from shoulders to shins. He held out his hands, and a pole the length of a man formed in his grip, ending in a razor sharp spear.

"I never wanted servants," he said, his voice returned. "I wished only for heroes to stand at my side." He held out the weapon. "You may need this, skald, before the end. I do not know what will happen." He blinked over and over, his eyes searching the night. "It's too strong…and there's no room…I don't know if I can control it much longer…" he clenched his jaw, and met Zaya's eyes. "Perhaps it is not just Yacat's day of judgment after all. Remember the courage of your people, daughter of ash. I will leave my neck unguarded."

Zaya took the weapon with trembling hands, then Ruka seized the wooden bars and roared, ripping them apart with nothing but his mailed fists. The slaves sprawled over each other to get away, and the shaman stepped from the cage with the sharp thud of iron on stone.

"Run and hide, little things!" he yelled to the square. "The night is black, and the sons of darkness come."

Chapter 29

Yacat fought for the first time in years without a moment of conflict. As a young warrior he had killed with idealism but little skill; as he'd gotten older, he had became a craftsman of death, but lost desire. Not today.

The sword felt a piece of his arm, his muscles fired with righteous purpose, all fear of death or error or misdeed some distant memory. In this moment, any man who came against him was the fallen servant of a lost god, and deserved no pity, mercy, or hesitation. Yacat gave them none.

Uncle Anatzi still lay dying at his feet, his look of surprise total. Yacat hoped to see him in the afterlife. He kicked a piece of the bonfire to scatter sparks and ash, then spun and charged the cowards trembling at the stairs. They wavered and all but closed their eyes as they thrust trembling spears towards their prince. Yacat deftly avoided the first shaft and hacked off the man's hand, then gouged the face of another on the upswing. He paced across the narrow stone kicking back the closest man, slashing any who dared climb until they'd fallen back from the platform.

More were coming from the stands. Yacat ran across and cut off a man's foot, then intercepted the closest stairway, slashing around swords and spears without touching anything but flesh. When these fell back he turned towards the priests, and his father's guard.

His gaze met High Priest Nahua's, the malicious fool backing away with wide, fearful eyes.

"Kill him! Or your crops, your children, your city—*Centnaz will destroy you all!*"

Yacat spit blood and charged. The guardsmen thrust their spears in his face and he was forced to turn, looking for any path through as he preserved his sword's edge. From the corner of his eye he saw fire and fighting towards the slave pens, but he had no time or attention to spare. There was only one left thing to him now, one way to serve his city before his doom—to kill Nahua, and as many of his lying minions as possible before they stopped him.

"Mahala, stop! *Please!*" The closest royal bodyguard's face twisted in horror, but Yacat ignored him. He ducked past the flimsy stab that followed, kicked another warrior aside, and leapt through to the inner circle. The priests tried to escape, some stumbling violently into guards or one another. Yacat hacked the closest down with two vicious swipes.

He heard a roar from behind him, a deep voice speaking in a language he didn't understand. He twisted and ducked a sword slashed for his throat, cutting the guardsman's calf as he fell away.

"Kill him!" Nahua's eyes were bulged and wild, one hand on the arm of a warrior, the other clutching a star-charm of his evil god as if it were a shield. A rank of men closed ahead of him and Yacat growled in frustration. He was almost surrounded.

A spear grazed his cheek and again he spun low and cut at unarmored legs, just trying to slow them down and create a gap. His sword deflected off the shaft of a spear, and he heard the crack of his flint edge snap.

The elite of House Mar had at last gathered their wits and moved with order, pinning him with spears and bodies in a narrowing circle. For a long moment Yacat breathed and recognized he was trapped and finished. He held his half-broken sword and met the eyes of resolved men, knowing it would be his final attack.

The strange roar got louder, and closer. Along with

most of his foes, Yacat looked out from the combat to see a metal giant charge. From the slave pens, this grey-blue monster crushed and knocked four men aside with a shield the size of a palace door. He smashed his way into the circle snapping guardsmen like dry reed until he stood inside facing Yacat. Golden eyes shone from the helmet.

Ruka's gaze moved up and down, as if inspecting Yacat for the first time, unimpressed by what they found. "You've broken your pathetic weapon," he growled, dropping a huge, metal mace to the stone before extending his hand. Sparks forced Yacat to squint as fire erupted from the air, and a long, thin blade seemed to grow from the giant's hand. "Here. This one will outlast you."

The giant tossed the blade as if it were nothing, and Yacat caught the handle. As the men around him kept their distance despite the shouting and chaos, he inspected the solid metal blade, astounded at the feel. As he did he realized the giant had again lifted his mace and turned to face the warriors, standing at Yacat's side.

"The priests," Yacat managed. "They're the ones who matter. Kill the priests."

Ruka snorted, seeming to shiver as he looked out at the square. "Priests. Soldiers. Kings. All are mine," he hissed. "Do you hear, little things? You are all *mine*."

By the voice alone Yacat at last knew for certain the pale giant was truly an evil spirit made flesh. But like the ancient spirits of the dead, or the fallen gods who ate souls, such spirits were only ever summoned by the deeds of man. They were a kind of dark justice, spawned by dark deed into the world. And Yacat knew in his heart they all deserved that judgment.

The battle resumed as quickly as it had begun. Ruka waded into a line of spears, breaking men with his impossible weapon and armor. Yacat swung his new blade with wild abandon, cutting spear shafts and sometimes hands without slowing his attack, taking another grazing wound to his arm from overextending. He cut through a man's spear and then his arm in the same blow, then stumbled forward in surprise. As he did the guardsmen pounced, and a sword cut hard and true towards his neck.

A thrown spear caught the guard in the chest, knocking him back too far to land the swing. When Yacat rose he glanced back to find Zaya in a ripped dress, a collection of stolen weapons draped on her back and hips. He wondered, then, was she an evil spirit too? Or perhaps a holy one?

He truly hoped it was the latter, but it made no difference now. With his back guarded by the foreigners or spirits, and his target ahead, Yacat breathed to clear his mind. He gave thanks to his ancestors for all the years of blood and war, sparing him and preparing him for this final moment of reckoning. For his city, his family, and for the olds ways that once guided a lost people, he would give these few high priests their justice.

* * *

Zaya's skin itched with sweaty paint and eyes as she crossed the square. As she watched the shaman and the prince battle alone against a growing army of guards, she knew it was a story in the book of legends. A piece of her wished only to stand close enough to watch, to record, to one day sing the song of their deaths. It was what her father would have done. But though she loved him, emulated him, and had the same song that moved through his blood, she knew then she was more than a skald.

Her stolen spear had sailed true, another man dead because of her. She followed in the shaman's wild wake and stepped into the circle until she stood at Yacat's side. As he met her eyes, she felt and shared his affection, but this wasn't why she'd come. He was her lover, and a good, strong man, who would be a worthy mate and father. But she had come because he stood against an evil deed—because he was a hero of the book, and whatever she was, whatever she might feel or wish or what the gods might demand, she knew her place was there beside him.

Then the guards were moving in, and Zaya waved the shaman's spear and cried out as she covered Yacat's flank. "Stay near Ruka!" she shouted, falling back to the growing pile of wounded and dead near the Godtongue. With every blow of his terrifying club, Ruka laughed or kicked the dying men as if in mockery, ignoring their blows against him, waving off spear thrusts as if swatting at flies. When he saw Zaya had entered the fray, he smiled and stepped towards her, then shook his head.

"Take this, and stay alive." He barked in a hoarse voice, handing her his shield. Then he moved rather purposefully away and turned back on the foreign warriors, another iron rod forming from fire in his spare hand, every blow felling some other poor, outmatched man.

The stands were emptying now. Copanoch elite were scattering in every direction as more and more warriors raced up the temple steps, or spilled from the palace. Zaya tried to protect Yacat's flank with the heavy shield, using it once or twice to bash away a man who came too close. Spear thrusts and wooden blades bounced uselessly against it, usually cracking in the attempt. Behind the incredible protection of it, Zaya had a moment to look at the dead and dying around her.

Some men crawled away, or simply lay and moaned in their agony. But even in the gloom of night and with the smoke from the bonfires, she knew something was wrong. A dark fog seemed to be growing from the Godtongue's corpses. Some were almost swallowed by it, and as she stared Zaya could have sworn she saw some of the lifeless bodies *move*.

"Shaman!" she called. "What's happening? Are you alright?"

Almost as in answer, the mighty runeshaman lifted his helmet, seized a man with a mailed fist, and picked him off the ground as if he weighed nothing. He brought him close as if he meant to whisper in the man's ear, then instead opened his jaw of jagged teeth, bit the man's cheek, and chewed.

A nearby warrior stabbed the shaman uselessly, spear snapping off against his armor. Ruka threw away his victim and laughed, crushing the would-be savior with another blow of his mace. He extended his arms, and Zaya could swear she saw dark wings forming from his back, obscured in the night and smoke.

"Do you feel it, brother?" he shouted in the Ascomi tongue. A wind blew hard through the square, scattering flames and throwing refuse from every side. Zaya squinted and tried to hold her shield against the gale but it seemed to come from all directions. Light bent and flickered towards the center of the square, towards Ruka, angled and low like dawn creeping over a new horizon. "Together," boomed the shaman's voice, not yelled yet echoing over the stone. "*We* will master life and death, light and shadow. Not the princes of paradise, not some ignorant enlightened, or the fools here at the end of the world. It is as it always has been. It is our destiny."

As he spoke, the corpses at his feet twitched and shook, inky darkness rising from their skin with red eyes and ebony claws. Ruka was laughing as the men before him scattered, his own golden eyes watching the shadows rise.

"Pitiful nothings. Come to me. Give purpose to your useless lives."

He reached out for the first with his hand, and Zaya sprung. She crossed the frozen scene of carnage, jamming her spear into the rising shadow. It hissed and withdrew, black maw opened to swallow the dark as it fell away.

The shaman turned on her with eyes wide, mailed fist extended to grasp her throat. "You dare, *insect*? Pitiful wretch. You are meat and weak bone and I will eat your limbs before you die."

His face contorted, and the reaching hand instead went to his face as he screamed, falling to a knee. He blinked and Zaya saw the eyes of the man she had known.

"Fight him, Ruka!" she called into the storm. "This is not who you are!"

Again the face twisted, the lips curling into a sneer. "Oh but it is, daughter of lies. My brother is the mask."

"I'm not speaking to you, creature." Zaya snarled. "I speak to Ruka, son of Beyla. What would your mother say to you now?"

The man's eyes widened and misted, the armored giant stilled as he stared at Zaya. All around him shadows had risen and circled like wolves, snarling and grasping at nearby guards, but seemingly unable to move too far.

"Would she see a legend of ash?" Zaya's heart pounded in her chest as the shaman stared. "Would she see the man who took her people across the sea? The man who brought an empire to its knees? You're not this monster, Ruka. You're a hero of the book."

Ruka's lips uncurled, his expression softening until wetness touched his eyes. "One day you may see," he gasped, "to become the second, you must be the first." He dropped his weapon and growled in agony, hands gripping his helmet as he screamed. The dark shadowy wings sprouted and firmed as they had on the ship, a black torso following, attached with bat-like tissue misted in shadow. A red eyed demon from hell grew from the shaman's back, attached with thin gold chain like some unholy umbilical cord, jangling with the creature's heavy step. It roared, and the shadow creatures charged from the square, leaping at men, women and children with equal fervor, their dark claws spraying blood.

The shaman collapsed, his huge shadow swaying as if dazed on its feet. Zaya had no idea what to do.

"Are we too late?" Yacat came to Zaya's side drenched in blood. He stared out at the shadows as if horrified but unsurprised. "Is this the price of my people's failure?"

The shaman's eyes were closed, but he had turned his face up, exposing his throat. Zaya felt the weight of the spear in her hands, but knew the gods would not approve. It wasn't for her to kill such a man, no matter what he said, not like this.

"We fail in only two ways." Zaya quoted the words, clutching her divine weapon. "We quit, or we die. Are you dead, Yacat, son of Mar?"

The prince's handsome face drew back.

"Stop thinking. Do what needs doing. Go and stop them."

Yacat looked to Zaya, his expression firming beneath the blood, and he was the man she much admired again. Like so many of the brave, he became who he truly was only with the closeness of deed, and danger.

They attacked the shadows together.

Chapter 30

Chang and his crew killed their way to the temple steps. Alongside their tribal allies, they had fought across Copanoch against small packs of confused, drunken soldiers, or men armed with kitchen knives. It seemed the shaman Pacal had been right—the valleymen had not feared attack, nor been prepared in any way. They had believed in their own superiority, obsessed with their own idols, confident in the walls they'd all but forgotten. Now all their lives and houses burned.

"How can we know the pilot's up there?" Chang panted and leaned on the temple steps. He glanced around for the captain, and found him dispatching a soldier in near silence nearby. Before the captain could answer, a man screamed from above, his body flung far from the temple steps to land badly on the cobblestone street.

Chang and the others stared at the broken man, then up at the square, which was very far for the man even to have run and jumped.

"Alright boys," Chang wiped sweat from his brow with a mailed sleeve. "We get ours, and we go. No looting or lollygagging. Ka?"

"Ka chief," Basko looked up the long flight of steep, railless stairs and swallowed. The Steerman moved up behind them with weapons drawn, his courage holding for now. Only Old Mata hadn't yet been wounded, everyone else oozing blood from hands, faces, or scalps. The pilot's armor had saved them all a dozen times from arrows and spears, but that didn't mean the attempts didn't hurt.

They ascended together. The temples were joined,

staircases linked in seamless joints of stone that allowed the enemy to race up every side. Already Chang could see forms in the dark moving up towards the square above. Screams and the sounds of fighting echoed along the sloped walls amidst the revelry, half the city still celebrating as the other half burned.

Arrows, javelins and stones hissed and clattered past or over them, hurled from both above and below, impossible to tell whether from friend or foe. Chang and his men held up their small shields and advanced with heads down, little else to do but move and pray. Their whole world became gasping breaths at the exertion, no room left for fear after a mad dash through the city, watching the once happy, fun-loving tribesmen become mad, bloody wolves trapped in a coop.

They reached the top and killed four men to step uncontested onto the square. Warriors fought in its center in a chaotic melee, impossible to tell apart save for the familiar, iron giant at its core. Civilians filled a kind of coliseum, some scrambling madly to escape, others oblivious, others cheering on the violence. Chang blinked and gripped his sword in anxious fear when he saw Zaya fighting at the pilot's side, seemingly two against an army of warriors. Then he saw the shadows.

"Dear spirits." The Steerman clutched his luck charm. "Is it like the ship, chief? Is it the pilot's doing?"

Chang glanced at Eka, whose masked face of course revealed nothing. "What do we do, Captain?" he yelled over the din.

The island assassin's knife tapped against his thigh —the only sign he felt a hint of the concern now surging through his men. He shrugged, and wiped the blade. "Protect our crew. We get them back."

Chang ground his teeth without noticing, his eyes sweeping the scene of death and madness without much comprehension. Still, his survival instinct had never failed him, and even now it warned there was only one place to stand in safety: the correct side of the barbarian warlord.

He rolled his neck and called in a courageous tone he did not feel. "Circle our crew, brothers," he shouted. "Kill any man, beast…or *spirit* that gets in your way."

His bowels trembled, his bladder so tight it almost leaked down his leg. A death on land would cost him his soul. Haumia, Goddess of the earth, would know Chang had betrayed her brother, the lord of the sea, and she would devour him without pity.

But there was nothing else for it now. The only thing 'Lucky' Chang could do now was step further into the square, and pray his men and namesake held.

* * *

Black, acidic blood splashed again over Zaya's shield as she pierced another shadow. Yet another leapt at her side, and she stumbled and nearly fell before Yacat took off its head.

The king's warriors, moments ago the biggest threat, fought desperately for their lives. Most hacked at the creatures in twos or threes, trying to pull them off their fallen comrades. Their weapons, it seemed, did almost nothing. Only the shaman's iron killed them with any speed.

Ruka had risen again, eyes open, growling and locked in some private war Zaya feared as much as the walking shadows. Any warrior of Copanoch that stepped too close to him was mobbed and ripped apart by darkness.

The huge, winged creature that sprouted from the shaman's back woke with him. Already it had grown since its appearance on *The Prince,* and it looked out at the temple square with malevolent eyes, burning like coal in a craftsman's forge. It raised a clawed hand, and purple flame erupted, forming a blade of darkness deeper than obsidian. A single word whispered in a long rasp in Zaya's ears, and she suspected in the ears of everyone else in the square, in a language Zaya did not speak, yet somehow understood.

"Diiiie."

The chaos, for a moment, stilled, then erupted. The shadows no longer stayed near the shaman, but left the square and raced into the stands, charging at guards and citizens alike. In moments they had killed men, women and children in scores with equal abandon, their claws and fangs spraying blood. Zaya blinked as the night shimmered. Two shadows leapt straight for her.

The first screamed as Yacat's sword lopped off its arm, then silenced when he took its head. The second crashed against Zaya's shield, claws screeching against the iron as the creature nearly shoved her over. She kept her feet and hurled it back, stabbing the shaman's spear through its neck. It fell away streaming black ooze, which slopped off Zaya's shield and hit the ground steaming.

"Be careful of their blood," Zaya shouted again to anyone who would listen.

Yacat had already moved on, racing across the square with the shaman's sword flashing like lightning, spraying dark gore with every stroke. Neither man nor shadow could touch him, both limbs of flesh and darkness falling away in defeat at every turn. Despite the horror and chaos, Zaya's spirit soared to watch him, a song close to her throat.

The huge, winged demon watched him, too.

With a hissing moan it stepped from the shaman's

side, dark sword spraying mist as it walked towards the prince.

"Shaman!" Zaya called as she tried to slow it down, plunging her spear into its side with almost no affect. "Help us!"

Ruka groaned as his eyes forced open. He turned and leapt at the demon with a feral growl, seizing its arm and holding it fast. It spun and hacked down with the dark blade, but fire blazed from the shaman's hand as his own sword formed and blocked the blow. They stared at each other and held, red eyes meeting gold, jagged teeth bared against fang.

"You. Will. *Obey*."

Ruka's deep voice filled the square, though which of the shaman's personas had spoken Zaya had no idea. The creature roared and hacked again, the sound of the blades meeting echoing off the pyramids as man and demon dueled, bound by a chain that held them together.

"Macha!"

Zaya blinked at the familiar word yelled from the East in a smoky baritone. She turned to see Chang and a line of warriors armed like ashmen in iron mail, crossing the square in formation. She was so surprised she nearly died to a shadow's claws as it leapt for her throat. A dark, impossibly fast thing caught it mid-air, two blades flashing as they sunk into its chest and pulled it down stabbing. What could only be the dangerous captain of *The Prince* rose in his silks, the briefest nod to Zaya as he raced towards the winged shadow at a speed that seemed inhuman.

Hope flooded Zaya's heart for the first time since the night began. That the crew had come at all seemed impossible, yet was true. If they could only deal with the giant creature, perhaps they could survive...if the shaman could win his private war, perhaps the creatures would simply fade away, and they could escape in the madness…

Zaya blinked as the first shadow she'd stabbed rose from the stone. It choked and spit blood as the wound in its throat simply closed, others already rising. The first creature Yacat had cut down stood as a new arm and head emerged from its body, twisting as smoke from a doused fire until it formed bone and sinew. A sound like a landslide of screaming children rung in Zaya's mind— and she paled as she understood the sound of the winged demon's laughter.

"Impossible," she whispered, not knowing who to tell. "We have to run." A little louder. "We have to get out of here!"

But she knew even as she said it there was no escape—that violence like this had no end save death.

The shaman's blows sprayed inky chunks of demonic flesh. Sparks of red and purple flew from the clash of his blade against the demon's, both roaring in rage and desperation as they tried and failed to bring the other down. All around them the smaller shadows were gathering to assist their master, leaping against Chang and his men, but always repelled. Zaya stood beside them, the hope fading but not her courage. She sang the song of the hero Egil to block out the feral cries, holding the heavy shield to protect her comrades with an arm already numb from use.

In another scene of insanity she couldn't comprehend, a huge black cat the size of a horse leapt up from the stairs, sending men and shadows scrambling away from the pirates. Half-naked tribesmen followed, throwing spears and shooting arrows at warriors and unarmed civilians and shadows as if all were equally their enemy.

Zaya watched it all, but saw no victory. No matter

who won the shadows would butcher them all unless the shaman's madness could be stopped. She looked again to the golden chain binding Ruka to the creature —the small links as much mist as substance, the small gaps no wider than the head of a spear.

She was for a moment protected by the ring of pirates, and tossed down her heavy shield. "The chain!" she shouted, hoping Yacat or Eka or *someone* could hear in the chaos, and understand. "Break the damn chain!"

For a moment she wondered if they could even see it —or if the gods had brought her here, and given her this gift of sight, just for this moment. Either way, she knew she must act.

Her target would have to be close. She leapt over a fallen warrior, holding the shaft of her spear along her stronger arm. The chain bounced and pulled between the two combatants like a ship caught in a storm. If the demon turned on her, she knew it could cut her in half with a single blow. She may get only one chance, and in any case didn't know what would happen if she succeeded.

As she closed she breathed and let the world blur and vanish save for her target. Everything faded but the bouncing chain. She saw as a vague blur the captain leap from the corner of her eye, stabbing at the creature's back. It pulled away, and the chain pulled taut and straight for just a moment before the shaman followed. Her test had arrived, and this time not to save a child or her pride, but to save them all. Zaya pulled back her arm, and threw the runic spear.

A sound like jangling coins followed sparks as the weapon struck, bending the link as it passed. It halted as it lost momentum, lodged firmly in the chain. It didn't break.

Red eyes followed the throw, fixing on Zaya. The

winged shadow charged, ignoring the shaman's sword as it tore another chunk from its breast. Zaya fell back as the dark blade slashed where her neck had been. She scrambled backwards, scraping her hands harshly on the stone as the demon followed with sword raised in fury.

Chang and two of his biggest men seized her spear and spun it like a rudder's wheel, and the chain snapped in two.

A pulse of light and wind erupted from the break. The force of it threw men, weapons and refuse all over the square, many shouts of agony or panic following the blast. The demon stared off into the night as if it had heard some distant bell, its eyes rolling back as its mouth slackened. The dark blade vanished as it howled, or maybe wept. Then it staggered away to the sounds of snapping bone. It smashed straight through the wooden stands, its smaller brethren chasing after with animal calls and keening, vanishing quickly into the night and the far side of the temple.

"Macha," came the smoky baritone, followed by a wet cough. "Take to sea."

Zaya's ears rang, and she spit blood as she stood. She found Chang laying beside her, somehow thrown from his feet and knocked some distance away. The pirate chief lay on his back on the stone, face bloodied and burnt, one of his arms twisted. He met her eyes before his head sunk. "Sweet Macha, small favor. Take Chang's body…to sea."

Two other pirates lay shattered nearby. The half-naked tribesmen were still fighting with city guard at the further stairwells, the other few people still left in the square trying to escape. Everywhere she looked there was corpses.

"The ship," a panting Eka rose to one knee, pulling off his singed mask. "The city is burning. We have to get to the ship."

Zaya looked to the armored, maybe unconscious form of the giant shaman, the many wounded sailors, and as yet saw no sign of the prince. While she had no desire to stay in Copanoch for another moment, especially at the temple, even now she saw the fires spreading across the cityscape below. She had no idea how they were going to go anywhere, or even how they'd get down the stairs.

Chapter 31

Yacat found his father ripped open by the altar of Centnaz. His glazed eyes scanned the stars, and when Yacat knelt beside him and extended his hands, he did not take them. The king of House Mar died as he had lived—strong, and unrepentant.

"I stayed where you told me, father." Zolya stepped from the temple wall pale and trembling, his eyes locked on his grandfather's corpse.

"Good boy. Good lad." Yacat took his son in an arm and kissed his brow.

"Is…Centnaz angry, father?" The boy's eyes were slick with tears. "Is it because I didn't…that we didn't…"

"No, son. It is the opposite. It's nothing to do with you, and everything to do with the men who would kill a child. Do you understand?" The boy nodded, though Yacat had no doubt he did not. It didn't matter. Very little did now.

The shadows had butchered half the elite or more of Copanoch, yet the slave-spirit called Ruka had fought them. He had fought to *protect* Yacat, and to protect his son. Why?

Yacat could see no reason save that he had stood against Centnaz. Perhaps this strange man and spirit was a herald of the ancient gods, just as Nahua was a herald of doom. Yet Yacat could see the flames, and the tribesmen. He looked out at his people's city and saw rebellion and destruction of men by other men—the ending of civilization.

He took his son and started walking, though he had no idea where. Across the square he found Ruka, and Zaya, then a crowd of armored men. The demonic blast had ended the melee save for a few clashes at the edge of the temple. Zaya's eyes were wide and frantic, the familiar panic of a warrior broken on the battlefield. Yacat knelt at her side, and took her arms. "You're alright, Zaya. Look at me. You're alright."

She stared and matched his breathing, pupils shrinking as she calmed.

"We have ship, Yacat, but…our men are wounded. It's far, and dark, and the shaman…" she trailed off, and though Yacat had no answers he squeezed her arms. If he could reach the soldiers he was sure many would still be loyal to him, but he could do nothing in this chaos. First, they had to get out of the city.

"Mahala."

Yacat rose with sword in hand to find a familiar face, though he couldn't remember from where. The man was painted for sacrifice, surrounded by slaves that must have come from the broken pens. The men carried looted weapons, and the familiar face saluted like a warrior. Yacat realized it was a captured soldier from many months ago—a man he'd spoken to and thought sacrificed.

"Nahu," he said as the name came to him. "From the Orino river. I thought you'd be long dead. You must be a hard man to kill."

The younger man stiffened at his name, and smiled. "The gods saw fit to spare me, prince." He looked around the square. "Honor demands my life still belongs to the sons of Mar. As far as I can see, you are the only one left alive. Command, and I will obey."

Yacat snorted, half expecting the men had come to kill him. He gestured at the dead king, the burning city. "The House of Mar is no more, Nahu. Your life is your own."

"Can you help us?" Zaya rose with a groan. "Can you

help carry wounded? Help escape?"

The young warrior's chin raised. "We would be honored."

Yacat shrugged and gestured at the fallen men, and the slaves gathered them on shoulders and backs, two men lifting Ruka. Fortunately, once the giant was on his feet he seemed to move on instinct, face contorted as if still enraged. Promising she was alright, Zaya helped carry one of the men. "What is best way out?" she stopped and stared at the burning city.

"Not that way," pointed a man garbed almost entirely in black cloth, his voice humming strangely. Yacat followed his hand and saw thousands of torches swarming the streets.

"West, then," said Yacat. "There is a gated tunnel built for nobility. It will get us under the wall."

The black garbed foreigner looked Yacat up and down. "Remove your royal dress, do it now," he hissed through his mask, his words echoing strangely but clearly in Yacat's ears. After so much blood and violence, Yacat's body still trembled with opposition, but he could see the sense. He stripped off his headdress and jewelry, and the strange man spoke again. "Stay close. Don't even look at the rebels."

Yacat nodded, holding his son with his least bloody hand. The boy shook and his eyes were wide with silent terror, but he kept moving, and Yacat was proud of him. He tried not to think of his wife and other children, of his dead father and brothers and the chaos that now enveloped his city. There was nothing he could do for them now. But he could still save his son.

His body faltered with fatigue and wounds, and he nearly stumbled on the rough stones as they made the long descent. All around him the other tired, wounded men grunted in exhaustion, but managed until they reached the main street heading West. In the dark it was difficult to tell, but he felt several shallow cuts on his limbs, and his back ached in waves of agony.

The street was all but abandoned. Fire and battle cries and screams could be heard clearly from the East, and to Yacat it seemed as if the entire countryside had risen in rebellion. They walked on carrying their wounded, and soon saw men dressed for war burning and pillaging. Yacat grit his teeth, choking back the rage of such desecration on a holy festival, which had held meaning to all long before the stolen rituals of Centnaz. The raiders moved nearly unchecked, ducking in and out of houses, murdering citizens and killing the few warriors sober and close enough to realize what was happening. Yacat expected that by the time whatever generals were still alive could gather an army, the city would be burned to the ground.

"My ancestors built this place," he said, mostly to himself. "It has stood for a thousand years."

No one answered him, and the dead could not complain. Yacat felt the weight of failure as he watched it burn. Untold generations had passed their labor down from father to son, father to son, until corruption and decadence had replaced reality, weakness with strength. He knew life was too cruel to let them learn from such mistakes. It was all over now.

In the wreckage of Copanoch, the valley would split apart as cities and tribes bickered over ancient feuds, fighting over the spoils. None knew now how to build a city-state; all alive had been given that miracle as a gift before they could stand. They had forgotten what it took. They had forgotten what had made them kings.

Some citizens still stood in the streets, a stunned hopelessness in their eyes. Families gathered with their belongings looking unsure where to go, and Yacat wanted to call out to them, to help them, to say 'follow me, I will lead you to safety'. But he didn't know if he could.

At last they reached the edge of the city, buildings turning to farmland, with only the road they'd follow East as far as possible, apparently to the sea. At the crossroads they found a party of tribesmen guards—painted warriors who stared and armed themselves as they lined up along the road.

"We are allies of mist tribes, and the shaman Pacal," called the black-garbed foreigner in his strange, echoed voice. "We are not your enemies."

The tribesmen seemed to understand, but did not clear the road. They inspected the group, careful eyes moving over everything, one speaking to the others, his eyes steady on Yacat. "We don't know you, though by your voice perhaps you are ally to Pacal. You may pass." He pointed a finger. "But that man is Prince Yacat, the great killer of House Mar. He has murdered and enslaved hundreds of our people."

Yacat slowly pushed his son behind Ruka, hoping they didn't recognize him too. He saw other tribesmen had heard the speech, at least twenty more approaching from the nearby fields. His heart ached at the thought of his son growing old without him, and witnessing his father killed here brutally. But often a man could do little enough but meet his fate with courage.

"I served my king," Yacat stepped forward. "Now he is dead, and so I have no quarrel with you. I never did."

The tribesman snorted, the awful excitement of revenge growing in his eyes. "But *we* have quarrel, Prince. Give him to us, stranger, and we will know the rest of you are allies as you claim."

Yacat did not wait for the inevitable betrayal. He took another step forward and unhooked his metal sword. "You want me? Here I am. Come and be the first to die."

"Take that bastard, brothers!" a man yelled from the group. A handful came forward with spears and drawn bows.

One of the armored men being carried who looked half dead coughed and spoke with a rasp. "I'm not an ambassador, friend, but I don't think they like you."

"Savage," whispered the masked man. "Can you fight? There's a great deal of them."

The giant spirit-man stirred and swayed on his feet, though he still looked as if he were *already* fighting. His breathing was ragged, and he used his spear as a crutch, golden-eyes webbed with veins. "Of course," he growled, then slumped to the dirt and groaned.

Yacat searched for something, *anything* else useful he might say to the angry tribesmen to stop the violence. Then the group of warriors ahead yelled, and charged.

* * *

Chang pushed off the men carrying him, drawing his sword with his good arm. With the one eye he could still open he watched the rising dawn, and the expressions of shock from the men as he steadied on his feet.

"Stop your staring," he barked through bloodied lips. "Stay together. Kill them all."

Basko looked about as red as Chang felt. He nodded and slapped the Steerman hard. "You heard him, kill the bastards!"

The only Oarmen left stepped ahead with his shield, dripping blood from deep bruises. Chang hadn't heard much of anything that was said since the explosion, but that didn't matter. Enemies were between his crew and the sea, and for that they would die.

The half naked tribesmen slammed spears, arrows and knives off the thin shields, chain links, and plates on Chang and his men. They struck a moment later, pushing against the line of iron, slashing their wooden swords as they tried to leap over the defences. They failed.

Chang jammed his sword into the first unarmored chest. Grunts and screams followed as the crew of *The Prince* showed the strength of the shaman's weapons. Wooden swords and spears smashed and broke against them, more arrows and rocks bouncing away without purpose. One ripped skin off Chang's burnt cheek and he roared in pain, stepping forward to hack another spearmen down. He could hardly see but he knew by their numbers the enemy were trying to wrap around his men's flanks. Made no difference. They were too outnumbered. All he could do was hope the others held.

The armor soon felt like an anchor tied to his back. His arm throbbed with agony that matched the waves of pain from his face, and he was very tired of fighting. He was in fact tired of landsmen and mosquitoes and words he couldn't understand. He wanted the feel of the sea, the sound of the ship as it creaked over the waves. He wanted what he was owed, or to go down to Roa and sleep until another life. But a good pirate needed stamina.

He stepped out from the line, sensing a man at his side he assumed was Basko. Two paces and he found another target, ignoring the spear that cracked on his shoulder to make another trench of blood. With a tired glance he realized the man beside him was the native prince. The foreigner swung his own metal sword and deflected another spear thrusting towards Chang's neck, then with an almost casual backstroke, cut open the man's gut.

Chang looked back to find Basko and the Oarman close behind, throwing men back with their shields as they followed. Chang kept his sword high as he advanced. That he was here in some strange land wearing armor like a damned infantryman made it all feel like a dream, or a nightmare. But Lucky Chang was not a man to dwell on how, and why.

The tribesmen fell back and scattered under the attack, but there were even more than Chang realized. Wave after wave, the pirates kept fighting. He didn't know how many he and his brothers cut down, the foreign prince soon in the lead, sidestepping arrows and spears, charging at enemies like a madman. He shouted words Chang didn't understand, but the meaning was clear: '*Follow me!*'.

The old crew of the Bahala, the last pirates of a dying age, howled like wild dogs as the enemy tried to stop them with rocks and arrows. They cried out in animal fury, mouths frothing in the dim light, nothing in their minds but survival. Chang saw Zaya skewering men with her spear as if she hunted wild boar; he saw the captain disappear in the fading darkness, his knives cutting men down before they could scream. As they emerged from the crossroads into flat, open ground, it was the worst, most terrible, most glorious moment of Chang's life.

Yet still the tribesmen harassed their flanks from the fields beside the road. The men lost their shapes and faces, becoming only limbs, and spears. More wounds and bruises filled Chang's armor like a patchwork of pain. His endurance flagged, his whole body a windless sail that drooped on the mast. Ahead he saw trees and maybe safety, but didn't think he could reach it. Every step was endless and impossible, every heartbeat a pleasant surprise.

Golden eyes stared back at him from the jungle. For a moment he couldn't understand how the shaman had got ahead of him, then he heard the familiar growl.

The enemy screamed as Wanchoo leapt from the darkness, crushing a man with its weight, raking bloody streaks across two others with huge claws. The lingering tribesmen scattered in panic in his presence, weapons forgotten in trembling hands.

Pacal emerged from the city behind them with a handful of warriors. They carried water and carts loaded with supplies, and began lifting wounded men on top without a word.

Chang collapsed into the men's arms without a struggle, watching the few remaining stars as they carried him. He looked to see the Boatswain beside him, dead eyes still open and staring from his bearded face. One of the Oarman was lost, and the Swabbies; Old Mata's toothless smile sat frozen on his lifeless face. Chang knew vengeance would never come. He had failed so many of his brothers he burned with shame, but not for a ship's weight in silver would he come back to this place.

He would give his dead brothers to the sea, for that was their home. And perhaps, if Roa was impatient, he would join them.

The foreigners marched them along the road, the others speaking but their words incomprehensible or at least lost to Chang's ears. His mind soon wrapped in fog, and he lost track of how long they carried him. The sun rose higher and higher until the smell of salt came with the sound of waves against the foreign beach. And here, at last, the goal in sight, Chang surrendered to sleep.

Chapter 32

"Your men are brave warriors. I can hardly believe this one still lives."

Zaya looked to the prince and tried to smile, emotions warring as she held Chang's hand. His breathing was steady, but he looked dreadful. At least one, maybe two of the other pirates lay dead on carts, Chang and another very close. Once on the long march the shaman had stumbled to them from his daze and forced the party to stop while he bound and inspected the wounds, saying 'it will do, but I need supplies from the ship.'

After a few hours of quick travel along the road, they reached the coast. Zaya saw no sign of the many villagers and farmers she had seen working when she traveled to Yacat's manor before. Now everything was quiet, a few corpses scattered through the fields and towns, some tribal warriors plundering houses with the calm banality of laborers.

The prince's eyes took everything in, though he remained silent. When it seemed he could stomach it no more he walked to Ruka's side.

"Those shadows. Will they perish on their own?"

The Godtongue's jaw clenched, and he shrugged. "I do not know."

"You mean even now they might be slaughtering people?" Yacat's eyes widened, the fury and harsh toil of the day thinning his skin, and perhaps his soul.

The shaman said nothing, and Yacat shook his head. "There's nothing to be done? No penance that can be paid?"

"You are not being punished," Ruka snapped, then

cooled. "I am not the master of such darkness. But I will seek answers. There are men across the sea who... *know* such things. I give you my oath, I will learn what I can, and return. You may come if you wish."

They had reached *The Prince* now anchored off the coast, her sails and masts repaired and perfect, bits of cloth fluttering in the breeze. Zaya was surprised at the lump of emotion that formed, the feeling of safety and longing at the sight, and her desire to return to the sea.

"Come with us," she said, turning to Yacat. "It's not safe here for you now."

He took a long breath and shook his head. "I am still a prince of House Mar. All my life I have had that privilege, and responsibility. What sort of traitor would I be to flee my people now? What other function of nobility than to face hardship?"

The land of ash had no royalty, no lords or kings—they were ruled by chiefs who gained their following by right of deed, and Zaya did not understand Yacat's heart. She shrugged, feeling helpless, wishing only that the man would come aboard.

"Our journey will take months," Ruka explained. "I will have to find you when I return. One or both of us may not survive."

"Our lives are in the hands of the gods," Yacat answered. "You will find me, or you will not."

Ruka growled as he turned from the sea. His golden eyes flicked over Yacat's body as if inspecting a horse. "Do not move," he murmured, closing his eyes, a huge hand moving to the prince's shoulder. After a long, strange pause—flame sparked from beneath his hand. The same outline of sparks that had created something from nothing in the long night of shadows traced Yacat's body. In moments, where there had been just a man in torn and bloody cloth, stood an armored warrior of the valley, the same cuirass and limb guards as the prince had always worn, this time in thin metal plates of blue-tinged iron.

Ruka grunted at his handiwork, and stepped away. "I have yet to see gods save men, but that armor might. Don't lose the sword."

Yacat had not flinched at the flames, but now stared at himself in wonder, eyes tracing the few symbols engraved on the iron. These were 'runes', or the ancient written language of the people of ash. As an educated woman, Zaya could read them.

"What do these mean?" Yacat whispered, but Ruka already turned away.

"A prince is made by deed alone," Zaya told him, not surprised that mighty Vol, god of men, had found another champion.

The leader of the tribesmen who had helped them stared in wide-eyed wonder at the metal, a thing like greed in his face. "I see your powers are not exaggerated," he spoke, his voice strange and echoing in Zaya's ears.

The Godtongue blinked and stared until Captain Eka stepped to the foreigner's side. "They have a…divine metal here, savage. It allows this man to speak any tongue, and who knows what else. I told him you would share your own knowledge of such miracles with him for his help. We would not have found you otherwise."

Ruka's eyes narrowed, but he nodded. "What has been promised, I will fulfill. But first I return to my own lands."

"You may never return," echoed the foreigner's voice, though he didn't seem particularly alarmed.

"You have my word," Eka soothed. "And when we do, we'll bring more warriors and supplies, and ambassadors from my king. This is but the beginning of our friendship, Pacal of the Mist."

The older man smiled and gestured. "I understand, my friends. We have already achieved more success than I could have hoped. We have burned the dread city of Copanoch, and destroyed the House of Mar."

"Not quite," Yacat spit, eyes snapping to the older man.

"I have no love of destruction," the older man raised a hand in peace. "Nor am I a fool. I know with the fall of the great city there will not be some paradise in its place. The tribes will quarrel and at best choose a new king." His voice firmed. "But your city had become monstrous and I will not apologize. Nor will any son of Mar be safe from the tribes, no matter what I say."

Yacat stared, but his anger faded, and he looked away.

The shaman turned from the coast and the transport that would take them to their ship. "Your pasts and petty hatreds are irrelevant. The best men are always those who could have been the worst, Pacal. Harmlessness is not a virtue. Go with him, prince. Try to survive. When I return, I will help you both." With that he stepped onto the transport and waited for the crew.

"My place is with the shaman." Zaya smiled sadly at Yacat.

He stepped closer and took her hand. "I understand." His jaw clenched and he spoke more softly. "Will you take my son?"

The boy had endured the night and march bravely, but he heard his father's words and his eyes widened in terror. "Don't send me away, father. I will stay with you, I don't know them."

The prince closed his eyes and breathed before he turned on the boy. "It isn't safe for you now, my son. Pacal is right. We are hated in these lands, and where I go—I can't protect you."

Tears leaked down the boy's cheeks, his body trembling as he nodded and looked at the ship.

"As you can see, he is strong, and disciplined. Tell your sailors he will earn his keep, and if you teach him he will…"

"Of course we'll take him." Zaya squeezed Yacat's hand. "And one day, return him."

The look of relief that flooded the man brought warmth to Zaya's chest, and she leaned forward and kissed him gently.

"Goodbye, *Tekit*." She smiled, hearing his song already forming in her mind.

The pirate crew took their men and a few supplies and loaded all into their transports, soon pushing off from the coast of the new world. Yacat and the tribesmen watched them go, some waving from the shore as *The Prince* set her sails and snapped her spars, and took to the strong East winds.

Zaya did not weep as she left a man she loved. She was a daughter of ash, warrior and skald to a great hero, and her place in this story was atop the waves until the gods deemed otherwise. She helped the wounded pirate crew prepare their ship, and looked to the sea.

* * *

Chang woke and slept for days in mixed delirium. He heard the waves and thought it must be a dream, then he'd see golden hair and grumble as a woman coaxed him up to drink and chew before he lay down and slept again. Then the fever was gone, and he remembered a new world and fighting with landsmen and felt the loss of two more brothers like daggers in his scar-scabbed heart.

The men cheered when he left his cabin. "Enough of that you cheeky bastards," he croaked, adjusting to the brightness of the world with his only working eye. He thought of Old Mata giving bits and pieces of himself for his men over the years, until finally he had given his life. Now, Chang supposed, it was his turn.

His arm, at least, had begun to mend. The shaman said the bone had set and with enough stretching and pain he would regain the use entirely. Zaya left him to stand on his own, wise enough it seemed to know a man had his pride. Soon enough he was back in his bunk.

Every day Zaya brought him food and water and helped him to the buckets. She sat with him and sang her songs, and when he realized no one in his whole life had given him such care he one day stopped her and took her hand, trying to find the words.

"You didn't leave us," she said first. "Me, and the shaman. Why not?"

Chang frowned, knowing he wouldn't have under any circumstances save the belief that they were dead and gone, no matter what he'd said.

"Because you're mine," he said, then rolled his eyes at her mocking grin. "You're my *crew*, Macha. You and the pilot. I don't leave my own."

"I have learned many things since leaving my homeland," she said with a smile. "I thought all chiefless men were scoundrels and thieves. I have since learned—there are many kinds of hero."

Chang squirmed under her gaze, to change the subject he told her of life amongst the tribesmen, and listened in fascination as she told him of her life in Copanoch. His jealousy flared when she told him plainly of lying with the prince, though he knew he had no right.

When she noticed his discomfort, she laughed. "Amongst my people, pirate, a woman takes whatever mate she chooses. There is no shame or insult. But she rarely takes two at a time save for brothers, for the men of ash are careful with honor."

With some chagrin Chang confessed his own tribal conquests, but here again she laughed with genuine amusement. "I do not blame them," she said, then left him in his bunk, stopping at the door. "You are a worthy man, *Lucky* Chang, on land or sea."

That night she returned and washed him, and with smiling eyes she'd leaned over his bunk and kissed his lips. They made love—very carefully, and still with at least as much pain as pleasure. Zaya slept naked in his bunk, nestled against his good arm without a hint of shame.

He found the experience…most enjoyable. And though he knew she didn't love him, the knowledge brought a kind of comfort, for he knew too he belonged to Roa and the sea and always would, and it wouldn't hurt her when he explained.

Still, by all the gods and spirits she was beautiful, and even in the dark he stared at her oh so welcome body in his bunk, hoping she stayed as long as possible. "Or until she comes to her senses," he whispered.

"Mmm?" she mumbled against him, but he shook his head. "Nothing, Macha, go back to sleep."

The voyage back across the Dark Sea was the most contradictory of Chang's life. Half filled with the pain of recovery, and the regret and loss of the crew; the other the pleasure and comfort of Zaya's company, both day and night. He had worried at first about Ruka, but the man seemed entirely changed since landfall. Whatever darkness had plagued him seemed gone, the almost child-like man intermixed with the brilliant pilot returned, the warlord not to be found. He nurtured the plants he'd taken, and took like a father to the foreign boy, teaching him the island tongue and many other things.

"I see you have a new shadow, pilot," Chang joked one morning on his first walk of the deck. But the big man stared so hard Chang retreated and dropped his smile.

The captain remained inscrutable and silent, smoking his cigars and watching the sea. He seemed content to let Chang manage the remaining crew, and for the pilot to guide them. The men grew restless as the voyage lingered, but to endure a known hardship was but a fraction of enduring the unknown. They knew they were going home, the ship soon to be theirs. To suffer the endless sea was nothing new and at least they knew why. A man with a good why could endure any how.

With fair winds and a single storm, the journey home from the new world took *The Prince* fifty-one days to the Western coast of the continent. Chang spent most nights in Zaya's cabin. With some awkwardness he addressed the chance of pregnancy, unable to say what he knew a woman would like to hear.

"And so?" she'd frowned.

"It's just...I am a sailor, Macha. My place is on the sea...I don't know if I could...if I would be of any use..."

"If I grow with child I'll return to my people, pirate, and become a matron with my own house."

Chang shrugged helplessly until Zaya rolled her eyes. "Where I am from a woman's children are hers alone. And I have told you I'm from a wealthy family. You needn't worry about me or my children."

He'd left it gratefully at that. After the many long days and blissful nights, the outline of Sri Kon—capital of the island nation of Pyu—finally formed on the blue horizon.

The pirate crew stared at the end of the long, dark sea.

"Home at last, Chiefy." Basko grinned and slurred a little—mostly drunk since he'd been back aboard.

"Aye," the Steerman almost shivered in relief as he clutched the rail. "Will we be rich, chief? Isn't that what the pilot said?"

Chang doubted it, but didn't say so. He was about to order the rudder turned North by North-East to reach the royal harbor, when the captain ordered them South. Chang frowned, utterly confused.

"We won't be stopping at Sri Kon," the captain explained between puffs. When the men all stared he glanced at them with perfect innocence, then said with an edge of contempt. "I don't work for the king."

Chang felt the blood draining from his face. His men were mostly confused, still not caught up to the sinking feeling of understanding Chang still needed to confirm. "But the prison. How did you get us out of prison?"

"I lied." Eka flicked the stub of his cigar into the sea, and waited.

"But the guards," Chang insisted, feeling his understanding turn to rage. "The guards let us out. They knew who you were."

"Yes, they're as gullible as you." Eka didn't smile, but Chang still sensed it and reached for his knife. His men sensed a killing and started moving behind him now.

"I should kill you," Chang whispered, thinking of Old Mata and the Oarman and the Swabbies, all dead because of this man. "I should kill you slow and dump your body for Roa. Why shouldn't I?"

The assassin stood at perfect ease against the rail, no weapons visible or anywhere close to his hands. He spoke without a hint of concern, or malice. "I like you, Master Chief. And so I strongly advise against trying."

The pilot had come down from his perch on the prow

to watch the exchange, looking no more concerned than the captain.

"And the ship?" Chang met his strange eyes. "Is that another lie, ashman?"

"No, Chang. The pirate lies, but I do not. This ship is yours, as promised, as soon as we reach the Batonian monastery."

"We're supposed to be rich!" almost squeaked the Steerman, a kind of panic threatening his nerve. "We've lost men, and there's no damn *money*!" he yelled, close to begging as he looked at Chang. "Old Mata never told us where the silver was. He never *told* us!"

Chang knew, of course, that it had been spent long ago, bribing a dozen kingsmen corsairs to spare old captain Mata's crew. They'd tortured him anyway, and near broken him as they'd broken so many. But he'd held on long enough, until the kingsmen tired and gave in, and for the location he'd bought mercy for Chang and his men.

His reverie broke as sparks flared from the pilot's hand. A square, metal chest formed from nothing as if forged from air before all their eyes. The men all stared in wonder, and the pilot flipped the lid to reveal at least a hundred silver coins of the highest weight and worth.

"For your oaths, both this ship, *and* its cargo, are yours," he said, and Chang managed to tear his eyes away from the small fortune in coin.

"What oaths, pilot?"

"First," the giant's eyes seemed to dig into Chang's skull. "You will not speak of the new world. Nothing but this ship could yet reach it with any safety, and the men of both continents are not ready." The giant did not pause to see if they agreed. "Second, aboard my ship you are not pirates." He turned his golden eyes to *The Prince*, inspecting the hull and sails. "You have the fastest, safest ship in the world, and enough coin to purchase whatever goods you wish. That should give you enough advantage to thrive as merchants. That is my bargain."

Chang said nothing, still angry at the captain's lies and now at being told what he could or couldn't do on his own ship. In any case what exactly a pirate *was* remained unclear, full of contradiction and hypocrisy from noble lords. He felt the moment linger too long, and the giant's eyes watched, and watched.

"When I have left Bato," the pilot continued, "I give you my word, the captain and I will go to Sri Kon and speak to the king about your pardon. But I wouldn't worry. The isles are in turmoil since the death of the old king. With so many problems, the new one is not going to worry much about you and your impossible ship."

There was truth in this, at least. Chang knew he should agree and let that be the end of it. He glanced at his men and saw his mood reflected in their eyes, a kind of petulance he wasn't yet willing to dismiss.

"Every man has a choice," the pilot's deep voice increased in volume, and perhaps menace. "Do as you wish, islanders, as you always have. I promise only that one day your ship will not be uncatchable. Use your power with cruelty, and one day you will find a greater thing on the sea than yourselves, and on that day *The Prince* will be your funeral pyre."

The threat was clear enough, and Chang nodded as he smiled politely at the strange, and terrifying man. "As you say, pilot. You have my oath."

"Then we part as friends." The ashman turned back to his cabin, the hint of violence gone from his face. The crew's stares all turned to Eka, who shrugged with his infuriating, endless apathy.

"I don't care what you do. Just hold course and

maintain sail, you can dock directly at Bato."

For the last time, they did what they were told. The journey to the island monastery was short—a small island just off the coast of Sri Kon, a patch of land ringed with mountains, the famous monastery and hotsprings at its center. The men dropped anchor near a small, rocky beach, and stuffed the transport with the shaman's things. Chang stood on the beach feeling as vulnerable as he always did on land, looking from Ruka to Zaya to the captain, unsure how or whether to say his farewells.

"Goodbye," the pilot announced and lifted a disturbingly large collection of crates full of plants and contraptions, walking away without a glance behind. The foreign boy was similarly loaded, struggling behind to keep up. Chang shook his head and grinned, but lost it when he saw Zaya staring at the man's back.

"Shaman!" she called, her face surprisingly torn, "what should I do?"

The giant turned with a furrowed brow. "What do you *want* to do, Zaya, daughter of Juchi? Or shall I pretend you'd listen?"

The woman suppressed her obvious pleasure as she looked at the horizon, then *The Prince*, and finally at Chang. "I think I'd like to see the isles," she said, allowing the grin. "Perhaps I'll learn the merchant's trade for a time. No doubt that would please my mother."

Ruka nodded and walked on, and the boy set down his boxes and returned with a sheepish glance before embracing Zaya's waist. "Thank you," he said in the island tongue. "Thank you for saving me."

She returned it, and called again to the pilot. "How will you return to the new world without your ship?"

The giant only snorted in response.

"Come, boy," he grumbled. "You too pirate. We have monks to question. They won't be pleased to see me."

Chang returned to the ship on the transport, Zaya quiet at his side. They hadn't discussed her coming with the crew—in fact it hadn't even entered Chang's mind as a possibility. They reached the ship and climbed the netting aboard, suddenly all standing on the deck and alone, the captain and pilot gone, the ship truly theirs. The crew glanced at each other without smiles, some unsure what to do with their hands.

They weren't sure about her presence, he knew. Old habits died hard for men of the sea, though things would be much different now if they truly became merchants. A pirate had to know the trade of the sea to know when and where to sail, so the prospect wasn't ridiculous.

"Well you can't keep your name," Chang announced in the silence, then frowned at Zaya. "And your hair's too bright and pretty, so wear a damn cloth or the sky god will kill us before Roa does. You hardly know anything so you're a Swabbie now, pay is three quarters share for the first year."

Zaya nodded without expression. "As you like. You superstitious pack of fools."

Chang grinned, and the men with him.

"Where to, Captain?" The Steerman took his place at the rudder now that the pilot was gone.

Chang made a show of thinking, but he already knew. The answer was simple: *anywhere we damn well please.*

"The wind is Northerly. Let's follow that."

"Sri Kon is North, Chiefy," Basko said without concern.

"Aye it is. So let's pass the royal port, and perhaps they'll chase us. Good to show 'em early just how useless that'd be."

The crew's grins broke into wide smiles, and the Pitman climbed a mast to make more sail as the Steerman turned into the wind. Chang took the helm and ran his hands along the rail.

"Swabbies don't stand near the captain, nor on the helm," he said softly when Zaya came to his side.

"As you say," she said without moving, and Chang repressed his smile. The woman's presence brought him a kind of pleasure he couldn't describe, and didn't care to anyway. He would still belong to Roa, of course, and one day go down to sleep amongst the fish. But not yet.

"Are you not the pilot's *'skald'*?" he teased. "Will you not need to sing of his heroics?"

She shrugged. "If so, the gods will bring us together again."

"The gods, and my ship," Chang answered, and Zaya patted his arm.

"We're not so different, you and I," she said, watching him until he turned. "We both have our faith."

Chang nodded, no desire to argue and anyway a good pirate ignored philosophy. *And a good merchant, too*, he decided.

He knew then he would keep his promise to the pilot. But then, if things went well, he might soon have other ships. And he never said he wouldn't *hunt* pirates. These days on the king's sea, there were a great deal of arrogant kingsmen who called themselves such. Very well, Chang thought, maybe he'd see how they liked to be hunted by a power they couldn't escape.

The thought vanished just as quick, blown away like smoke in the breeze. The future was wide, and open, and tomorrow everything or nothing might change, just as the sea god intended. Chang closed his eyes to the cool spray as the incredible vessel cut a deadly swath through the waves. The wind was always perfect if you went where it blew.

"But it's a shit name," he whispered, and ignored Zaya's questioning brow. All seamen knew ships were feminine and not masculine, and to call this magnificent creature *Prince* was so insulting Chang had hardly endured it. He yelled so his voice would cover the ship. "The next man who calls my beauty *Prince* gets a damn flogging!"

A few yelled 'Aye, Captain.'

Chang didn't need to see the crew to know they'd be relieved. Islanders didn't name their ships for the same reason they didn't name themselves. But Chang wasn't concerned, and a piss cutting she-devil like this one shouldn't be nameless. One day he'd tell them, but not today. Chang's ship needn't fear the waves anymore than him because she was his, and he was Roa's, and together they'd cross the seas without rules or purpose save for their own. Chang smiled as he clutched her metal rail, so strong and perfect like her lines and hull and sail.

Sometimes a good pirate had to be sentimental.

"Not to worry, beauty," Chang whispered for her and her alone. "You'll have your name. Lucky Chang will call you *Freedom*."

THE END

Epilogue

Yacat, son of Mar, waded through the burnt rubble of his ancestors' city. The 'holy' festival of stars was supposed to bring Copanoch good fortune, blessings from the pantheon of gods, and especially the Devourer. Instead, it had brought destruction.

As he'd left the jungle and the tribesmen behind, the 'shaman' Pacal had warned him the countryside was in chaos and filled with men who would kill him if they could. "You should stay with us. There are many tribes," he'd warned, "none will see you as anything but their enemy."

I have not feared death for many years now, Yacat had thought, but did not say. Instead he had forced himself to extend an arm in a friendly gesture, the warriors all tense as they put hands to their spears.

"Thank you for helping my son to the coast," he said honestly. The older man nodded and took his arm.

"What will you do?" he asked, with a concerned tone he failed to hide.

"I'll find my family." Yacat shrugged. "I'll do what I can to help."

Pacal had called to his back as he walked away.

"This land will need men who know what it is to rule, and win battles, Lord General. A son of Mar can never be king again, but you could help us crown our own. The name *Mahala* still strikes respect and fear across this valley."

Yacat had turned, scanning the line of tribesmen who watched him, feeling nothing for them but pity and regret, no desire to ever serve a king again.

"You were right before, Pacal. The House of Mar is

gone, and Mahala with it. May the gods watch over you, men of the mists, and men of the mountains. I can promise you only this: despite what you have done, I am not your enemy. Goodbye."

With that he had trekked through leagues of jungle, sweating in the strange armor summoned by a foreign spirit-man. He had drunk and washed in clean rivers forgotten by his people, floating as he stared through a window in the canopy, mind clear and humming with a quiet numbness. That false peace had gone when he left the jungle.

Smoke rose across the horizon, mixed so deeply with the gray sky it was as if the heavens themselves invaded the earth. Yacat crossed trampled, looted, and neglected farmland, empty villages and corpse-ridden roads. Distant wails of sorrow, the hum of insects, and the songs of the birds, were the only sounds.

As Yacat neared Copanoch, the stone walls and distant temples gave the illusion that all was well. The gates, however, were open, corpses piled on either side. Yacat stood for a long time at the gate, feet for a moment refusing to step inside. He'd taken a thin cloak to try and cover his armor, but he knew he might be challenged and forced to kill within the walls. Still, he had to see.

Buildings everywhere had been reduced to stone pillars and ash. A thousand years and more the city had stood and weathered plague and storm, war and famine. But in two nights and days of oil and fire, it had burned to the ground.

The dead lay everywhere, many burnt to cinders, like the blackened leavings of a raging forest fire. Yacat walked on, eyes locked on the untouched stone beyond. Because of the rampant fires, there was little enough left to plunder in the city. Some few tribesmen and citizens moved about the wreckage, some perhaps looking for survivors, others for metal trinkets, or anything of value they could take. Fires continued to burn, waves of heat and smoke washing over Yacat in the wind as he pulled the cloak against his face.

"You there! Who are you?" yelled a young voice, the accent from some far-flung jungle tribe. Yacat turned and pulled back his hood, letting the iron armor show. Every muscle in his body trembled with the need to kill for the fall of his city, and only will and practicality kept his hand firmly on the hilt of his sword. The tribesmen who'd challenged him was no more than a boy. He stood wide-eyed in the rubble as he inspected his intended victim, then turned and ran.

Yacat walked on.

He knew the hastily cobbled, amateur army of the tribes would have no plan in success. With the loss of their mutual enemy they would scatter, every chief with his own mind on how to proceed. Yacat had fought in too many wars not to know what was coming: endless civil strife; starvation; and chaos none alive had ever known. There was no stopping any of that now.

The palace gates were shut and barred, and for a moment Yacat felt a hope that perhaps his family had taken refuge in the inner walls. Then he saw the sidegates—their bronze bars bent and broken, sagging useless from their catches. With a deep breath, he carried on.

Dead tribesmen, and the looted corpses of palace guard cluttered the halls—scenes of violence following the newly decorated corridors like another form of morbid art. None had been spared. Yacat stepped over as many women and servants as he did soldiers, all with a stone heart, his mind turned to the royal halls ahead.

King Etzil Mar's throne was destroyed. Several hammers still lay near the limestone, rock, wood, and papers strewn about the hall. Anything that looked valuable had been taken, including all the pottery and even the furniture. A few pages blew against Yacat's leg in a breeze from the hall, and he lifted them up. When he realized what they were he sought others, and soon held a collection of land deeds and titles, including his own.

'*Lord Yacat Mar,*' it read, followed by the king's seal, '*Baron of the Eastern ricelands running from the Swift South River to the King's road.*'

If his heart had not been stone, he might have laughed. Three days before the world had been shaped by such words—soil or slaves claimed by the swipe of a royal quill. Even this was backed by men with spears and swords—men like Yacat, who spattered and sealed such paper with blood. Now the thin veneer of civilization was gone.

Yacat forced himself towards the harem. He expected it too would be looted—the royal children slaughtered, the women taken. He could only pray Maretzi and his children had somehow escaped the festival and the city. His stone heart helped him onward, but it beat faster when he heard voices and then crashing sounds from the end of the corridor.

He ran to the turn to find the harem gates were barred, several men that looked like a mix of tribesmen and just bandits trying to get in. They were hammering at the wall and the gates and looked as if they'd been at it for some time. When Yacat rounded the corner, clanging his armor against the wall, they turned.

"Well now," said the closest. "Who the hell are you?"

Yacat drew his sword, trembling with a thing like lust but darker, a need to punish men like these for all the horror he had seen.

"Death."

He raced forward before the men realized their peril. The man who'd spoken scrambled for a nearby spear, fumbling a jab at nothing as Yacat cut him down and stepped past without pause. He swept his blade once, twice, and again into the men with hammers, growling as he hacked off a hand then took the wielder's throats. He stabbed through the heart of the last man, who tried to run. Then there was only the sound of his ragged breaths, and the last, gurgling gasps of the dying hammerers, their eyes wide and frantic as they bled out.

"Mahala? Is that you?"

Yacat blinked and returned from the killing trance. He saw eyes watched him from a hole in the gate.

"It is," he managed to say as the heat of violence cooled. "The men are gone. Have no fear."

Wooden latches and metal locks clicked and released until the gates opened. Beyond, a group of Eagle and Panther warriors waited by a table filled with dice—as if they'd been almost bored until they saw Yacat. All stood at attention and saluted.

"Cuexta." Yacat could hardly believe any soldiers were alive and still here—let alone one of the army's heroes—still guarding the harem. He stepped forward and took the big man's arm. "Where is my family?"

Cuexta's lips tightened, his eyes roaming Yacat's sword and armor before pulling back. "I'm sorry, Mahala, I do not know. Most of your house fled North to the other great cities. We stayed at our posts, hoping reinforcements would come." The warrior's eyes unfocused and looked far away. "For two days and nights we have smelled the smoke, and heard the screams."

"Who is still here, Cuexta? What families?"

"Mostly the wives, concubines, and young children of

the king, Mahala. Most of your brothers took their families. They told us little."

Yacat ground his teeth, thinking of his brothers leaving their father's children and the men who guarded them. "The king is dead, Cuexta. I watched him fall."

The big man's face drooped with the exhaustion he clearly fought. Yacat felt like a liar not telling the man the truth of what he had done at the festival of stars—that he would be seen as a traitor by any of his kin. But the spirit-man Ruka had been right, such things made no difference now.

"Do you yet serve the House of Mar?" Yacat said, looking to all the warriors, and not just Cuexta. As one their backs straightened with the promise of purpose.

"Until death, Mahala." Cuexta's face lowered in respect as he held the warrior's salute, and Yacat put a hand to his shoulder.

"Then your task is this: collect the remaining women and children from their rooms, and go North East. Their only hope now is to seek refuge in the noble houses of Tlanopan."

With that, Yacat turned, his mind already leaving the palace.

"Will you not come with us, my prince? Let us protect you."

Yacat smiled, gripping the hard pommel of his impossible sword. Even now he felt the eyes of the ancient gods upon him like the golden orbs of their foreign herald, impatient, in judgment. "Prince Yacat is dead," he told them. "He died in the fire with his city and his house. There is an enemy in this land, that is true, but it isn't the tribesmen. While the chiefs and kings of the valley bicker over power, someone must hunt that true enemy down."

The men stared in incomprehension, but it made no

difference. Yacat walked over the corpses and back through the halls. He would have liked to see the temples of the gods and paid homage, but he had no wish to see the scene of corruption and slaughter for a second time. Instead he walked to the broken gates and left the palace, no intention of ever returning. He covered his face against the heat and ash and walked North along the main road, empty now save for the leavings of destruction. A few looters and tribesmen yet moved nearby, but none challenged him, so busy with their tasks and largely hidden in the ruin.

At last at the outer gates, a voice and the silhouette of a man in the smoke stopped him. He turned with a hand on his sword, only to see Cuexta emerge with a cloth over his face, weapons and a large pack draped over his shoulders. He caught up, then stooped and coughed several times as he wiped sweat from his brow.

"Long have I served the House of Mar," he said between breaths. "On the battlefield I have killed or captured twenty men, and fought in many battles. Never have I served a greater or more honorable general than you, Mahala. Whatever your path, let me come with you."

Despite the stone he had used to replace his heart, Yacat felt a touch of emotion. He had no desire to lead the man to his death, but nor did he wish to turn him away.

"So be it. Kneel."

The eagle warrior dropped instantly to the road, scarred face squinting against the heat still blowing on the wind. Yacat wasn't sure what he intended. The oaths of loyalty taken by his house were great affairs attended by half the nobility. A man swore his life and the lives of his sons to his lord in a hall surrounded by wealth and tradition. Yet here, amid the destruction of all he had known, Yacat felt it somehow right—the perfect place for new oaths, and unlikely renewal.

"Swear to me now, and be my brother: you will reject Centnaz, the Devourer, and all his teachings. You will reject all kings and city-states, and the authority of other men. You will follow your own heart, wherever it leads, even unto death."

Cuexta blinked in surprise, but nodded. "I so swear."

"Then rise, my friend," Yacat dragged him to his feet. "For we are equals now. And today, like me, you are a knight of the old gods. Come." He turned away and smiled, more pleased than he'd expected to have a companion before the end.

"Where do we go, lord?" Cuexta asked, and Yacat didn't bother to correct him.

"To our doom," he smiled, pleased the other man didn't look the slightest bit surprised or worried. "We hunt living shadows, going amongst one people who will despise us, and another who will call me traitor. If we succeed, and survive the road, we will fight demons that can not die."

Cuexta's face took on the same squint Yacat had thought discomfort, and he adjusted his pack.

"I should have asked before the oath."

Yacat's stone heart cracked, and he nearly laughed as he left the gate of his home for the last time. "That you should have. Now come, my friend, we leave a ruined city. But the worst is yet to come." He looked out at the open road, trying and failing to stop his mind from asking again if his wife and children had escaped the city in time, or wondering at the insanity of his task. He spoke again, whispering this time, perhaps only for own benefit. "The worst is yet to come."

314

Where to Find More...

1. Want to learn about Ruka, Eka, and read the original Ash and Sand series? The completed trilogy is available on Amazon, starting with Kings of Paradise.

2. Check out my flintlock fantasy, starting with The God King Chronicles, also available on Amazon.

3. Remember choose your own adventure books? I have a scifi/fantasy 'playbook' story you can check out on your phone or tablet in an app called 'The Living Library' (on Google and Apple).

4. Sign up to my newsletter for news, and the occasional freebie, at www.richardnell.com.

Get in touch...

Email: email@richardnell.com

Locals: https://richardnell.locals.com

Twitter: @rnell2

Goodreads: Link here, or just search for my name

On Reddit: you can usually find me on r/fantasy (as richnell2)

About the author

Richard Nell concerned family and friends by quitting his real job in 2014 to 'write full-time'. He is a Canadian author of fantasy, living in one of the flattest, coldest places on earth with his begrudging wife, who makes sure he eats. He's been a dishwasher, brick-layer, bin-sweeper, floor-waxer, factory-worker, government employee, and managed a few teams in the bloody *insurance* business. He went to school for none of those things. He has one eye, a few useless English degrees, enjoys history and video-games and learning of all kinds, because what he really loves are ideas.

He writes fantasy because the real world can use a little sprucing up. His stories are often intense and complex, just as reality is, plucked believably from the real vagaries of history. But there is always hope, or love, or greatness. Or at least glory. He hopes you like them.

Visit his website here: http://www.richardnell.com
Or contact him at: email@richardnell.com

Made in United States
Orlando, FL
14 February 2024

43681991R00190